"Got you [...] little brot[...]

Tyler gave him a withering look.

"Well, I must thank Rita for leaving Tyler all those years ago." Saira singsonged in that dangerous tone Tyler knew all too well. "That breakup was most *definitely* to my advantage."

"Sweetheart." Tyler pretended to chide her as he laughed to himself. *Do not mess with Saira Rawal.*

"Rita is more than happy with the Hart brother she's got," Colton retorted.

"To each their own, I suppose." Saira shrugged.

"Mom wants us to come over at seven tomorrow," Colton said.

Tyler glanced at Saira, then back at Colton. "We'll see her another time. We don't want to steal your thunder."

Colton scoffed. "As if you could."

"Whatever. You two—" He stopped as Saira nudged him and held out her phone. There was a message from his mom.

Don't even think about letting Tyler miss this dinner.

His shoulders dropped as he glanced up at Colton's victorious face, then looked at Saira. She flicked those brown eyes at him, agitated, but resigned.

They were going to his mother's tomorrow night.

To announce their engagement.

Dear Reader,

Let the games and shenanigans begin! I'm so excited you've chosen to play along with Saira and Tyler!

I LOVE a fake relationship, but this one has a twist! No spoiler here—just read away! Saira and Tyler are also dealing with family members and a secret from the past, as well as Saira's panic attacks. But there's a very mischievous puppy—hence shenanigans!

Saira is trying to build a relationship with her estranged father, even though her brother is against it. At the same time, her panic attacks are getting worse as graduation approaches. Tyler has always been in competition with his estranged brother, so when his brother shows up engaged to one of Tyler's exes, Tyler fakes his engagement to Saira.

This is the last book in the Once Upon a Wedding series. If this is the first one you're picking up, there are a bunch—all stand-alone—but don't be surprised if you see familiar faces pop up here and there!

I've had so much fun incorporating elements of Indian weddings in these books, as weddings in general are so fun and always add to the drama! I look forward to adding different elements of Indian culture in future books.

Enjoy the journey! And as always, I'd love to connect with you! I'm most easily found on IG: @MonaShroffAuthor or FB: Mona Shroff, Author.

Happy Reading!

Mona Shroff

THE DATING GAME

MONA SHROFF

SPECIAL EDITION

Harlequin®
SPECIAL
EDITION™

Recycling programs
for this product may
not exist in your area.

ISBN-13: 978-1-335-18022-3

The Dating Game

Harlequin Enterprises ULC
22 Adelaide St. West, 41st Floor
Toronto, Ontario M5H 4E3, Canada
www.Harlequin.com

HarperCollins Publishers
Macken House, 39/40 Mayor Street Upper,
Dublin 1, D01 C9W8, Ireland
www.HarperCollins.com

Printed in Lithuania

Mona Shroff has always been obsessed with everything romantic. If she's not writing, she's making melt-in-your-mouth chocolate truffles or doing her favorite thing, reading. Alone time *is* precious, but Mona is just as likely to be raising a glass of wine or her favorite gin and tonic with friends and family. She travels whenever she can, but when she's not out and about, she cuddles up with her romance-loving husband and their rescue dog, Nala, in Maryland.

Books by Mona Shroff

Harlequin Special Edition

Road Trip Rivalry

Destination: Forever

The Dating Game

Once Upon a Wedding

The Five-Day Reunion
Matched by Masala
No Rings Attached
The Business Between Them
Their Accidental Honeymoon
If You Can't Stand the Heat...

Visit the Author Profile page
at Harlequin.com for more titles.

To Nya, You asked and I heard you.

Chapter One

Saira

Saira Rawal adjusted her deep blue lehenga and the matching dupatta. She side-eyed her brother, Aneel, who was the groom. He was resplendent in his cream sherwani. Thin red thread made a subtle pattern throughout the outfit, with just the slightest bit of sparkle. He wore a matching red turban to complete the outfit.

She beamed at him as her heart swelled with love for him. He was everything to her. He had been father, mother and brother to her for as long as she could remember. Today was his day. He and Karina Mistry were two sides of the same coin, and Saira couldn't be happier that they had decided to get married sooner rather than later. Not to mention, she had never seen a happier, more handsome groom.

"Stop fiddling with your buttons," she admonished, slapping his hand away from them.

Aneel barely glanced at her.

Saira stood between her brother and the mirror, and reached up, putting her hands on either side of his face so he had to look at her. "You look amazing—Karina and Tracy Auntie saw to that. Everything will be fine."

He smiled. "Of course it will." Her brother inhaled and relaxed some. "Where the hell is—"

"Right here." Tyler Hart's deep and familiar voice came from the door. "Ring in hand, ready to watch you finally do something for yourself."

Tyler Hart was her brother's best friend and best man. He was basically her best friend too, since they had all grown up together. Saira did a double take as Tyler entered the room. No denying Tyler was a handsome man, but he was breathtaking in this moment in the deep blue sherwani the groomsmen were wearing. It fit his taller leaner build perfectly and Saira could not help but notice the deep blue of the sherwani perfectly matched his eyes. She swallowed hard and forced her gaze away from Tyler, internally shaking her head. This was Tyler, not some random hot guy. What was she doing, gawking at him?

It had to be the wedding vibes. Love and hooking up was foremost in everyone's mind. Must be getting to her as well. Weddings made everyone believe in love. Well, everyone but her. She believed in hard work. She believed love existed, just not for her.

"All set?" Tyler asked.

Aneel turned to face his friend. "You better believe it." Her brother glowed with happiness, and it made her heart sing.

"It's almost time," Tyler said. "The DJ is just about finished setting up."

They were heading out for the groom's jaan—Saira's absolute favorite part. They would dance the groom's procession to the doors of the hall where Karina's family would greet him, and the wedding ceremony would begin.

Saira's heart started to thud in her chest. Her palms started to sweat. *No! Not right now.*

"You okay, Sai?" Tyler furrowed his brow. "You look pale."

Aneel spun around to look at her. Concern dimmed the happy glow on his face. "What's the matter, Saira?"

She forced a huge smile onto her face. "Nothing. I don't know what Tyler's on about." She glared at Tyler over Aneel's head. Tyler put his hands up in surrender. "You two better get down there. I'll join you in a second."

Aneel's brow remained furrowed. "You sure?"

"Can I use the bathroom in peace?" She put as much sass as she could into her words, even as heart rate continued to race. If they didn't leave soon, they would see her have a full-blown panic attack. And that was the last thing Aneel needed today. Or any day.

Tyler wrapped an arm around her brother's shoulders, steering him toward the door. "Can't have the groom late to his own jaan." Tyler glanced over his shoulder, concern in those gorgeous blue eyes, even as he ushered Aneel from the room.

She widened her eyes at him, trying hard to convey the message: *I'm fine.*

He didn't believe her. She saw Tyler hesitate just a fraction. He wanted to stay with her. And deep down, she wanted him to. But he needed to be there for Aneel. This was Aneel's day. She steeled herself. She needed Aneel to get to his wedding. Aneel needed his best man by his side.

"I promise I'm fine."

The dhol beat floated up from outside, beckoning them to the jaan. Aneel's face lit back up. "It's time.

Tyler left with Aneel, but not before throwing her another glance. No sooner had they left than she shut the door and collapsed on the bed. Her hands were shaking, she suddenly found it difficult to breathe and she was sweating. She was going to ruin her brother's wedding. She tugged at her jewelry, suddenly finding the ornate necklace and bangles stifling.

She had no idea how long she was there. Music from the DJ joined the dhol and she heard cheering. The jaan had started. Aneel would be looking for her. But she couldn't breathe. She took off the dupatta and unbuttoned her blouse. She covered her ears. The music felt so loud it seemed like it was inside her.

The dhol beat accused her of being a bad sister. She needed to get down there, but she did not know how.

"Sai? Sai! Saira?" Tyler's voice came to her as if from a tunnel. "What are you doing on the floor?" She felt him sit next to her.

She wanted to hide this from him. She wanted it to just go away. But she couldn't breathe. And it was so loud. "I… I… can't breathe." She managed between labored breaths.

"Okay. Wait." Tyler left and came back in a minute. He handed her a paper bag. "Inhale and exhale into this." He held the bag for her, and she tried to follow his direction. It took a few minutes, but she was finally able to inhale and exhale steadily into the bag. Her heart rate lowered. She felt less hot, and the feeling of doom slowly dissipated.

"You need to go back to Aneel," she said. "I'm coming." She tried to stand and wobbled a bit. Tyler caught her and helped her to sit on the bed.

"I'm not leaving you here. What happened?"

"Nothing."

He pressed his lips together as he studied her, clearly not believing her. "Uh-huh." That was Tyler-speak for *we will discuss this later.*

Not if she could help it. "I'm fine. Let's go," She stood and this time, her legs held her. She felt better already.

Tyler looked at her. "Um…you might want to…" He waved in the direction of her chest.

She looked down to see her blouse open and lacy bra exposed. She flushed and hastily hooked the blouse shut and tried to adjust her dupatta.

"Here. I can pin that." Tyler took the scarf and proceeded to make perfect pleats before pinning it to her blouse.

"Impressive."

"Your mom taught me."

Saira froze as heartache came over her. Her mom should have

been here for this. For her son's wedding. For Saira's graduation. Hollowness so deep and strong overtook her and threatened to trigger another panic attack.

Tyler took her hand. "Shall we join this jaan and show them who can dance?"

Tyler's hand in hers was reassuring, strong. She leaned into that, and she calmed, nodded her head. "I'm game if you are.

Chapter Two

Tyler

Tyler danced to near exhaustion in Aneel's jaan. The weather was pleasantly warm, but he was sweating from dancing. An April shower would have been welcome. Saira never left his side. They had planned some of the steps beforehand, so there was that, but they were just naturally in tune with each other, after having grown up together. She seemed fine, no sign of the panic attack he had witnessed earlier. It must have been a panic attack; he'd never seen Saira so out of sorts. Made sense that she would be on edge, given that her brother was getting married. Not only that, but she was close to graduation and still looking for a job, and had just moved out of her apartment with Aneel so that she was living on her own for the first time.

Anyone might freak out a bit.

Still, he couldn't help keeping an eye on her. It was just concern for a woman he had known all his life. It wasn't because he was desperately in love with her.

That would be ridiculous.

The image of her exposed lacy bra had not helped.

Especially since he planned on meeting someone tonight.

"Tyler, if you don't tell that girl how you feel, I will," his mother muttered to him as they approached the bride's family. His mom was standing in for Aneel's mom.

"For the last time, Mom. There is nothing to tell," he muttered back, his smile never faltering.

"You were up there—"

"She was freaking out a bit. I couldn't just leave her there on her own."

His mom looked at him. "Is she all right?" Concern filled her blue eyes. Saira might as well be hers. She and Malti Auntie had been best friends.

"She's fine. Big day, that's all. To be expected." He brushed off her concern. Saira would not appreciate everyone knowing her business.

"You're sure?" she asked again.

"Yes, Mom." He nodded, then changed the subject. "You look spectacular in that purple lehenga. No one would believe your sons are thirty-two years old." He spotted Saira approaching. "Ask Saira if you don't believe me." She really did look great. Tracy Hart looked nowhere near her age; Tyler hoped the youth genes were passed down same as eye color. "You should try to hook up." He chuckled.

She smacked his arm. "Tyler Hart, I am not going to *hook up* at this wedding. What is the matter with you?"

"Oh! Tracy Auntie. I saw the cutest guy for you. I'll scope it out, make sure he's single," Saira added. "His name is Raj something. He's a friend of Karina's dad, I think."

"What's the matter with you two?" His mom was flushed, but Tyler saw her run her gaze over the crowd as if looking for this Raj person she'd never met.

The priest approached.

"We're up, Mom," Tyler said. "Stop scoping out guys." He grinned as she glared at him. She stood on one side of Aneel, while Saira stood on the other. Tyler stood just behind Aneel.

Karina's father and sisters welcomed them with the aid of the priest, and they all proceeded inside. Aneel took off his shoes as he prepared to enter the mandap. One of Karina's sisters, the youngest, Rani, grabbed them. Tyler made a half-hearted grab for them, before Rani handed them off to a young girl.

The festivities began and Tyler gave himself over to celebrating Aneel and Karina's happiness. He did his best to push aside all thoughts and concerns for Saira, but found himself constantly aware of her presence, as he always had been, and likely always would be.

Chapter Three

Saira

Three weeks later

Saira Rawal drew her gaze around the small nearly destroyed studio apartment. Pillow stuffing was everywhere. A lamp lay on the ground. A small pile of poop was off to the side—on the carpet, of course—right next to the tile of the small kitchen. Beside it was a wet spot that could only be pee.

Of course, Kiara had done her business on the carpet next to the tile instead of straight up on the tile. She was a baby queen as her name implied, so she did what she wanted. The sofa was slightly shredded. The little vandal looked up at her, tail wagging, tongue hanging out, eyes bright, with no idea that her antics had just made them homeless. Or maybe she absolutely knew and was putting in the effort to be extra cute because of it.

Either way, Saira Rawal was screwed.

Because at the door her landlord fumed at her.

"You will clean this up before you leave. And no deposit back!" the burly middle-aged man barked at her.

Saira opened her mouth to explain she had nowhere to go, but the fury rippling off her landlord kept her mouth shut. Besides, she was starting to sweat. He had been very clear when she moved in that pets were a complete no-no.

"Yes," was all she managed as she attempted to glare at her little puppy. She couldn't help it; a smile came over her face as she knelt down to pick up Kiara. "You are naughty," she whispered, holding the puppy close. Her heart rate was starting to rise. Where was she going to go?

"Cleaning supplies are in the hallway." Her landlord harrumphed and walked out.

Saira watched the man leave, then turned to assess the mess, all the while holding baby Kiara close. "It wasn't your fault, was it, baby? No...you're just a baby." Holding Kiara was calming. Her heart rate slowed as she held the puppy. Even though the puppy was part of the reason she was fighting a panic attack, the attacks were the reason she had Kiara to begin with.

As a veterinary student, she should have known better than to walk into an animal shelter. Because of course, she wanted to bring them all home. The fact that she only brought home Kiara showed a high level of restraint on her part. She knew the rule about pets at this apartment, but the panic attacks had been coming more frequently lately, so she had brought Kiara home. It was mutually beneficial. Kiara needed a home, and everyone knew dogs were great for anxiety.

The mess wasn't so bad; she'd have it clean in no time. Saira waited for her heart rate to regulate, for the feeling of being overwhelmed to leave her before she put down Kiara and went to fetch cleaning supplies. It worked. Perfect. Dogs were helpful for people with panic attacks. A known fact.

Problem solved. She grinned to herself. And no one knew.

Well, maybe Tyler. But he didn't count.

As she cleaned, she logically contemplated her options of where to go. She had found that logic sometimes helped her handle that feeling of being overwhelmed, which frequently led to the panic attacks.

She could go to her brother's new place. They had finally decided to leave the small apartment they had grown up in, to each get their own place. Saira had wanted to be closer to school, and Aneel wanted to be closer to the restaurant where he was the head chef. Not to mention, he now had a wife, who also had the cutest son, Veer.

Her brother currently had a townhome that was closer to the suburbs since Karina needed to be close to her son's school. Probably plenty of room, but Saira really did not want to third-wheel it over there. They'd only been married like three weeks. Besides, her brother had spent his entire life so far taking care of her—he'd practically raised her—he deserved and needed this time with Karina without his younger sister—and her dog—skulking about.

She finished scrubbing the carpet of Kiara's "gifts" and vac-uumed up the fluff from the pillows. She sighed as she realized she would have to replace the pillows as well. She worked part-time at the veterinary clinic, so she had some money, but her hours were limited by school, so it wasn't a lot.

Aneel had offered her a hostess position at Fusion where he was head chef, that paid more, but the busy and stressful res-taurant seemed more likely to cause panic attacks than work-ing in the clinic where she was comfortable, so she had turned down the offer and continued at the clinic. Not to mention, the clinic had offered her a full-time job that was hers as long she passed the board.

Everything she owned fit into two suitcases and a few boxes. She had only been here six weeks, and she was at school all day, so she didn't need much. The furniture belonged to the apartment.

She sat on the torn sofa and stared at her phone. Her father might be an option. He had only recently reentered her life, however, and was also newly married. He would be more than happy to take her in; she just wasn't quite sure she was ready for all that. A few coffees and a lunch or two didn't heal all the wounds, even if she had attended his wedding.

She sighed as she came to the conclusion she always did. She would simply call Tyler.

Her heart thudded in her chest. She had been avoiding even considering this possibility if she didn't have to. Certainly, Tyler Hart would take her in. She and Tyler had grown up together, along with her brother, and had more sleepovers than she could even count. She had stayed with him for a few weeks a couple months ago and that had worked out fine. Well, sort of.

She might even still have his key.

It was just that now she had Kiara.

Her thumb hovered over his name as she contemplated other options. There was her friend Lin from school, but Lin was married and had a son as well. She didn't want to call Lin at 9:00 p.m. on a Wednesday and ask for a place to stay.

Tyler was her best option.

She tapped her phone.

Chapter Four

Tyler

Tyler clinked glasses with the beautiful woman across from him and laughed. Jackie was funny, highly intelligent and drop-dead gorgeous. Long red curls bounced when she tossed her hair, and she had beautiful green eyes that could be warm one second and cutting in the next. Jackie was everything, including kind, which was a rarity in his chosen field of corporate law.

They had attended law school together, she had been a year behind him, and he remembered having the most interesting debates with her. She had returned to Baltimore upon securing a new job and had reached out to him for drinks.

"You know, I always had the biggest crush on you in law school," she said, some mischief in her green eyes.

"Seriously?"

She shook her head. "No. But you believed me so easily. Were you hoping it was true?" She laughed.

Drinks had turned to dinner, and he could not remember the last time he had enjoyed himself like this.

Well, he could, but the whole point was to *not* think about Saira Rawal.

He pushed the thought of her away as quickly as it came. He was on an actual date. He was enjoying himself. This was what he wanted.

He did not need to be thinking about his best friend's sister, even if she was his friend as well. He needed to just. Stop. Thinking about her.

Period.

"Tyler?" Jackie raised a perfectly manicured eyebrow. "Where did you wander off to?"

"Oh Sorry." *Damn it.* "Just had a thought about a case. I know, classic workaholic." He smiled. "Won't happen again."

She shrugged. "No problem. Tell me about it—or whatever you can. I have no problem discussing work."

Tyler grinned at her. She really was amazing. "Well, if you insist."

They spent the next couple hours talking about work, occasionally hitting other topics, but returning to the career that they loved each time.

Tyler got the bill, with much protest from Jackie. "I get paid, you know."

"I asked you out, it's only fair," Tyler insisted.

"My treat then next time." Jackie eyed him with a half smile.

"Next time." This was fabulous. There was going to be a next time. Jackie was turning out to be exactly what he needed.

They pulled up their calendars on their phones and made a second date for two weeks from now while they waited for her Uber.

"Two weeks seems like a long time," Jackie said as they stood by the curb.

"It does." Tyler smiled at her and met her eyes. He stepped closer to her. "You could cancel your Uber. I live a few blocks away."

She grinned up at him, her body grazing his. "I never called one."

"Perfect." He offered her his arm and led her toward his building. The evening was a bit cool for May, but it was pleasant enough. His phone buzzed in his pocket. He ignored it. Whatever it was could wait until morning.

* * *

They walked the few blocks, continuing their conversation, floating from topic to topic. They made it up to his condo. Jackie sidled up to him as he got his card key out and kissed him. She tasted sweet like wine, and he kissed her back as he unlocked the door. He pulled her close and walked her in, still kissing her. He was so distracted by her mouth and wandering hands that he hardly noticed the apartment lights were on.

"Oh, shoot! I'm so sorry!" Saira's voice broke him from his occupation with Jackie and he turned to see Saira standing in his small foyer while a small ball of black fur zoomed in circles.

He widened his eyes in disbelief. "Saira!"

"Hey!" Saira waved, a sheepish look on her face. "Don't mind us. We'll just go back…" She thumbed toward the hallway where "her" room was. Her eyes widened as she took in Jackie and assessed the situation. "Hi, I'm Saira. I'm not a girl. I mean I am a girl, like I identify as a girl, but I'm not—"

Tyler glared at her. *What the hell?*

"What I mean is Tyler and I are only friends. We grew up together."

"I'm Jackie." She looked at Tyler. "I didn't realize you had a roommate."

"I don't—not usually." He glared at Saira. How was he supposed to move on from his secret crush on her when she was always around?

Saira laughed. "He's telling the truth. I just needed a place to crash for a couple nights, I got kicked out because of…" She pointed in the direction of the fur ball, which on closer inspection turned out to be a puppy. Who was currently using his white rug as a toilet.

His very white rug! As a toilet!

"Oh. No. Kiara!" Saira exclaimed as she moved to clean the mess. "I'm sorry. I tried to call and text, but you didn't respond…and my landlord was really mad," she explained as she cleaned the mess.

She picked up Kiara. "But of course you have other things on your mind. I'll just leave Kiara in my room. I'm meeting someone for a late drink, anyway. Just leave the door shut and she won't bother you." She wiggled her eyebrows at Tyler. "Nice meeting you, Jackie."

Tyler stood speechless as Saira took charge of the room, as usual. He should be angry that she had interrupted his date, but his only thought was, *Who was she meeting for a drink? Was it some guy from school? A new guy? Who?*

She was in her room before he could say another word.

What the actual hell?

Chapter Five

Saira

Saira closed her bedroom door behind her and gently dropped Kiara on the floor. She inhaled deeply. Wow. Tyler bringing a woman home. Good for him. She couldn't remember the last time he'd talked about going on a date, though maybe it happened all the time and he just didn't talk about it with her? She was not privy to his dating life. Jackie was gorgeous. Beautiful curly red hair, green eyes to kill for, perfect porcelain skin and tall. Taller than Saira. Perfect height for Tyler, since his date—Jenny? Julie?—came to his jawline.

The image of his mouth on the woman's while her fingers had been threaded into his thick brown hair was permanently tattooed in her brain.

She grabbed her shoes and made sure Kiara was settled into her little doggy donut bed before tiptoeing out.

She hadn't lied to Tyler; she was meeting someone. She was meeting her dad. And it was barely 9:30 p.m. anyway.

No sign of Tyler and Janice(?) as she left. They were likely already in his bedroom. She shook her head to clear it of *that* image and quietly shut the door behind her.

Her schedule was crazy with it being her last year of veterinary school, so she sometimes had to squeeze things in. She hadn't seen her father in a couple months. He had gotten married six months ago, then he was traveling. Now that he was back, they were trying to meet once a week, to rebuild their relationship, as it were.

She walked to the neighborhood bar, just a couple blocks away. It was far from the dives she frequented with her school friends. Being in this nice Locust Point neighborhood, the bar was very clean and light and offered meals as well as the full bar. Her dad was already waiting when she got there. Tall and lean, with a small paunch, he had a head full of salt-and-pepper hair and was always clean-shaven when she saw him.

"Hey," she said. She still hadn't gotten around to calling him *Dad* to his face, but it felt rude to call him by his given name, so she avoided names altogether.

"Hi." He lit up when he saw her and stood while she sat down.

She settled in.

"You are staring." His accent was slight, but undeniable.

"I just can't get over how much Aneel looks like you." Her brother would age well, if the man across from her was any indication.

Yogesh Rawal chuckled. "It's good to see you. How are things? You look a bit frazzled."

"Oh." She waved a hand, trying erase the image of Tyler and Jamie(?) from her mind. "I'm good. Just busy with school and all that."

They ordered a round of drinks. Gin and tonic for her, club with lime for him.

"How was the honeymoon?" she asked as she took her first sip. Gulp. Whatever. It was calming.

"Greece is always lovely, very relaxing." His eyes drifted briefly to her glass, before settling on her face. "But it's time to get back to work."

Her father was a self-made businessman. He owned a business that retrofit Sprinters vans for mobile health services. It was still awkward talking to him. She had so many questions. Another sip.

"Go on. Ask away," he said, as if he could read her mind. This was their deal. He got to be part of her life, and she got all the answers she wanted.

"Why did you drink so much?" Her curls tumbled forward toward her drink. She tucked them behind her ear.

"At the time, I did not know why. All I knew was that I felt better when I did. I used to get panic attacks—sometimes they were debilitating."

Saira paused and stared at him, wondering if that was something she'd inherited. But then, lots of people got panic attacks. It didn't mean anything. She tossed the similarity from her head.

He was still talking. "I found that alcohol helped me deal with them in the moment. After I became sober, I was diagnosed with depression." He looked her in the eye and explained all this as if they were talking about the weather. "Apparently, alcohol allowed me to dull the effects of the depression, to ignore it."

She leaned into him. "Depression?" She eyed her drink. She had Kiara to help with the panic. That was much healthier than depending on alcohol. And she never felt depressed. She was different. She was not her father.

"I'm okay now. Finally went to a therapist all those years ago and I take meds for my depression. Still see the therapist when I need." He was eyeing her as if hunting for any signs of panic attacks or depression on her part. He'd never get it from her. She was master of her mask.

"You never came back for us." Her hair tumbled forward again. She pulled it up and back and secured it with a hair tie. She smoothed it away, her fingers stopping to trace the small scar at her hairline. She'd had that scar as long as she could remember. No idea how it got there. But she used it as a marker whenever she put her hair up without a mirror, which was always, since the curls had a mind of their own.

He shifted his gaze. "Well…that is true."

"Why not?"

He passed his gaze over her face and suddenly seemed to have trouble looking her in the eye. "I don't know. Maybe I was just afraid. Your mom and I were divorced…"

This was the first time she'd had the courage to ask him why he had never come home to them, and she wasn't fully satisfied with the answer. She wanted to press but decided to leave it for another day. Maybe she didn't really want to know what he obviously did not want to share.

He was the only parent she had left. Her mother had died of cancer ten years ago, when Saira was seventeen. She and Aneel had been devastated by her loss, and she knew Aneel, twenty-three at the time and of legal age, had lived in fear of their father showing up and trying to take young Saira away from him, as she was technically a minor. Social services had officially made Aneel her guardian when no one showed up. Aneel saw to it that she went to college and then vet school, even if they occasionally had to wait a bit to save more money for tuition.

She still missed her mother, particularly when it came to things like panic attacks. Aneel, while a fabulous brother, was a worrywart, which kept her from confiding in him, since she didn't want to add to his stress.

When her father showed up seven months ago, she had been curious. Aneel had been angry, but Saira could not find anger in her toward this man. Just a hunger to know *why*.

She nodded and changed the subject. Another sip. She was feeling quite calm now. Maybe she should order food. She signaled the waiter. "Okay. Tell me one thing about you."

This was a game they played to see if they had any common ground. So far, they knew that they both loved animals.

"My favorite fruit is mango."

She chuckled. "Well, I love mango too, but I don't think that counts." The waiter came by, and she ordered a burger with fries. She loved a good burger with fries. She bet ol' Janie(?) upstairs with Tyler never had a burger and fries *and* ate the bun. Saira was going to devour the whole thing. Her father's shoulders seemed to relax. He had said at their first meeting that he wanted to make up for all the time he hadn't been around to feed her.

"Fine," he chuckled. "You go."

"I like to paint. But I'm no good at it."

He stared at her. "Seriously?"

"Yes. I'm crap at painting, but I find it very relaxing." She bit into her burger. Delicious. Who would not want to enjoy this?

He pulled out his phone and scrolled and then turned it to face her. She was looking at a painted landscape. A very badly painted landscape. She grinned as she looked from the phone to him.

"No way."

"I'm sorry to say yes. I painted that."

"It's terrible." She laughed.

"I know. But I love doing it—very therapeutic." His smile was broad and proud, despite the fact that the painting was terrible.

Saira had many other things she wanted—needed—to know from him, but it was too much to get into tonight. She simply reveled in the idea that she and her father were both terrible painters, but they still loved it. Neither one of them seemed embarrassed by their lack of art skills either. Huh.

And they liked mangoes.

She giggled. "Next time, we'll go to one of those paint-and-sip places. No sipping for you, but we can paint together."

"Deal." He chuckled and the sound warmed her. Though try as she might, she could not make it trigger a memory. It was as if she had never heard it before.

Maybe she hadn't.

"I should go." She finished her burger, packed the fries into a to-go box and stood. She'd only been gone an hour. Hopefully Kiara was okay. She'd have to tiptoe back in and not disturb Tyler and his date.

"Next time," her father said.

"Next time." She nodded and left. She walked back the two blocks, thinking about her dad so she did not have to think about Tyler and the redhead who were probably naked in the condo.

She let herself in, being careful to unlock the door quietly. She needn't have bothered, since as soon as she opened the door, she saw a frazzled Tyler holding Kiara, while the condo looked like a hurricane had blown through.

"What the—?"

"Exactly." Tyler glared at her.

Chapter Six

Tyler

Jackie had hightailed it out of his apartment so fast she was a blur. He had no idea when Saira had left. He had knocked on her door and then slightly opened it, and that had been his biggest mistake.

Kiara had come flying out of the room like she was fleeing hell, then there was a small dog peeing on his carpet. Peeing! On his very white carpet! Again! He had tried to catch the little monster, but she was too fast.

He had spent the past hour trying to apprehend the puppy who now thought he was playing a game and ran faster. He finally caught up with her, but not before she had pooped and knocked over end tables.

"What happened?" Saira asked.

"Where did you go?"

"I was meeting my… Yogesh for a drink. I was only gone an hour and I left her in my room. I thought you had a hot date here anyway." Saira sounded accusatory, like this was all somehow his fault.

"You went to see your dad?" He hated the relief that came over him at the thought that she hadn't been on a date. "Jackie left. Almost immediately upon seeing you." Tyler did not bother leaving the accusation out of his voice.

"How is that my fault?" Saira asked.

"Because I had no idea you were here when I decided to bring a woman home," Tyler shot at her.

Saira widened her eyes. "Whatever. Still not my fault. I texted you." She avoided looking at the apartment, which clearly was her fault. "Why did you let Kiara out of my room?"

"I did not let her out. I didn't realize you'd left, and I came to check on you." He was losing his patience with her. He hadn't had sex with the amazing Jackie, and he had spent the last hour being terrorized by this beast and wondering whom Saira was having a drink with.

"Why?"

"Because I wanted to know why you're here."

"I need a place to stay for a few days. I'll buy groceries, help with chores. I'm not looking for a handout."

He narrowed his eyes at her. "What's wrong with your place?"

She avoided his eyes. "I might have gotten kicked out."

"Dare I ask why?"

"You probably should not." Saira finally looked up, her brown eyes meeting his with no apology. "But I promise Kiara and I will be out of your hair in a few days. You can call Jenny back and have all the noisy sex you want."

"Jackie."

"Ah! Jackie. Sorry. Could not remember her name."

"This is not a dog-friendly building," Tyler said.

"Um, well. Actually, it is." Saira nodded.

"It's my building, I would know,"

"Well, you don't because your neighbors have dogs." She raised her eyebrows at him.

Tyler stared at her. She might be right. He was never really home, so he didn't even know who his neighbors were, much less if they had pets. On the other hand, he had also known Saira his whole life, and he was well aware that she had the tendency of stretching the truth when it suited her. She literally got through life being confident. People then backed down. He wasn't people. "Nice try, but I know for a fact that this place is not pet friendly."

"Fine," she capitulated. "I promise to keep Kiara hidden. It's only for a few days, I promise."

"Hidden? She has used my carpet as her personal toilet."

"We're still working on potty-training. She's just a baby, Tyler." Saira actually chided him. In his own home, while her little monster defecated all over his very white condo. "Have a heart."

Tyler shook his head. That would not work on him either. "No. I'm sorry. You can stay—but give Kiara to Aneel for a couple days."

"He's never home. Besides—" she grinned at him "—you and Kiara are already great friends."

Tyler looked down at the pup in his hands. She had curled herself into a tiny black fur ball and fallen asleep in his arms. She was kind of cute. He sighed. Who was he kidding? Of course they were both staying. There was no universe in which he did not do whatever Saira wanted.

He was totally screwed.

Chapter Seven

Saira

"Sit down. I'll take care of the mess." Saira quickly cleaned up and set up newspapers in a corner. "She'll be potty-trained in no time. I will be a veterinarian in a matter of months, you know."

Though what kind of veterinarian would she be if she couldn't potty-train one little puppy? She glanced at Kiara and swore she saw the little mischief-maker smirk at her before falling back asleep.

Tyler looked up at her from where he sat on his very white sofa with Kiara fast asleep in his arms, exasperated.

"How about a…snack?" She pursed her lips and raised an eyebrow, and she was rewarded with a resigned sigh from Tyler. Food always put Tyler in a better mood. Not that she cared about his mood; she just needed to ensure that she and Kiara had a place to stay for a bit.

Besides, Saira was feeling surprisingly good since *Jackie* had left without getting some.

"I have all the stuff for our usual." The beginnings of a smile twitched at his mouth. He had a very nice mouth. Near-perfect lips.

What was she thinking? This was Tyler. She didn't think about his mouth or his lips. Maybe it was because she had caught him kissing Jackie? Whatever. She turned and proceeded to take out the ingredients for her nacho concoction, which had been born when they were children sleeping over at each other's houses. Saira had craved nachos one night, but there were no chips or salsa to be found, so she had put together this odd concoction. Aneel wasn't the only one who knew his way around a kitchen.

She ripped up a flour tortilla into small "chips" and laid them on a plate, which she then sprinkled with cheese and set in the broiler until the cheese was melted and bubbly. She topped it with tabasco and brought it over to Tyler to share.

It should have been horrible. But it was delicious.

"How was your drink with your dad?" Tyler asked. She popped a "chip" into his mouth for him since his hands were full of Kiara. He was still wearing his date clothes. She ran a quick gaze over him. He looked good. His blue dress shirt brought out the blue in his eyes—she had to stop.

"It was…good." She shrugged.

"What does that mean?"

"That means we share little bits of our lives with each other because we both want a connection."

"But…"

"But he still won't tell me why he never came back to see us all those years." She counted on her fingers. "He got sober. He got a proper therapist, is dealing with his depression. Got a proper job, is doing well. So why did he never even try to see us? So what if Mom had custody? He could have tried to get a visitation, once he was better, right?" She shoved some food in her mouth. This was what she needed even after that burger. More carbs.

Tyler simply shook his head. "He came to the hospital when your mom was sick and Aneel kicked him out."

"I know that. I mean before that. According to his timeline, he was dealing with everything, and already doing much better, about five years after he left."

"What does he say when you ask?"

"He doesn't."

"Give him time maybe?" Tyler said quietly.

She nodded. Tyler was right. He was probably the most level-headed person she knew. Her brother led with emotion, but Tyler led with logic and sometimes that was what was needed.

"At least your father is reaching out and showing interest in you now," Tyler said. He was right—and she knew from his own experience that it could be worse. Tyler's own father lived in New York and was a lawyer with a successful divorce practice. He barely reached out to Tyler once he became an adult. Not to mention, he never even offered Tyler a job in his firm.

She scrunched closer to Tyler, so their arms and legs touched. She felt him stiffen briefly before he relaxed. They always sat like this. She was a touchy-feely person and everyone knew it. It was part of the reason why she had gotten the dog.

"You're right. I am grateful for that. I just kind of feel like he's hiding something though, you know?"

"Maybe he's just not ready to tell you everything," Tyler said wisely. He clicked on the TV and, no surprise to Saira, a Bollywood movie was on.

"Tyler. Your addiction to Bollywood is becoming a problem." Saira smirked.

"Whatever. The music is awesome."

They sat together for a while and chatted about everything and nothing while the movie played in the background. She pulled up apartment listings on her computer and they debated the ones she should see, until finally she needed to get some sleep. She had class tomorrow, after all.

"Here, I'll take her out." She stood and held out her hands for Kiara.

"I got her." Tyler stood.

"You sure?" she asked, though she handed him the leash.

He grinned as he shook his head and hooked the leash to Kiara's tiny collar. "Be right back."

Chapter Eight

Tyler

Tyler was making coffee when Saira returned with Kiara from a quick morning walk. The apartment still smelled like rug cleaner, but the smell was fading. He poured some coffee into a to-go cup for Saira. She grabbed the cup, placed her backpack on her back and started to leave.

"Uh…what about the monster?" He nodded at Kiara.

"I have clinic all day. She hasn't had all her shots, so she can't be near other dogs."

"You're a vet. Give her the shots today." Sounded logical to him.

"She's too little. Another week," Saira said as if this was a matter of common knowledge. "And she's not a monster. She will pick up on your animosity," Saira warned.

"You were gone for one hour last night and my apartment was destroyed. I have calls all day."

"You'll be fine. Just take her out every two hours."

"Every two hours? Are you out of your mind?" No, no, no. He had a very busy day.

"It's not that bad, Tyler. You always said you wanted a dog."

"No. No I didn't. I never said that," Tyler insisted. He was dog-indifferent.

"I'm going to be late. Bye." She laughed as she ran out the door. Silence filled the apartment.

Tyler looked down at Kiara. "Just because you're cute does not mean you can do whatever you want."

Aneel FaceTimed him. "Hey. Saira texted that she's staying with you."

"Yes." Tyler picked up Kiara and her dog bed and took her to his office while he talked to Aneel. "She got kicked out of her building. Because of this little monster." He held Kiara up to the phone.

"Oh my god! My sister!"

"It's fine," Tyler said. It was not fine.

"How can it be fine when she's collecting dogs?" Aneel said.

"She's not collecting dogs. She has one small puppy." One small very mischievous puppy. Beast.

"You always defend her," Aneel said.

"You always try to tell her what to do," Tyler countered.

"That's my job. I'm her brother."

"She's a grown woman."

"Don't use those words to describe my little sister. She got kicked out of her apartment. She should return the dog and get a proper place, not mooch off you."

"She's not mooching. I have plenty of room. Though *white* was probably not the best design choice I ever made." Tyler sighed. This was just one of many arguments he and Aneel had about Sai. "I'm happy to have her." *He loved her.* "She's my family."

"You're a saint." Aneel furrowed his brow. "Sorry, I just got a text. I need to deal with this." He ended the call.

Tyler placed Kiara into her dog bed. She sat up and tilted her head at him. "It's just a crush. It'll go away soon," he said heavily. "It has to because being in love with Saira is not going to lead to anything good. Aneel might as well be my brother, since my real brother wants nothing to do with me. But I doubt that Aneel will be anywhere near happy if he knew how I felt about Saira. He and Saira and Mom are all the family I have."

He leaned down and scratched under Kiara's chin. "And Dad? Well…he's made it clear who is the heir and who is the spare." He pointed to himself. "Spare. In any case, everyone finding out that I have a crush on Saira would not be good. And it is just a crush. I'll get over it soon enough." Kiara curled up into her doggy donut and fell asleep. Why was he telling this to a dog? He shook his head.

He went to his desk and opened his laptop. He had a call in fifteen minutes. His phone buzzed. Mom.

Mom: Just checking in, Ty.

Tyler: All good, Mom.

Mom: Have you heard from Colton?

Colton was his twin brother who had lived with their father in NYC since their parents' divorce when they were children. He was the *heir*.

Tyler: Of course not.

Mom: He might be coming to Baltimore.

Dread filled every part of him. Colton's visits were basically little stopovers for Colton to tell Tyler how wildly successful he was and how Tyler should consider joining Dad's firm. No, thanks. Tyler was happy where he was; he loved his work. It paid for this beautiful condo in the Locust Point area of Baltimore—a beautiful view of what used to be the Key Bridge, anyway.

Tyler knew all this, but Colton's visits still had a way of making him question everything in his life.

Tyler: Call starting, gotta go.

He muted his phone and gave his attention to his screen as his colleagues popped up in the Zoom call.

For now, thoughts of Colton were all but forgotten.

Chapter Nine

Saira

It was later than she had expected to be. Clinic had run long and she had stopped off to check out a couple apartments, which ended up being no-goes. She had tried texting Tyler a few times to see how he was doing with Kiara, but he never got back to her. Must be busy with calls.

She picked up Tyler's favorite sushi and white wine as a thank-you/forgive-my-dog peace offering and opened the door to his apartment with a loud, "Honey! I'm home!"

Her first thought was that she and Kiara were about to be homeless again.

Tyler was standing in the middle of the room while Kiara sat sleeping in his arms. His hair was pleasantly disheveled, the sleeves on his very wrinkled dress shirt were rolled up, the top two buttons undone, his tie nowhere to be seen. Of course, he was wearing shorts because today had been a Zoom-from-home day.

Her heart sank into her belly as she noted fluff from a pillow or two scattered around the floor like a layer of snow, along with an overturned ottoman. All the glass end tables were in a corner. The pillows alone were a few hundred dollars each. She knew because she had helped Tyler pick them out and he hadn't batted an eyelash at the cost. Thankfully she didn't see any poo or pee.

"I cleaned the messes just a few minutes ago," he said as if he could read her mind.

"I'm sorry. I went to see some apartments—"

The way Tyler's eyes lit up was almost offensive. "AND…"

"And nothing. They were dumps." She shook her head. "But I brought you sushi and wine," she said sheepishly. It seemed lame compared to the mayhem that surrounded her.

"This dog is not normal." Tyler sounded weary.

"She's a puppy." Saira started taking out the sushi and a couple glasses for wine.

"She's a maniac. Give her to Aneel or a friend until you find a place. At this rate, the condo police will find out and I'm done for."

"Here." She handed him a glass of wine. "There aren't any condo police. This place is pet friendly."

Tyler took it with his free hand, even as he glared at her. "Not true."

"Fine." She held up her hands. "I'll keep looking, but I really don't want to dump her on Aneel and Karina."

"But you can dump her on me?" Tyler raised an eyebrow.

"You're not my brother." Saira reached for Kiara. "I can hold her."

"She's sleeping. Don't wake the beast," Tyler said as he moved Kiara out of her reach. She did not miss the look of caring on his face as he glanced at the puppy.

Ha! Tyler loved the dog. She had known he would.

Chapter Ten

Tyler

The Beast, as he would always call her, lay dormant and sleeping like an innocent little puppy in his arms. He could see the appeal. But after the events of today, when he missed three important meetings and was forced to leave another early, he saw Kiara for what she really was—a beast disguised as a puppy. Adorable as all get-out, but a beast for sure. His door buzzed. He put down his wineglass and pressed the button. "Hello."

"Hey, Ty! It's me! And I have a huge surprise for you!" the voice called over the speaker.

What the hell was happening today? Was it a full moon?

"Is that Colton?" Saira asked, her eyes immediately hardening.

Colton Hart was his twin. Fraternal twins. It was always important to—both of them—to make that distinction. They were split between their parents when they divorced, *Parent Trap*–style, except they saw each other whenever each parent had them both. His stomach tightened as it always did when Colton was in the vicinity. Tyler closed his eyes. "Yes."

"Did you know he was coming?"

"No." Tyler shook his head. But quickly remembered his mother saying something. "Yes. Maybe." His brother popped in on him from time to time; Tyler never really knew when. Sometimes he got a text, but usually not. Colton would crash at his place for a day or so until he was done with his work, then he'd leave.

To say that Tyler felt inadequate around his brother was an understatement. If Tyler played soccer, Colton's team won the championship. When Tyler helped build houses for the home-less, Colton was given an award for raising the most money to send to inner-city after-school projects. Tyler graduated at the top of his law school class, Colton did as well. Colton never seemed to miss a moment to rub it in.

Tyler became a lawyer in a big firm on the partner track, after not even being offered a position at Hart Law. Not that Tyler wanted to be a divorce lawyer, but he hadn't even been asked. *The Spare.* Colton was a lawyer and worked in their father's firm. He lived in a fancy condo in New York. Tyler's condo was fancy, but Colton's was nicer.

He could not imagine what this "surprise" visit was about, but whatever it was, Tyler braced himself. Colton was about to rub something in his face.

"Well, let him in, I suppose. The sooner he gets to brag, the sooner this is all over," Saira said.

Tyler grinned at Saira as he pressed the button. She was fierce in her loyalty, and between Colton and him, Saira's loy-alty was always his. She had never been taken in by the looks or whatever he said he was up to these days. His other friends growing up always thought Colton was the bomb, many of them showing up only when his charismatic brother dropped by. "Come on up."

No sooner did he press the button than there was a knock at his door. He was still holding Kiara when he opened the door.

"Took you a while to buzz me in, but your neighbor let me in," Colton said as he entered the room. Colton took up space in any room, and Tyler's condo was no exception.

Colton grinned as he walked in. Where Tyler had brown hair, Colton's was nearly black. Tyler's eyes were blue, so of course,

Colton's were green. Tyler was lean and muscular like a swimmer; Colton had the physique of a quarterback.

"Hey there, little brother." Colton also never let Tyler forget that he was one minute older. Behind Colton, a beautiful woman with long dark hair and olive skin entered and then stopped. They were holding hands. "This is my fiancée—"

"Rita?" Tyler's eyes widened and his heart plummeted. No way was Rita Biltmore standing in his apartment. Holding hands with *Colton*.

Tyler had dated Rita in law school. For almost a year. Probably the longest relationship he'd ever had. She was the first woman he had really cared about, aside from Saira. With Rita, he had been able to put Saira out of his mind for a time. They were together almost all of second year, before she ended it.

Tyler had been devastated.

But here, now, he felt even worse. This was probably the single most humiliating thing that had ever happened. His asshole brother engaged to his ex-girlfriend and announcing it while he smelled like dog pee and probably looked like he spent the day at the zoo. Which as far as he was concerned, he kind of had.

At the mention of her name, he felt Saira stiffen beside him. She knew who Rita was—he shouldn't have been surprised that she remembered.

Rita's perfectly manicured eyebrows were raised, an expression of mingled surprise and horror on her beautiful face. "I had no idea that Colton was your brother."

"He is," Tyler said lamely. He didn't know what else to say.

"It's good to see you," she said, but it came out as a question.

"Wait." Colton looked from Rita to him. "You two know each other?" His eyes narrowed. It was the first time Tyler had ever seen anything resembling confusion in Colton.

"Well, it's been a while—" started Rita.

Tyler snapped out of it. "That's right!" He grinned and literally threw Kiara at Saira. As he reached for Rita and hugged her. "It has been a while, hasn't it?" he said as he pulled back. He was aware that he might smell like dog. Or dog pee.

Rita smiled at Colton. "Tyler and I dated in law school," she said, meeting his eyes. Colton paused as he looked at her, reading something there. Whatever it was satisfied him and he turned to Tyler.

"Too much for you, eh?" He grinned.

Of course, Colton would make out that he had won some sort of competition.

"Congratulations on your engagement," Saira said from beside him.

Tyler started. He had almost forgotten that she was standing beside him. In as much as he could ever forget about Saira Rawal.

"And who is this?" asked Rita.

"This," Tyler said, stepping back to stand by her, "is Saira."

"Oh, honey. Tell them the truth," Saira said as she leaned her whole body into the side of his, taking his hand in hers and threading their fingers together. "We can't keep it a secret forever. I'm his fiancée."

Tyler froze with a smile on his face. In all the ways he might have imagined that Saira became his, this was definitely not on the list. She looked up at him, her eyes narrowed, the message clear. Kiara stays and she'll be the doting fiancée.

Colton's jaw dropped.

Tyler squeezed her hand, agreeing to the deal. He would have agreed to anything right now. This was the first time he'd ever seen his brother speechless.

Saira grinned in triumph before turning to the couple. "It's true. Tyler proposed just last night. We haven't had a chance to tell anyone or even get a ring." She turned and looked at him fondly. "It was just time. We could just *feel* it, you know?"

Who knew Saira was such an actor. If he hadn't known better, he'd believe her too. She leaned into him, resting her head on his shoulder. It fit perfectly, and her floral scent surrounded him.

Colton recovered quickly. "Wow! Ty, you finally got—"

"Found the right woman," he quickly finished. Colton had teased him about his feelings for Saira for years, though Tyler had never confirmed his brother's suspicions. Tyler fixed his brother in his gaze, daring him to say more.

Tyler fully expected Colton to continue his thought. To let the room know that *he had finally gotten the woman he loved.*

"Right. Well, congratulations," Colton said, smiling at Saira, throwing a quick furtive glance in Tyler's direction.

Tyler was floored. He inhaled, unable to believe that his brother had actually taken the hint and spared him further humiliation.

Rita grinned. "This is so fun."

Yeah. It was a damn comedy show around here.

"What brings you to town, Colton?" Tyler asked as they entered the condo. He noticed that Colton had a suitcase and that Rita also had a small suitcase on wheels.

"I have some clients to meet here, and I wanted to introduce Rita to Mom. Rita works for a nonprofit, and there are people here she can learn from. So we're doing it all."

"Mom hasn't met her yet?" Tyler raised his eyebrows.

"Well, it all happened so fast." He turned what even Tyler would call a sappy smile on Rita and shrugged. "When you know, you know. And Rita is the perfect woman for me. I'm just lucky that she wants me too."

Tyler just stared at him, speechless. He hoped that his face was frozen in a look of support because inside he was gagging. Of course Rita wanted Colton. Everyone wanted Colton. And no one wanted Tyler.

"You're choosy about your ring, huh?" Colton asked, nodding at Saira, a small smile on his face. "So was Rita. Luckily I didn't have a top limit, so she could get whatever she wanted."

Rita held out her left hand. A rock the size of a dime glistened on her ring finger.

"Wow!" Saira exclaimed. "That is some rock!"

Rita grinned. "Right? We'll have to take you shopping."

"Oh, I'm good. I have the diamond picked out. I just need the perfect setting."

Rita nodded knowingly. "Truth. You need a setting that will do your rock justice. What did you get?"

Tyler opened his mouth—but to say what, he had no idea. This line of conversation simply needed to end.

"Asscher cut, 1.2k, so smaller than yours, but my fingers are tiny." She waved her fingers. "The clarity is VVS2, and the color is E, so a quality diamond for sure."

Tyler stared at her. He had no idea what the words she was using meant, but she sounded like she knew what she was talking about.

"Solitaire?" asked Rita.

"Of course," Saira answered with confidence.

Colton chuckled. "Tyler looks like he's been hit by a truck."

Saira grinned at Colton, then at Tyler. "You have no idea."

Chapter Eleven

Saira

Tyler did indeed smell like dog pee, and he had looked better. She took Kiara from him. "Why don't you freshen up, and I'll take care of things out here."

Tyler met her eyes and nodded his gratitude. Well, they had a deal now. Good thing they'd known each other long enough that they easily communicated without words. "Yeah. It's been a day." He chuckled and left.

Saira wouldn't let Tyler down, and besides, she really couldn't stand Colton. He'd always treated Tyler like crap and Saira hated it.

"Who would have thought you'd both get engaged at the same time?" she exclaimed as Tyler left.

"Well, we are twins," Colton said.

"Fraternal though," Saira reminded him. "And Tyler's the good-looking one."

Colton rolled his eyes. "Still shared a womb."

Saira shook her head. Whatever. Colton always liked to remind people that he and Tyler had shared a womb. It was weird.

"Of course!" She tucked Kiara under one arm and reached for a couple more wineglasses. "We must celebrate, but before we do—" she turned to Rita and Colton as she grabbed Kiara's leash "—could you two be amazing and just take Kiara for a quick walk around the block outside? Doesn't look like Tyler had a chance to do so in a while."

"Oh, I…uh, don't really do dogs," Rita sputtered, standing there awkwardly in her stiletto heels and tight skirt.

"No worries, I'm sure Colton's a pro. Like he always says, there isn't anything he can't do." She grinned as she shoved the dog and the leash into their hands and almost pushed them out the door.

She shut the door and got to work. First, since Colton and Rita were going to be staying here, she'd need to empty that second bedroom of her stuff. She tossed all of it into Tyler's room without thinking about it too much. His room was bigger, with a bed and sitting area with a small sofa.

She changed the sheets in the spare room, did a quick dust and vacuum, so there were no Kiara traces, and lit a scented candle. The pillows were fluffed and fresh towels hung in their bathroom.

She then picked up all the fluff from the pillows Kiara had wrecked in the family room and ran the vacuum quickly. She moved all the furniture into an upright position and again fluffed the pillows and lit another scented candle. Tyler had scoffed when she had purchased these. But see what use they were now? If someone held Kiara all night, they should be good.

Saira was putting the finishing touches on the family room when Tyler walked into the kitchen looking fresh, his hair still damp from his shower, wearing a long sleeve T-shirt with the sleeves rolled up and jeans.

He looked…*good*. Huh.

He glanced at her. "Your stuff is in my room."

"Duh. Colton and Rita need my room."

He stared at her a minute, then nodded. "Right." He set to work pouring wine.

She was still watching him pour wine when the door buzzed. She let Colton and Rita back in. They looked a bit windblown, but Kiara seemed fine.

"Thank you," Saira said, unhooking the leash.

"She poops a lot," Rita said.

Saira shrugged. "Better out than in, I guess."

Chapter Twelve

Tyler

This was a nightmare. Surely he would wake from it sooner than later. But no luck so far. Colton was on his sofa, drinking wine, with Rita almost in his lap. Saira was in the one chair, sipping her wine and downing sushi.

Tyler had ordered more sushi and he was just bringing it out, when Kiara ran past. At least she was moving. She couldn't pee or poop while she was running. He met Saira's gaze and she started to stand.

"It's fine," he said, leaving the tray of sushi on the coffee table. "I'll get her."

"Got you wrapped around her little finger, eh, little brother?" Colton chuckled. "Rita, was he that whipped with you?"

Tyler gave him a withering look and turned to follow Kiara.

"For my part, I must thank Rita for leaving Tyler all those years ago," Saira singsonged in that dangerous tone Tyler knew all too well. "That break up was most *definitely* to my advantage. And he's wrapped around much more than my little finger, if you know what I mean. I mean one time I had him almost completely wrapped—"

"Sweetheart." Tyler pretended to chide her for revealing too much, but the reality was he didn't think he could handle the sexy picture she was about to paint. Still, he took pleasure in noting that Colton looked even more uncomfortable than Tyler felt. He laughed to himself. Do not mess with Saira Rawal.

Though he swallowed hard at the thought of what she had been about to say.

"Rita is more than happy with the Hart brother she's got." Colton's voice reached him as he picked up Kiara from her favorite hiding spot, behind his ottoman.

"To each their own, I suppose," Saira said.

Tyler sat down on the arm of Saira's chair and Kiara jumped into her lap and curled up. The Beast was growing on him.

"Mom wants us to come over at seven tomorrow," Colton said.

Tyler glanced at Saira, then back at Colton. "You two go on over. We'll see her another time. We don't want to steal your thunder."

Colton scoffed. "As if you could."

"Whatever. You two—" He stopped as Saira nudged him and held out her phone. There was a message from his mom.

Colton is engaged and I expect both you and Tyler to show up and celebrate. Aneel and Karina are coming. Don't even think about not coming.

His shoulders dropped as he glanced up at Colton's victorious face, then looked at Saira. She flicked those brown eyes at him, agitated but resigned.

They were going to his mother's tomorrow night.

To announce their engagement—even though they weren't actually engaged.

Shortly after their late dinner, Rita and Colton retired. Tyler and Saira finished cleaning up, not saying much.

His bedroom was relatively large, plenty of room for his king-sized bed while still including an area large enough for a small sofa and table and of course his master bath—complete with a shower and soaking tub. He'd paid extra for all these things.

Saira came out of the bathroom in shorts and a tank top. He felt his jaw go slack and quickly found great interest in his lamp.

He certainly had plenty of room. What he did not have room for was Saira Rawal.

There was enough physical *space* for her. There just wasn't enough room for him to be this close without losing his mind. All that space, and yet he could not get far enough away from her, which he needed to do before he did something ridiculous like pull her into his arms and kiss her.

It was ridiculous because they had grown up with sleepovers.

But they were all grown up now, and there was nothing innocent or childlike about the thoughts running through his head of her in his bed. With him. Definitely not sleeping.

"You okay on that sofa?" she asked.

She never said that in his imagination.

"Yeah. I'm good." He pulled a blanket over himself. "It's a comfortable sofa."

"You know we have shared a bed a few hundred times before," she said.

"Yeah. I know." He shrugged. "But those few hundred times taught me that you kick." It wasn't a lie. She had kicked. One time.

"That was one time."

"Whatever. I'm fine here," he said.

"More room for me." She shrugged and got in the bed.

He turned off the light. Within seconds he heard the steady rhythm of Saira's breathing. He stared at the ceiling in the dark.

It was going to be a long night.

Chapter Thirteen

Saira

Saira had not thought this through. This was her only thought as the four of them exited the Uber in front of Tracy Hart's building. Well, not her only thought, but certainly the predominant one.

She had thought she would let Colton and Rita believe she and Tyler were engaged for a day or so, and in return she and Kiara would have a place to stay until she could find another apartment. It was a bit mean to capitalize on Tyler's pride and discomfort, but he had agreed. Truth was, she would have faked the engagement simply for that look of pure astonishment on that asshole Colton's face.

Now, however, she was lying to Tracy Auntie as well. Tracy Auntie was like a second mother to her. Her mom and Tracy Auntie had been best friends for years, since before Saira could remember, up until her mother had passed. There wasn't a time Saira could remember without Tracy Auntie. Or without Tyler, for that matter. Both single moms, they had shared childcare often, been each other's family when they had no other.

Lying to Colton was standing up for Tyler, which Saira would always do. But just the thought of lying to his mom was making her sick to her stomach.

"Let's just make tonight about you two," Tyler said to Colton as they went up the elevator. "We'll tell mom after I buy the ring."

Saira nodded agreement. "No need getting her all excited when we don't even have a ring," Saira added while they approached the door to Tracy Auntie's apartment, as if this was really the most logical path.

The door opened before either Colton or Rita could respond.

"My boys!" Tracy Auntie said by way of greeting, her blue eyes shiny with instant happy tears.

"Mom!" Colton exclaimed as they all entered the space. Aromas of cooking food surrounded them, and Saira was immediately taken back to her childhood. Aneel had cooked for as long as she could remember, and Tracy Auntie was always asking him to teach her new things. Saira definitely smelled her brother's chicken jalfrezi.

Colton wrapped his mother in a huge hug before stepping back. "I want you to meet Rita Biltmore. My fiancée."

If Saira was not mistaken, Colton looked slightly apprehensive. Like he wanted his mother to like Rita. Like he was concerned that she might not.

In all the years she had known Colton, she had never once seen him look so...vulnerable.

Tracy Auntie pulled back from her son and rested her gaze on Rita. Rita held out her hand in greeting.

"So nice to finally meet you, Ms. Hart. I've heard so many wonderful things."

Tracy Auntie's smile was instant as she reached her arms around Rita, passed her extended hand, and enveloped her in what Saira knew was one of the best hugs on the planet.

Rita's eyes widened in surprise and she gasped, but to her credit, she melted into the embrace and immediately hugged Tracy Auntie back. Saira caught Tyler's eye. Colton and Rita were as good as married now.

Tyler smiled, genuine affection on his face as he took in the two women in front of him.

Tracy Auntie finally pulled back, ushering them all into the apartment. Her coloring was the same as Tyler's. Thick brown wavy hair and bright blue eyes. Saira always figured Colton looked like his father.

The space was not large, not small, but very welcoming with plenty of room for them all. Tracy Auntie hugged each of them in turn.

"I told Aneel to bring Karina by since you were all going to be here. I never get to see that boy, he's so busy."

"That's perfect," Colton said, "considering Saira and Tyler have news of their own."

"What? No. We don't," Saira started at the same time that Tyler did.

"You guys," Rita said. "It's okay. We can all celebrate together."

Tracy Auntie looked from one face to the other. "Celebrate what, dear?"

Saira looked at Tyler. *What the hell were they going to do?*

Before Tyler could do any more than nod, her brother's voice boomed from behind them. "Hey! Did I hear you all say something about celebrating?" he asked, Karina right behind him.

"Well come in from the hallway first," chided Tracy Auntie as she stepped back and they all entered the apartment. "Let me hug you."

"Tyler, honey. What is your news?" Tracy Auntie asked. All eyes were on them. Tyler looked at her. Saira had known him since she was five years old. She could read him like a book. He was going to tell the truth.

Made sense. This was going too far. Probably best to take the momentary humiliation of Colton knowing they had lied as opposed to lying to Aneel and Tracy Auntie. She nodded her agreement.

Tyler opened his mouth. "Well. We have a confession to make."

"They're engaged!" Colton burst out. "Sorry, little brother, I just couldn't help it."

"No. NO. That's not it," Tyler started. "We're not—"

"You're what?" Aneel turned to both of them, his face contorted in anger.

Saira reached for her brother. He stepped back, shaking his head at her. "No. Aneel, you don't understand—" Tyler began.

"They're in love. Isn't it obvious?" Colton said. "And they're getting married."

"What?" Tracy Auntie clapped her hands together in what could only be described as glee. "Saira. My baby. Tyler." She reached for her son, even as Tyler continued to sputter, still trying to tell the truth.

"You cannot possibly be engaged. When were you two even dating?" Aneel asked.

Saira opened her mouth. She would have to fix this.

"You two were dating and neither one of you said one word to me?" Aneel plowed forward, passed his hurt and angry gaze between Saira and Tyler. "You couldn't have mentioned this—" he waved a hand between them "—before actually getting engaged. You never said anything." He met Tyler's eyes and then Saira's. "Seriously, Saira, what are you thinking? And Tyler—I don't even know what to say to you. I'm sure keeping the secret was her idea, but how could you cut me out like this?" He paused. "My sister." He glared at Saira. "And my best friend." He turned his glare onto Tyler and shook his head. "I don't know which of you makes me angrier. My best friend, who didn't even have the decency to tell me he was even thinking about dating my little sister," he growled at Tyler. "Or my little sister for the same thing."

"How well would you have taken it?" Saira asked, her eyes narrowing.

"I… I… Well, we'll never know because you didn't tell me," Aneel sputtered.

Saira stepped toward him. She was tired of this. She was twenty-seven years old. She was not the five-year-old he had to take care of after their dad left, or even the seventeen-year-old whose mother just died. She was about to be a doctor in a few months. A damn good one, in fact. "My name. Is. Saira. And I can do whatever—and *whoever*—I want." She enjoyed his flinch when she said *whoever*. "I am a grown woman. I do not need your approval or your consent to date whoever I want. One hundred percent you would not have approved of this, so obviously you were not told. Consider yourself lucky that you know now. You know what, Bhaiya?" Saira narrowed her eyes at her brother. "I happen to be a grown-up, capable of making my own decisions."

"And the decision you made was *Tyler*?" Aneel shot back.

"Hey!" Tyler called from behind her. "What the hell does that mean?"

Saira's eyes bugged open. "Are you serious?"

"Yes. I am quite serious. Tyler hasn't held down a relationship since..." Aneel cut his eyes to Rita.

"Well, he's doing just fine right now. Maybe he just needed to find the right girl," Saira said, barely controlling her rage.

"*You're* the right girl? For Tyler?" Aneel furrowed his brow.

"It would seem that I am since we are engaged," Saira hissed at him.

"He's a playboy, Saira. Come on."

"Aneel. Are you serious right now?" Tyler approached and looked at Aneel. "Aren't you supposed to be my best friend?" Saira had never seen Tyler look quite this agitated, or quite this hurt. Tyler usually took everything in stride. Clearly being insulted by his best friend did not sit well with him.

"Exactly, which is why I know everything about you," Aneel said.

Tyler shook his head at Aneel, hurt and disgust on his face. "Unbelievable. All this time I thought— Never mind."

"Boys. Saira." Tracy Auntie did not hide the reprimand from her voice. Her bright blue eyes narrowed at her children. She was not their second mother for no reason. "That is enough."

Pouting like she was still a seventeen-year-old, Saira turned to Tracy Auntie. "But—"

"But nothing." She shook her head. "Not a word, Tyler." She turned to Aneel. "You need to take a step back before you say another word."

Aneel looked like he wanted to say something, but he held his tongue.

"This is a happy occasion," Tracy Auntie said, tossing back her brown locks along with the tension on her face. Then she turned to Karina as if Saira and Aneel hadn't just been arguing. "Karina, so good to see you. Come in, sit down."

She turned to Saira. "You can help me get the wine."

Saira sighed and followed her. Tyler stopped her and leaned close. "You okay?"

She nodded. "Yeah, sure. My brother insults my fiancé every day." She smirked at him. "You?"

"I'll be fine after I punch your brother in the face." Tyler grinned, but she saw the pain in his eyes. Sometimes Aneel was a complete ass.

"Saira. Your brother needs a moment." Tracy Auntie did not waste time once they were in the kitchen.

Saira huffed. "He needs many moments. I'm tired of him trying to run my life."

"He is not trying to run your life. He just feels left out. You three have been tight for years. Quite honestly, I'm a bit shocked he didn't know either."

"Didn't you hear what he said about Tyler? About me?" Saira asked.

"Your brother has always protected you and put everything else behind that. Even Tyler." Tracy Auntie's eyes zeroed in on her as she spoke to Saira.

"Still, it's not right for him to talk about Tyler that way—or to act like I'm not smart enough to know what I want."

Tracy Auntie bent over, searching for something in the wine fridge. "Just give Aneel some time. He'll come around. You mean the world to him."

Saira shrugged. Right now, she was simply tired of him making her decisions for her.

"Ahh. Here it is." She stood up, pulling two bottles from the fridge. "I've been saving these for a special occasion." Tracy Auntie put her arm around Saira's shoulders. "Come on, now. This is all happy news. You, Tyler and Aneel can work things out later."

Saira grabbed the glasses and followed her out.

Chapter Fourteen

Tyler

What the hell was going on? He and Saira had decided to come clean, and now they were toasting their engagement. Saira seemed distant, but she was probably still mad at Aneel.

Truth was, so was he. Aneel had always been a brother to him, and it hurt to hear his low opinion of him. As if he wasn't good enough for Saira.

That might be true. But Aneel didn't have to say it.

Tyler made his way over to Saira. "We have to tell him the truth."

"No. We don't," she hissed at him.

"It's not fair—plus it's not true, so…"

"We are not telling him, okay?" She wasn't even looking at him. "I am done with him telling me what to do. And he can't talk to you that way."

"Fine. But that doesn't mean we have to lie to him."

"I'm not telling him."

"I can't believe both of my boys are taking that next step." Tracy Auntie raised her glass in a toast. "You two ladies have your work cut out for you. I may have birthed them, but you are doing this by choice." Everyone laughed and raised their glasses.

"Colton, Tyler, go on and bring the apps in."

Tyler followed his brother into the kitchen.

"I'm not surprised Aneel is pissed," Colton said as they unwrapped the charcuterie board and the hummus platter.

"What do you know about it?" Tyler snapped at Colton.

"You're engaged to his sister, and he didn't even know you were dating? Come on now. Any brother would be put out over that," Colton said. "Besides, if you know anything about Aneel, it's that no one would ever be good enough for his sister. He basically raised her."

Since when was Colton reasonable?

"You don't have to tell me—I was there."

"I know you have had a thing for Saira for years." Colton picked a piece of meat from the board and started munching. "Am I wrong, little brother?"

Tyler could not stand the way Colton called him *little brother*.

"Boys! Do not eat the platters. Bring them for everyone," their mom called.

Tyler pointed to Colton's tray. "Busted." He picked up the hummus platter and took it out to the family room.

Chapter Fifteen

Saira

"Isn't that fabulous?" Tracy Auntie said. "Both my boys getting engaged at the same time." She shrugged. "They say that happens sometimes with twins. Come, let's sit, get to know one another."

Then on cue, as if reading Saira's mind, Kiara opened her mouth and started to vomit.

Rita screamed.

Saira side-eyed her, but looked to the closest person to her, who was Aneel. "Bhaiya. Some paper towels, please."

But it was Tyler who stood and got to the paper towels before Aneel reached them. Saira tried to keep Kiara from eating the vomit.

"Oh, nasty," Rita said, shuddering.

This was the girl Tyler had been head over heels for in law school? He dodged a bullet, for sure.

"She probably ate something she shouldn't have." Saira cleaned up and stood with Kiara in her hands. "I should take her home, just in case she does it again."

"I'll go with you," Tyler said.

"No," she said. Maybe too quickly. "Stay, enjoy. I'll take care of Kiara."

"Tyler. Go home with your fiancée," his mother ordered.

Tyler looked at her and shrugged. *Mom's orders.*

Saira shrugged one shoulder. *Whatever.*

* * *

Thankfully, Kiara did not vomit in the Uber. In fact, she passed out in Saira's arms as if nothing had happened. Tyler was quiet, which was fine, since she was still processing her brother's anger.

It was almost too much. Her heart rate increased slightly, so she held Kiara closer and focused on the puppy and how good she felt in her arms. Tyler turned to her. "Are you okay?"

She nodded.

Tyler's phone buzzed and he looked at it. "Aneel is not happy. Tell me again why we aren't just telling him the truth. You and Kiara can stay in my apartment regardless."

"He just came barreling in there, all pissed because I didn't tell him all the details of my love life. He was out of line." She glanced out the window at the passing lights. "Then he was mean to you."

"Fake details." He sighed. "But, yes." He looked out the window and Saira could see that he had been hurt by Aneel's words.

"It's okay to be angry at him," she said softly.

"I know. I am, believe me," Tyler said, and she heard the edge in his voice. "We could end all this by telling him."

She narrowed her eyes at him. "Do you really want to tell him? Or would you rather he suffer thinking we're together and that we should not be?"

"You're being petty." He smirked at her and she noticed again how handsome he was. Way better-looking than Colton.

"I know and I don't care." She was too angry to be reasonable. "He can just be pissed. He doesn't like that I see our dad, and now he doesn't like that we're engaged. I'm tired of him thinking he gets to decide who is in my life."

Tyler said nothing. They arrived at his building and entered the apartment without further discussion. She took Kiara into his room and lay her on the bed. The puppy did not budge.

Tyler stood in the door. She entered the bathroom and got

ready for bed. She came out to find Tyler changed into shorts and a T-shirt, making up his bed on the sofa.

"We have shared a bed before," Saira said. "It's no big deal."

"We were like ten." He looked at her from underneath his lock of hair and Saira did a double take. When did Tyler get sexy?

"Whatever. Fine, I'll take the sofa then, since I'm responsible for all of this."

"Like I would let the queen of messes sleep on my white sofa."

"I'm not messy!" Her indignation was unwarranted. She was messy. If there was a way to spill or drop or otherwise mess a thing up, she found it. She had inadvertently gotten paint on a white sofa cushion when she had stayed here last time. Tyler had had to buy a whole new $200 cushion.

She glanced at him again in his sleeping T-shirt, a faded one from the private high school he'd attended, courtesy of his dad. No way Tracy Auntie could have sent him there on her social worker's salary. He had filled out considerably since high school, so the T-shirt, which had been loose when he was a teenager, was now hugging shoulder muscles and chest muscles and biceps. She suspected he only had on a T-shirt because she was in the room. Maybe he only had shorts on because she was in the room as well.

She dropped her gaze to his shorts and caught herself. She shook her head to dispel the image of Tyler sleeping naked. What was going on with her? Tyler had always been family— someone she trusted, someone she knew she could rely on. Not someone she fantasized about.

Aneel and Tyler were like brothers. Aneel was more of a brother to Tyler than the jackass Colton. They even fought like brothers. She suspected that the things Aneel had said today hurt Tyler more than he was letting on precisely for that reason.

Who was Tyler to her, then? To be sure, she'd never thought of him as a brother herself. She used to think he was the coolest kid *ever* when they were little. She distinctly remembered a phase in which everything Tyler said was fact and truth. She might have been around seven years old. She had been enthralled with the blue of his eyes. Not that she hadn't seen blue eyes before, but his had seemed more intense, more *blue* than the others she had seen.

"What?" he asked, facing her.

"What?" she repeated.

"You're staring at me, and not speaking. My experience tells me that is not a good sign. You have something to say, might as well say it." He gave her a half grin and fixed those intense blue eyes on her.

It was as if he knew she had been thinking about his eyes. She shook her head and shrugged. "Nothing." She pulled back the covers. "Just, your eyes are nicer than Colton's."

Tyler just stared at her. "Thank you?"

"I'm serious. Colton is not better than you. He makes you feel like he is, but he's not."

"The spare," Tyler said. "I feel like the spare."

Saira stared at him. "You are not the spare, Tyler Hart. You are the sweetest, kindest man I know."

Tyler looked at her like he'd never heard anyone say that before. Maybe he hadn't. "We should sleep."

She nodded and got into bed. *Tyler's bed.* Whatever. It had been Tyler's bed yesterday too, and she'd survived sleeping in it then, even though the sheets smelled like him. Cucumber Dove soap and the remnants of his musky aftershave. Or maybe cologne, he had been sporting a light scruff for a while.

"Aneel loves you, you know." She spoke softly into the dark.

"Yes." Tyler sighed. "I'm just not good enough for his sister, it turns out."

"Well, then I guess it's a good thing that we're faking," Saira said.

Tyler was silent for a moment. "Right," he agreed, but his words lacked enthusiasm. "Of course."

Silence again, during which she thought maybe Tyler had fallen asleep.

"Sai?"

"Hmm?"

"I won't tell him." His voice was low and calm, but Saira caught the vestiges of pain her brother had caused.

She almost sat up in bed. "Why?"

"Because you asked me not to."

This was the first time he had chosen her over Aneel. He must really be angry with Aneel.

"That's new."

Tyler made a grunting sound that indicated it wasn't so new. "Though for the record," he added, "I think we should just tell him."

"What about Colton?" she asked, yawning.

"After he leaves, we'll just say we broke up."

She pursed her lips together. "Perfect. We'll tell my brother, when we tell yours." She curled up inside the comforter that smelled like him and turned away. "Tomorrow is a workday."

Chapter Sixteen

Tyler

The sofa was not conducive to sleep. Tyler woke groggy and exhausted when his alarm went off in the morning. He opened one eye to find his bed neatly made, and no sign of the Beast. It was only seven o'clock. His first meeting was not until 9:00 a.m. If he skipped the gym, he could get a whole hour of extra sleep.

On his bed.

Yes! He slid into his bed, immediately noticing that it smelled of Saira's floral lotion. He set an alarm for an hour and a half—he could eat after the meeting—and closed his eyes as he sank into the comfort of his bed.

"Tyler!" Saira's sharp voice came to him along with the gorgeous aroma of cardamom, cinnamon and clove. Chai.

He bolted up in bed. "What?" An incessant beeping was coming from somewhere.

"You have a meeting in ten minutes." She tapped his phone, and the beeping stopped.

"No. I have a meeting at nine. It's only seven."

She put his phone in his face. 8:50 a.m.

He jumped out of bed. "I didn't hear the alarm."

"Why did you move over to the bed?"

He was still dazed with sleep. "What? I was so tired." Still groggy, he moved past her to the bathroom and started brushing his teeth.

"Why?"

He spat and rinsed. "Sofa. Too short." He moved past her again. Why was she constantly in his way? Though she was still holding the chai.

"Is that for me?" He looked down at the mug, hopeful.

She held it out to him.

"You're the best." He sipped the warm chai and started to come to life. "No matter what names Aneel calls you behind your back."

She rolled her eyes as he grabbed a clean pressed shirt and a tie.

"I have this meeting in two minutes…"

She held up her hands. "You're welcome."

"Thanks. You're the best." He leaned down and kissed her cheek without thinking.

She froze. Her eyes darted to his face. And she…flushed?

It wasn't the first time he had kissed her cheek. True he did not do it all the time, but it had definitely happened before—and yet this was the first time she'd looked at him like that.

He pulled back and she looked away.

"Your…meeting," she said as she backed her way out the door.

"Right," he said, momentarily stymied. He watched her leave, trying to make sense of what had happened.

"Your meeting!" she called from the other side of the door.

Right. He turned on his computer and knotted his tie as he logged on.

He finished his morning session of meetings, ever grateful for the chai that Saira had given him before she left. There had been no sign of the Beast, so she must have gone with Saira.

At 1:00 p.m., he emerged, still in his sleep shorts and a dress shirt. He loosened the tie as he approached his kitchen to forage for food. The sun lit the apartment from the floor-to-ceiling window. He glanced out at the view.

"Your view is incredible," Colton said from the kitchen. "Even from our room. I bet you never get tired of it."

Tyler turned. "We don't." He walked into the kitchen. "You making sandwiches?"

"Yes," Colton said. "You hungry?"

"I could eat."

"Here." He slid a sandwich in Tyler's direction.

Tyler did not remember ever getting food from Colton. Usually it was every man for themselves around Colton.

"Did you poison it?" Legit question.

Colton laughed like it was a great joke. "Of course not. Can't a guy make his brother a sandwich?"

Tyler eyed him. "Yes. But you don't do that."

"Do what?"

"Things for other people." *Things for Tyler.*

Colton stopped slicing onions and fixed his gaze on Tyler and pursed his lips. Tyler waited for the put-down, the snarky remark that defined the Colton he knew.

"I'm not that guy. Not really." Colton's voice was serious as he resumed his chopping. "Not anymore, anyway."

Tyler wasn't buying it. This was Colton. *Mr. Dad Picked Me.* "Since when? I have distinct memories of you stealing my food and teasing me. And we were not children when it happened. We were like twenty-five."

"Okay. I'm working on not being that guy anymore." He pushed the plate closer to Tyler as he bit into his own sandwich. "At least not with you."

Tyler had picked up the sandwich, but now his jaw dropped. "Where is my real twin?"

Colton laughed and swallowed. Tyler finally bit into his sandwich. It was really good. But last he checked, he did not have the ingredients for this sandwich. "Did you go shopping?"

"Duh. You have nothing in here." He pressed his lips together in irritation. "They have grocery delivery, you know."

"Yeah, but for just one—" Tyler stopped himself because technically Saira "lived" here now "—or two things, doesn't seem worth it."

"What do you eat?"

"Aneel fills my freezer." It was the truth. Aneel usually did fill his freezer, so Tyler almost never had to cook for himself. "This is a very good sandwich. Thank you." Tyler was cautious. "Did you spit in it?"

"I'm not twelve."

"I knew it!" Tyler grinned and pointed a finger at Colton. "You did spit in my sandwich that time."

Colton took another bite of his sandwich but chuckled. "We were kids."

They ate in silence for a bit.

Tyler glanced at Colton. "Why the big change? What's going on?"

Colton shrugged.

"Is it because of Rita?" Tyler asked as he continued to inhale his sandwich.

"Well, yeah. She does make me want to be…better," Colton admitted with what Tyler could only describe as a shy smile. His brother was *blushing*!

"She makes you want to stop spitting in other people's food? She's a keeper," Tyler deadpanned.

"Just so you know, I had no idea that *she* was the 'Rita from law school,'" Colton said.

"Would it have mattered?"

"Yes. It would have mattered." Colton met his eyes and his expression was *earnest*. "Rita has this huge family and they're super close. Seeing them together…it got me thinking…about family."

Tyler stared at him, not sure what to make of it all. But Colton sounded genuine. "What about you and Saira?" Colton asked as he finished up his last bite.

"What about us?" Tyler was suddenly interested in the crumbs on his plate.

"You getting that ring or what?" Colton asked.

"No rush."

"Hey." The front door opened and Aneel walked in, bringing with him what Tyler could only think of as a dark cloud.

Tyler swallowed and stood, eyeing Aneel. Aneel's shoulders were tight, his jaw set, nothing like the relaxed and happy man Tyler knew. "Colton. Good to see you. Again." Aneel was polite yet terse.

"You too. It was…fun…last night." Colton stood and gathered both plates.

Aneel stared at him for a minute. "Not really."

"Right." Colton placed the dishes in the sink. "Well, on that note, I have a meeting, and you two need… Anyway, there's an extra sandwich." Colton nodded at the sandwich left on the cutting board and went to his room.

"What the hell are you doing with my sister?" Aneel wasted no time, nor did he waste energy trying to be diplomatic.

Tyler stood and put the extra sandwich away as a way to stall while he thought of how to defuse the situation. Aneel was pissed about something based on a lie—but he'd promised Saira he wouldn't tell Aneel the truth. Therefore, the best thing would be to not engage.

It didn't work.

He couldn't stop wondering, what if he really had been with Saira? Was this the reaction they were to expect from Aneel?

Tyler narrowed his eyes at Aneel, barely containing the hurt and betrayal he felt at Aneel's words from the night before. "You know, all these years, I considered you nothing less than a brother, someone who had my back. What I did not know was how little you thought of me."

"That's not true. You are a brother to me—"

"Save it. I heard exactly what you said last night. That I'm not good enough for Saira. That I'm a man-whore who doesn't understand commitment." Tyler was not the type to raise his voice. He did the opposite. The angrier he got, the quieter his voice became. As if he were a live volcano that could erupt at any moment. "The truth comes out." He fixed his gaze on Aneel, anger and pain seething from his pores as he stepped closer to Aneel. "I have no desire to tell you anything about me and Saira. Except this." Tyler stared at Aneel and told him the truth. "I would burn down the world for her."

Aneel stared at Tyler. "You hurt her—"

"Stop right there. How dare you even think that I would ever do anything that would hurt Saira?" Tyler was letting loose the volcano.

"Are you kidding me? You're the one who is always advocating to let her to do risky things."

"I advocate for her to live her life. You can't keep her in a bubble forever."

"You let her on the monkey bars with a broken arm." Aneel waved his arm at Tyler.

"We were twelve!"

"I know she came to your dorm more than once when she was drunk in high school."

"I took care of her."

"But you didn't tell me, and you didn't tell her to stop."

"Why would I do that? She was having fun, like a normal kid."

Aneel shook his head. "No. She is my sister, and she's my responsibility. I'm all she has."

"She has me too." Tyler sighed as his heart broke. "But it seems you don't see that as a good thing." He waved a hand, dejected. "Just go, Aneel, before this gets any worse." Though he could not imagine how it could get worse than your best friend thinking you would never be good enough for his sister, who you already happened to be in love with.

Chapter Seventeen

Saira

"**S**aira." Lin Irving's hushed voice and elbow jab to the ribs beckoned her from her thoughts. Saira turned to glare at Lin.

"What?" she whispered.

Lin's dark eyes widened as she nodded her head toward the professor.

"I believe, Ms. Rawal, that Ms. Irving is trying to tell you that I asked a question. It seems your thoughts are elsewhere today," her professor stated.

"Sorry, I...would you mind repeating the question?"

"I would in fact." She turned to another student and nodded.

Saira turned to Lin with a look of apology. Lin just rolled her eyes. Saira and Lin had met on the first day of veterinary school. Saira had been excited to start vet school but was a bit overwhelmed by all of it. Lin seemed so completely sure of herself. Especially when she sat down next to Saira in their first class on the second day of the term and pronounced herself Saira's friend.

"I watched you yesterday. You're not like all the other students here, are you?" Lin had said with a confidence that Saira admired.

Saira had no idea what she was talking about.

"When did you graduate from college?"

"A couple years ago."

Lin grinned. "Me too."

Saira had returned the smile. "I needed time to save up."

"I feel that. I needed time to grow up." Lin had laughed.

"That too," chuckled Saira.

"Got any pets?" Lin had asked.

"Can't. No pets in our building." Saira had sighed.

"Same," Lin said had with a heavy sigh. "Some vets we'll make."

They became friends almost instantly, though mostly due to Lin's persistence. Saira was forever grateful.

The bell saved them. Lin stood and gathered her bag. "Where were you?" She raised a nicely manicured eyebrow.

"Right here," Saira said, though she knew exactly what Lin was asking.

"Fine don't tell me. But I have never seen you so preoccupied in class." Lin walked out, Saira behind her. "Not since that jackass Dhruv." Lin spun around, her straight dark flipping behind her. "It's a guy, isn't it? That's what you're thinking so hard about."

"It's not a guy," Saira said. *Tyler* did not qualify as a *guy*. Well, he hadn't until she saw him in his sleep clothes last night. Clothes that were too tight on him.

Saira looked at her friend. She could tell Lin. Lin was safe and nonjudgmental. But telling Lin would make it all too real.

Saira squinted in the sun as they walked outside. She fumbled and found her sunglasses. The air was warm, and the sun felt great after being in the AC all morning. "I need a new apartment—fast. Kiara is going to destroy Tyler's place."

"I can't believe you moved in with Hot Tyler again." Lin smirked at her.

"That's not really his name."

"Says you. I don't know why you don't hit that. That man is fine!" Lin spoke with authority.

"Is he? I hadn't noticed." A small voice in her head shouted out, *Liar!*

Lin chuckled again. "Girl, *I* noticed, and I'm married to a *woman*! For someone as smart as you, Miss Number One in Class, you are completely out of touch with your feelings."

Saira rolled her eyes as they walked and sighed heavily.

"You can roll your eyes all you want, but ever since you stayed with Hot Tyler—"

"Not his name."

"—a few months ago, you get all flushed whenever he's around or I say his name," Lin finished as if Saira hadn't spoken.

Clearly telling Lin about her current "fake engagement" with Tyler was not going to help when it came to getting her friend to stop teasing her. "Lora is super sweet to watch Kiara for me." Saira changed the subject to one she knew Lin loved.

Lin lit up at the mention of her wife. "She loves animals. As soon as I lock down a job, we're selling the townhome and getting a house with a huge yard and then having all the pets we want."

They approached the small house where Lin and Lora lived with their three-year-old son, Andrew. The door opened as they approached. Lora, who was usually quite put together and calm, had stains all over her clothes, and her usually immaculate ponytail was askew. Lin kissed her quickly on the lips as they entered.

Lora took the kiss and smiled. "Hi, honey."

"I'm home," said Lin. Both women giggled at their little joke greeting. No matter how many times she heard it, it always filled Saira's heart with warmth. Lin and Lora were the cutest. She wanted love like that. Lora turned to throw a glare Saira's way as Kiara came bounding over.

"That is no dog. That is a beast," Lora said as Saira picked Kiara up.

"Yeah. That's what Tyler calls her. The Beast."

Lora's eyes widened and she grinned. "Oooh. Hot Tyler?"

Saira narrowed her eyes at Lora. "Aren't you two married? To each other?"

"Don't put us in a box, Saira," Lora said. "We can appreciate a good-looking man without wanting to sleep with him. It just means we have working eyes. And my working eyes tell me that your puppy is a monster. She has destroyed the house. It would be easier to move at this point."

Saira cringed. "I'll send over dinner as a thank-you. Or a cleaning service?"

"Dinner would be great," Lora said. "We usually get food from your sister-in-law, but somebody forgot to place the order this week." Lora fixed her pretty brown eyes on Lin.

"Where's the baby?" Lin asked, pointedly ignoring her wife.

Saira grinned.

"Sleeping," Lora answered.

"Okay. Then I'll just go with Saira and walk the Beast, so you can nap. Be back in a few."

"You're the best." Lora leaned up and kissed Lin. "Take your time. He just went down."

"Can I help you clean?" Saira asked.

Lora shook her head. "Don't worry about it."

Saira set down the now-squirming Kiara and fastened her leash. Lin fell into step beside her.

"So, tell me more about moving in with Hot Tyler," Lin said as Kiara stopped to poop. "Why didn't you go to your brother's when your landlord kicked you out?"

"Aneel just got married."

"You could have come here."

"It was late—I didn't want to disturb you. Although maybe I should have put more thought into what I might be disturbing by going to Tyler…"

Lin perked up, sensing juicy gossip. "What happened?"

"He wasn't home, and he wasn't answering my texts, so I let myself in and tried to settle Kiara. Then he showed up with a date." A stunning woman who he had planned on having sex with.

Lin widened her eyes. "The date, she left after she saw you, right?"

"Yes." Saira shrugged.

Lin smirked and nodded. "Uh-huh."

Saira walked Lin home, grateful for the beautiful day, and arranged for a food delivery service to bring them dinner. Then she headed for home—Tyler's place.

"Hey," Tyler said as she entered with Kiara under one arm and her bags in the other. "Where was the Beast today?"

Tyler moved toward her, taking the bags. First the lunch bag, then the computer bag, then Kiara's bag. Saira was finally left with only Kiara.

"Lora watched her," Saira confessed as she removed her shoes and put Kiara on the ground. She made a beeline for Tyler, wagging her tail. Saira grinned. *Good choice, little one. He's a good guy.*

Tyler's eyes widened as he emptied her lunch bag. "You put that sweet woman through a day with the Beast?"

"Lora's pretty tough," Saira countered. She plopped herself onto the sofa. "But Kiara did a number on her. Still, I figured you had enough on your plate as it was."

"Aneel came by." Tyler's face dropped as he came over and sat down beside her, Kiara now in his arms. This dog was getting spoiled.

She flicked her gaze to Tyler's. "Yeah?"

"He's pretty upset." Tyler's mouth was set in a line. Not an expression he wore often.

"What about you?" she asked softly. Aneel didn't get angry like this often, but she knew Tyler was hurt.

Tyler landed his gaze on her. "Don't worry about me."

"He said some pretty nasty things about you last night."

"You noticed, huh?" Tyler smirked.

"Everyone noticed."

Tyler did not respond. She knew from experience that meant he did not wish to discuss it any further.

"Did Colton leave?" A change of subject was in order.

Tyler shook his head. "They are hunkering down. He made me a sandwich."

Saira's mouth gaped open. "Did he spit in it?"

"He says he didn't. It was really good."

"Well, okay. They're really not in a hurry to rush back to *the city*?"

"Doesn't seem that way." He shrugged. "Something must be going on. I just have to wait until Colton's ready to tell me what it is."

Chapter Eighteen

Tyler

Tyler's legs hung off the end of the couch. He pulled them in and tried getting comfortable in the fetal position, but while that was not bad for the legs, now his back was twisted and his head hit the arm. He sat up and fluffed his pillow for the tenth time. Maybe he should try the living room sofa. It was longer. But if Colton saw him, he'd have to explain it. Maybe he could just dangle his legs—

"I can hear you tossing and turning," Saira said.

"I'm fine."

"I thought Boy Scouts could sleep anywhere," she taunted him.

"We can. But that rule ends when we turn thirty-two apparently."

"We can share the bed," Saira said.

Tyler froze. "That's okay." He preferred navigating this tiny couch to navigating sharing a bed with Saira.

"What's the big deal? We have shared a bed before."

"You keep saying that and I keep reminding you that we were children at the time, and as such were a lot smaller." Right. Because the reason they couldn't share a bed was because they were too big now. Not because the thought of sleeping next to Sai was the sweetest form of torture there was.

"So now we're not." She sighed. "Up to you. But work is

going to be rough if you don't get a good night's sleep, right? Aren't you tired?"

He really was. This sofa was not meant for sleeping on. "Fine. But don't kick me."

"As if." He knew she rolled her eyes even if he couldn't see it in the dark.

He stood from the sofa and swore he heard something click in his back. He gingerly got in the bed, trying to take up as little space as possible and not get anywhere near Sai. Luckily, Saira was squarely on one side, with Kiara at her feet in her little dog bed.

"Some Boy Scout you are," she teased.

"Shut up," he countered. He knew she was smiling, because he was too.

He settled in, being sure to keep at least two feet of distance between them. He swore he could feel her body heat anyway, and the floral scent of her shampoo drifted to him. He made himself a blanket cocoon around his body, so he couldn't accidentally touch her. He lay there for five minutes, willing sleep to come.

Maybe he should go back to the sofa.

"Tyler." Saira spoke with clearly no clue as to his grand discomfort.

"Hm?"

"Whatever happened between you and Rita?"

"It didn't work out," Tyler responded. "I told you."

"Yes. But you never said why it didn't work out."

Tyler stared at the ceiling. *Because Rita figured out that I was in love with you.* "Sometimes things are just not meant to be."

"Did you love her?"

Tyler sighed. "I thought so at the time. But I think it was the kind of love you learn from, you know?"

"What did you learn?" Saira's voice was soft, nonjudgmental.

"I don't know. Nothing concrete. Maybe just that Rita was not the one for me. Hers was not the soul that spoke to mine." Only he and Rita knew the details of their breakup. Rita had been kind and gentle. She told him that she knew Tyler had feelings for Saira, and she did not want to be second to anyone. She was right. "Rita taught me that everyone wants to be wanted. Everyone wants to be number one to someone."

"Who broke it off?"

"Why the sudden interest in Rita?" He turned his head toward her. A sliver of light came in from above the blinds on her side. Tyler took in her silhouette. She was staring at the ceiling.

"Well, don't you think it's the kind of thing that your fiancée would know? And now that I think about it, we haven't really ever talked about her since…well since that night that Dhruv broke it off with me."

"You were pretty upset that night," he said softly. Instinct had him lifting his hand as if to caress her face. Reason had him fisting his hand and putting it back down at his side. On that night, Sai had thrown things, ranted and finally cried her heart out on his shoulder.

"So were you." She turned her head toward him.

He couldn't see her eyes. "I didn't like seeing you hurting. That was what had me upset, more than my breakup with Rita. It wasn't a big fight or anything like that. She just wanted different things from what I could offer her. She wanted someone who would burn down the world for her. Someone who would love her completely. She deserves that. But that guy was not me."

Saira nodded in the dark. "I was so distraught over Dhruv I hardly even listened to you. Which is why I don't even know who dumped who." She made eye contact. "I'm sorry about that. You needed a friend, and you got a hot mess."

"Your heart was broken. Rita and I… Well, she was braver than me. I would have kept moving forward with her and it would have been a disaster. She was tough enough to call it when she did."

"But now she's marrying Colton." Saira made a gagging sound, and he chuckled as he rolled onto his back.

"True, it does feel awkward. But they're so happy."

"Well, she and Colton absolutely cannot see you single. He would jump at the chance to rub it in." She rolled over onto her back.

The Colton he had known his entire life had never missed an opportunity to one-up him. It really did not feel like Colton was in that place right now, but he wasn't completely sure he could trust this new version of his twin. With that, on top of being in a fight with Aneel, he felt the need to play it safe. "Truth."

Silence floated in the darkness and Tyler thought Saira had fallen asleep, when he felt her turn toward him again.

"That's pretty intense," she said softly. "'Burn down the world for her.' You ever think you could love someone like that?"

Tyler turned his head to find Saira's eyes fixed on him. "If I did, she would be it for me. The One."

Chapter Nineteen

Saira

Saira had a rare early finish at the clinic the next day. She was interning at this clinic as part of her requirements, but they had already offered her a full-time vet job that could begin as soon as her boards scores came in.

She had taken the boards in April, and they generally sent out the score in late June. A passing score on the board exam was required in order to be a licensed veterinarian. No license, no job.

Maryland was granting them a proper spring this year, so Saira considered going home and changing out of her navy scrubs and into a dress. A quick glance at her phone told her she hadn't gotten off *that* early. She enjoyed a quick walk to the restaurant where she was meeting her father for dinner.

Yogesh was waiting in a booth when she arrived. She ordered a white wine; he ordered his standard, club and lime.

She glanced at her wine as the waiter put it on the table. *Would she abuse it the way her father had?* No. She knew better.

"So—" he met her eyes "—your brother actually contacted me. Well, he texted. But still." Yogesh just looked at her, waiting for her to say something.

Saira waited. Had her brother reconsidered his feelings toward their father? Hope lightened her mood.

"You're engaged?" He raised his eyebrows.

Her stomach fluttered, and hope for her brother and father melted away. This lie was getting bigger and bigger. "Yes."

"You never even mentioned that you were dating." His tone was calm, curious, not accusatory. Actually, it reminded her of the way her brother spoke when he wasn't being a complete jerk.

She took the defensive anyway. "I can't tell you everything in a few hours a week."

He sighed. To his credit, he smiled a little and nodded. He looked almost…amused. "That's true, but still. Relationships—serious ones—usually come up."

She did not know him well enough to discern if he was being sarcastic, or if he was implying her relationship with Tyler wasn't serious.

Yogesh inhaled. When he realized that she would not be forthcoming with further information, he simply asked, "Well, who is he?"

"His name is Tyler. He and I grew up together. His mom and Mom were like besties and so we spent a lot of time together, while growing up. He and Aneel have always been like brothers." She paused and smiled. "He's my family." It was true. Tyler was her family. The loss of her mother had never decreased the amount of time they spent with Tracy Auntie and Tyler. It had never even occurred to Saira that there could ever be a time when Tyler wasn't around.

"But the truth is… I never felt like he was a brother. He was just Tyler. Solid, steady, always there." She had never really vocalized her feelings about Tyler. Giving them voice somehow made her dig deeper to see what was there. "I had a serious boyfriend a few years ago and when he broke up with me, I was devastated. I had thought he was the one, but nope." She glanced at Yogesh. He was watching her intently, no judgment on his face. His brow was furrowed in concern, which she found touching and annoying all at once.

"Tyler was the one I went to. He sat up all night with me while I threw things, ranted, paced and finally cried. He had also just gotten out of a long-term relationship, but he never let

on how much that had hurt him. Not that night, for sure. No…
that night he was there for me and only me." She was now simply reciting, she realized. There was almost no pain associated
with her past relationship any longer. Huh.

"Was it after that that you began to look at him with different eyes?" Yogesh asked softly.

Saira snapped her gaze to him. "No, actually. I was in no
emotional state to be open to anyone new. No." She played with
her drink. "I didn't start to see Tyler differently until recently."
Very recently. Like right now.

Not true, the little voice in the back of her head niggled.

"It is clear from your face, that you are quite smitten and happy.
So congratulations. I wish you all the best. I'm sure Aneel will
come around." Yogesh smiled. That was easier than expected.

"Thank you. Did Aneel seem angry in his text?" Saira tried
to sound nonchalant, but she was sure she failed.

"He was…unhappy that he was out of the loop and concerned that you make the right decision." Yogesh knew how
to be diplomatic. "Does Aneel have any reason to be unhappy
with this union?"

Saira sighed and leaned in. "My brother is unhappy whenever I do something he doesn't think I should do. That's the
only reason why he is unhappy with my engagement." Saying it out loud made the pain of it more intense. What if this
was for real? What if she and Tyler really loved each other and
wanted to get married? Was this how Aneel would react? Saira
was lost in this awful thought so she didn't hear Yogesh until
he repeated his question.

"Saira? Do I get to meet him?"

"Oh. Um. Well, uh…sure. At some point."

"Nothing formal, just a quick hello. I'd like to see the man
who has clearly stolen my daughter's heart." He grinned at her,
looking like an older version of her brother.

He really had no idea who she was if he thought she was really smitten with Tyler Hart—or that Tyler wanted a romance with her. She had felt Tyler's discomfort as he lay next to her last night. He had not wanted to share a bed with her. No, there was clearly no chemistry between them. Good thing they wouldn't have to fake it for much longer. Colton and Rita would be gone soon, and then they'd find a way out of this farce, which she had now included Yogesh in.

"Hey." Tyler's familiar deep voice startled her so she nearly jumped out of her seat. That's why her heart hammered in her chest.

No other reason.

"Hey?" She turned. "What are you doing here?" A smile popped onto her face just at the sight of him. He had on a T-shirt and khaki shorts for the pleasantly warm spring day. He ran his fingers through his hair as it flopped over one eye. Her heart rate came back to normal. He grinned at her and it rocketed up again.

"Just taking Kiara for a walk. And I saw you here." He picked up the puppy and held her like a football. Kiara seemed very content. He widened his eyes at her and flicked his gaze to Yogesh.

"Oh, Tyler. This is my…this is Yogesh Rawal. My father," she stammered out.

Tyler widened his grin and extended a hand. "Nice to meet you, sir."

"You wouldn't happen to be the Tyler who is also her fiancé?" Yogesh shook Tyler's hand and a smile spread across his face.

She felt Tyler hesitate and tense next to her. She leaned into him. "Word gets around."

Tyler nodded as he shook her father's hand. "Guilty as charged."

Yogesh waved a hand at the empty chair. "Please join us."

"Oh, that's very kind of you. I would—" Tyler started to sit. Saira pinched what she could reach of his leg under the table. He startled a bit but did a smooth pivot. "Love to, except for the fact that I have a bunch of calls starting in ten minutes. Thank you, Mr. Rawal, but Kiara and I are just on a quick break. I will most definitely take a rain check."

"Quite understandable." Yogesh smiled. "In fact—" he looked at Saira "—our time is about up now, isn't it?"

She nodded. "Until next time."

"I look forward to it." Yogesh stood. "You are welcome to join us whenever you wish, as long as Saira has given her blessing, of course."

"That sounds great. Thank you," Tyler said.

Saira waited for Yogesh to leave. Then she stood and turned to Tyler. "Thanks. I can take her."

Tyler rubbed his leg. "Easy with the pinching." He handed her the leash and gently set Kiara on the ground.

Saira shook her head. "You can't sit down and chat up my dad."

"He wanted to meet your fiancé," Tyler insisted.

"Fake fiancé." She rolled her eyes as they started walking the two blocks to his place.

"She's done her business, but her poop was looser than normal," Tyler updated her.

Saira furrowed her brow. "We haven't changed her food. Maybe it's from the new treats?"

She paused as she took in the fact that Tyler had noticed the consistency of Kiara stools. It wasn't really the kind of detail anyone but a concerned pet parent would notice.

"Well, I just got her these organic sweet potato treats from that pet store." He held up a bag and tilted his head in the direction of the upscale pet store that was half a block away. "Maybe we should try those instead?"

Saira stared at him a moment. "Yeah. Okay." She paused. "You know that place is overpriced. You could likely buy those treats online for a lot less."

"Well, yes." Tyler nodded. "But this way we have them

today." The sun was nowhere near setting and the warmth was wonderful.

They made it up to his condo, and Saira held her breath as he opened the door, waiting to see what havoc Kiara had wreaked this time.

The place was—in order. Except for Kiara's dog bed, there was no evidence of a dog, let alone the destructive beast that was Kiara.

"You didn't have to clean before I got home. I can clean up Kiara's messes." Saira turned to him. The sun was coming through the large windows, lighting the condo beautifully.

"I didn't." Tyler grinned. "I moved my meetings to when you got home, and I spent the day with Kiara." He bent and unclicked her leash. "Kiara," he said firmly, "sit." He held up his fist in the air. The puppy looked at him for a moment. Tyler did not move.

She sat.

Tyler gave her a treat and tousled the top of her head. "Good girl," he said in a tone that could only be described as baby talk. "You were right. She just needed some training."

Tyler Hart with a puppy was just about the cutest thing Saira had ever seen. Her heart warmed and thudded in her chest. "I… I can't believe you spent time training her. How did you know what to do?"

"You left some of your books out. There was a basic dog training one among them." He shrugged.

"So you spent the whole day working with her? Instead of lawyering?"

"Well—" he checked his phone "—I have to go be a lawyer in ten minutes and I still have to change my shirt. So you're up." He walked away toward his room. "We're working on 'place' right now," he called as he removed his T-shirt, revealing his muscular bare back.

Hot Tyler, indeed.

Chapter Twenty

Tyler

Tyler put on his dress shirt and tie and clicked the Zoom link just in time for his 5:30 p.m. meeting. He sat in meetings with the west coast clients for a couple hours, then spent time catching up on paperwork and emails. By the time Tyler finished up it was close to 10:00 p.m. That's what he got for being a lawyer and delaying his day. Though rather than exhausted, he was surprisingly pumped.

He came out to the family room to find Saira and Kiara snuggled up and asleep on his sofa. Well, at least this sofa was comfortable enough to sleep on for Saira who was at least six inches shorter than him. He indulged in a moment of just looking at her. She had released her curls from their ponytail prison and had spread them over the throw pillow almost in a frame around her face. Her lips were full and plush, and in the innocence of sleep, it was hard to recall that Saira could have an acerbic tongue. She was so beautiful; it made his heart ache.

He did not remember the moment he fell in love with her, but he longed for the moment that he would fall *out* of love with her. Because one thing was certain: She would never see him as anything other than the guy she grew up with.

Tyler was draping a blanket over Saira and Kiara when the door lock clicked and Colton and Rita entered. Before he could shush them, Kiara woke and ran over to them with a bark and wag of her tail.

Saira sat up, groggy, but smiled as Kiara tried to jump up to greet Colton and Rita.

Tyler commanded Kiara with, "Off," but Rita had already picked her up for a cuddle. Clearly even Rita could not resist Kiara's cuteness.

Tyler gave a heavy sigh and shook his head as he caught Saira's eye. She gave him a commiserating smile, knowing that he was annoyed that Rita had rewarded the bad behavior, undermining Tyler's training.

Saira stood. "I'm beat. I have an early day. Good night." She started to grab Kiara's leash for her nighttime walk.

"I'll get that." Tyler jumped in. Saira looked exhausted. "You go on to bed."

Saira froze and stared at him a moment.

"Damn, girl. He must really love you," Colton said.

"What does that mean?" Tyler turned on his brother.

"Tyler is not a dog person," Colton explained. "Before the… when we were little, our neighbors had a dog. Tyler was scared to death of that dog."

"He barked all the time at me, and he was huge. And I was not scared to death." Heat rushed to his face. Yes, he had been. "But whatever, that's all—"

"Tyler was so scared he wet his pants once." Colton chuckled.

Tyler was going to commit fratricide. Right now. He would be an only child. Life would be good. He narrowed his eyes. Before he could speak, Rita spoke up.

"Colton!" she chided him, her brow furrowed. "What is the matter with you? Why would you reveal something like that in front of his fiancée?"

Colton actually seemed abashed. "What? I'm sure she knows already." He turned to Saira.

Saira shook her head, but she looked angry rather than amused.

"Oh." Colton's eyes widened. Then he looked at Tyler. "Oh." He seemed to understand what he had done. "I'm sorry, I just assumed—" He turned to Saira. "In his defense, it was a pretty big mean-looking German shepherd. And we were like six years old."

Tyler raised his eyebrows. It had been a golden retriever, only half grown. But it had been mean, and they had been six at the time.

Rita grabbed her fiancé's arm, clearly agitated with him. "Come on." She shook her head in Saira and Tyler's direction. "I'm going to take him to bed before he can do further damage."

"I'm just saying it's a sign of true love, that he walks the dog," Colton said as he was led to their room. "When he used to be afraid of them."

Tyler attached the leash and took Kiara for a walk. Any exuberance he'd had before was now long gone, but he wasn't going to neglect Kiara just because he felt tired and embarrassed. When he returned to the apartment, it was dark save the pinpoint lights from the harbor visible through his window and a small night-light he kept in the kitchen. Saira was probably asleep. Thank god.

He picked up Kiara and gently placed her in her dog bed at Saira's feet before using the bathroom. The line of light from the moon that came through the blinds was just enough for him to navigate the bedroom. He was debating the sofa versus the bed when Saira spoke in the dark.

"Was it really a German shepherd?" she asked, amusement in her voice.

He sighed. "No."

"What was it?" she asked, patting the empty half of the bed beside her.

"A golden retriever. Not even fully grown. In my defense I was six and I was small for my age."

"Whatever. You were there when I peed in my pants when that snake found its way to the playground."

He chuckled as he sat down on the bed, remembering that.

"Good thing it turned out to be a garden snake." His eyes had adjusted to the dark and he now saw that Saira was lying on her side looking at him. Her hair tumbled to the side. The sheet slipped, revealing the tiny strap of her shirt and glow of her bare shoulder in the moonlight.

"Whatever. It was huge," she defended herself.

"Aren't you going to be a vet?" he questioned.

"I'm okay with snakes now, though admittedly I will not be bringing one home anytime soon."

"I should hope not. Because I was terrified of that snake and I am not a vet."

"You were terrified?" She leaned toward him, and more of the sheet slipped, revealing just the slightest curve of her breast. Tyler's breath caught and he lost focus on her words.

She was still talking. "Tyler?"

He inhaled and closed his eyes, but that didn't help to calm him down at all, because now his imagination just kicked in.

"Tyler? You okay?" Saira asked again.

"Yep. Yeah. Sorry, you were saying?" He swallowed hard.

"I was just saying that you didn't seem like you were afraid of that snake and you were like eight?"

"I was nine." He gathered himself. "Besides, you were clearly terrified, and I felt like if I let my fear show, you would only get more scared." He shrugged. Even then he had cared about how she perceived him.

She lay back down. *Thank goodness.* "Get in bed. Long day tomorrow."

He got in bed, making sure to make his little fort of blankets around him.

Silence reigned as they both seemed lost in their own thoughts.

"You're great with Kiara," she said softly and yawned. "Colton is an idiot. You are totally a dog person."

What he was, was more in love with Saira than ever.

Chapter Twenty-One

Saira

Saira woke at 6:00 a.m. the next day, while Tyler was still sound asleep. He was handsome even in sleep. His face had some scruff, which really only served to make him hotter. She resisted the urge to run her hand along his jaw.

She had to report to the clinic for 8:00 a.m. patients and wanted to get a quick run in first. Though there wasn't really anything quick about her run. Other women, like Rita, probably ran fast, light on their feet, their breath rhythmic, their sweat beaded.

Saira ran a like a wild animal. And not the graceful kind. Her steps were slow and heavy, her breath came hard and sweat literally poured from her body. Her goal was fitness and strong cardio, and on the days she didn't run, she tried to squeeze in a lifting session. Her job required her to be able to lift heavy animals from time to time and she needed to be prepared for that.

The morning was crisp but promised that Maryland humidity. She returned sweaty and hot from her run to find that Kiara had left her dog bed and was cuddled into Tyler's torso, his arm draped over the puppy. This brought a huge smile to her face. If that wasn't the cutest, sexiest—whoa! What? Stop. It was cute. That's all.

She left them to it while she made herself some eggs. She was taking ingredients from the fridge when Colton joined her in the kitchen.

"Sorry about last night," he said as he poured coffee. In all the time she had known him, he had never ever apologized for anything.

She snapped her head to him and raised disbelieving eyebrows at him before she returned her focus to the food, placing onions and bell pepper on the chopping board.

"I wasn't trying to embarrass him." Colton glanced up at her from where he was hunched over his coffee.

Saira huffed before starting her chopping. "Yet, somehow you managed it. Must be a reflex," she snarked. This was how she and Colton communicated.

"Really, I was just appreciating the fact that he loved you enough to do things he probably doesn't like." Colton's voice turned soft and earnest, and Saira heard the similarity to Tyler's. "Though I'm sure that's not all he does."

Saira sprayed the pan and added her egg mixture without saying anything. She opened the fridge and found a new bottle of her favorite hot sauce. She grinned. Not all he did, indeed.

"Want some eggs?" she asked Colton.

He grinned at her, relief playing across his face. "That'd be great. Can I help?"

She shook her head. "I'm good." She studied Colton for a minute. He did seem different. Like he wasn't trying to take up all the air in the room anymore. "So why this sudden niceness toward Tyler?" she asked as the eggs cooked.

"It's not sudden." He sipped his coffee.

She turned to give him her best withering look.

"Well, okay I haven't always been the best brother."

"No argument here." She harrumphed her agreement.

"I just…want to fix things…between us. He is my brother… and…" Something in his voice made her turn all the way around.

"Are you dying?"

"What? No." He chuckled. "No. it's nothing like that." He paused. "It's complicated." He tucked into the eggs that Saira had plated for him. "This is amazing. If you haven't poisoned mine, I'd say you and I are off to a great start."

"Just because I don't kill you with eggs, doesn't mean you and I are okay," she said, narrowing her eyes at him. "If you truly want to mend things with Tyler, I will be your biggest cheerleader. But if you mess with his head, you're going to beg me for the mercy of poisoned eggs." There was true menace in her voice, and she realized that she meant every word. This guy—brother or not—was not going to mess with Tyler on her watch. Tyler was one of the best men she knew, and he deserved nothing but the best.

"Whoa, whoa!" Tyler's voice came to them as he walked out holding Kiara like a football. "Who is killing who with eggs?" His gaze landed on her before she could change her look to nonchalance. Whatever he saw there furrowed his brow.

"No one, little brother," Colton said as he nodded at Saira. "Just getting to know your fiancée better."

"Be careful." Tyler grinned. "She bites."

Colton nodded. "Apparently."

"I can take Kiara," Saira offered.

"You have to leave in fifteen minutes, and while I love you in every iteration, *that*—" he nodded at her running outfit, which was really just leggings and an oversized T-shirt "—will not fly in the clinic. I got Kiara. You go get ready for work."

Her heart warmed and a smile appeared on her face. Without thought, she stood on her tiptoes. She intended to kiss his cheek but found her lips grazing his mouth instead. Electric current shot through her body, zinging parts of her while melting others. Her eyes closed and she leaned into him, her mind devoid of all thought as he gently pressed against her mouth before pulling back. The kiss lasted a split second, a quick peck by any standard, but Saira was dazed, convinced that time had stood still for a moment. Certainly, her body was still charged. She met his gaze and saw that the confusion in his beautiful blue eyes mirrored what she was experiencing too. Had he felt the electricity as well?

"You two have kissed before, haven't you?" Colton said, half chuckling.

"Of course we have!"

"Duh, we're engaged."

They both responded just a tad too loud and a tad too quickly.

Colton put up his hands in surrender. "Okay, okay. Just for a second there, it looked like that was the first time."

"I'm going to take Kiara out." Tyler busied himself with the dog's leash.

"I'm going to shower—clinic and all." Saira could not leave the kitchen fast enough. She could still feel Tyler's lips on hers.

Colton was more observant than she had given him credit for. It *had* been their first time kissing—no matter how accidentally.

Did she want it to be their last?

Chapter Twenty-Two

Tyler

What the hell? Had she just kissed him? No, she had clearly been going for the peck on the cheek and he, not realizing, had turned his face to her at the wrong moment. Her lips, softer, more tender than he had imagined, had rested on his in what should have been the most chaste of kisses, but the spark from that touch had zinged completely through his body. It had been unexpected and delicious, and taken all his self-control to not wrap her in his arms and kiss her properly.

He barely remembered walking Kiara and was still preoccupied with that kiss when he returned to his apartment, to find that Sai had left for school.

To distract himself, Tyler occupied himself with feeding Kiara. *Maybe we should consider fresh food instead of kibble. Might be healthier for her. Something to discuss with Saira when she had a moment. Something other than kissing.*

"You listening? Or you daydreaming about your girl?" Colton's voice interrupted his thoughts.

"Huh? Sorry I was just rethinking Kiara's food."

Colton smirked at him. "Okay. Let's call it that."

"What did you want, Colton?" Tyler let his agitation show.

Colton looked back to his room, and then turned back to Tyler. "Listen." He lowered his voice, pushing his plate away and sipping from his mug. "I have to tell you something, and I want you to know that I am not making this up."

Tyler was immediately wary. Colton had a certain love of drama. Over the years, Tyler had learned to not get too worked up about what Colton had to say.

"Spit it out, Colton." He set the bowl down in front of Kiara and then poured himself some coffee. He stirred in the creamer as Colton watched him.

"It's about Dad."

Tyler looked up. That was new.

"Something is not right at Hart Law," Colton said, his voice almost a whisper. He clearly did not want Rita to hear him.

Despite his better judgment, Tyler leaned in.

"A few months ago, I heard Dad and another man having an argument—low tones of course, but I could tell both men were agitated. They were talking about a DUI that happened years ago. I really couldn't make out the conversation, but this man was clearly trying to see where he stood."

"Was he trying to blackmail Dad? Or sue for a retrial?"

Colton shook his head. "I don't know. But the man was clearly unhappy with how Dad handled things. He said things like… I know what I did, and I paid the price. I just want to know if…something…still stands. He said something about making amends."

"Who needs to make amends? Dad? Or this other man?" Tyler's heart thudded in his chest. His Dad was a shrewd lawyer. Any lawyer who handled divorces needed to be. Sometimes, yes, a lawyer took advantage of vulnerabilities to get a better outcome for his clients. But he hadn't thought his dad was the type to do anything unethical. Tread the line sometimes, but…

"No idea. But Dad seemed agitated when he left the room." Colton's leg was pumping up and down. Dad wasn't the only one agitated.

"Did you ask him about it?"

"Absolutely. He didn't really answer. Just waved his hand."

Colton waved his hand in a dismissive gesture that was an accurate imitation of their father.

Tyler stared at his brother while a hundred different scenarios played in his mind. Colton nodded. "You're thinking about what it could all mean, aren't you?" he asked. "Yeah. Do that for a week or two and you'll be where I am now."

"Why so serious?" Rita had come out of their room, startling both of them.

Colton eyed Tyler before plastering a smile on his face and turning to her. "Good morning, sweetheart. Sleep okay?"

"Fantastic." She wrapped her arms around Colton's torso and rested her head on his chest as she turned to Tyler. "That mattress is amazing. You'll have to tell me the brand. I'm going to want it in our new place."

"You two are moving?" Tyler asked. Colton had a fabulous loft in New York, well-located, gorgeous view, all the bells and whistles Hart Law could afford, which was quite a bit.

"Yes." Colton beamed. "We want something a bit cozier. That loft is fabulous, no doubt, but it's a bit sterile." He looked at Rita and Tyler had to look away from them for a second because the love on Colton's face was almost too intimate to witness. "It doesn't feel like me anymore. It doesn't feel like who I want to be."

Tyler's jaw dropped. "Where is my real brother?"

Colton laughed. "I'm here. Honestly, I never really liked the loft. Dad bought it for me, and it seemed like the kind of place I was supposed to have, so I thought what the heck. But it's really not me. I just never had any reason to leave." He looked at Rita. "Now, I have a great reason."

Their Dad had bought that loft for Colton? Tyler tried to mask his expression, but he knew some form of anger played on it.

"What?" asked Colton.

"I didn't know Dad bought that for you," Tyler managed. He was being ridiculous. He was a grown man, did well for himself. He took pride in the fact that he had purchased this condo on his own. He didn't need a thing from his dad.

"It was part of the package with the job," Colton said slowly. "You didn't take the job—"

"I was never offered the job," Tyler said flatly.

Colton's eyes widened. He was not acting. "You were never—?"

Tyler shook his head.

"Aw, jeez. Dad can be such an asshole." Colton looked at Tyler in apology. "I had no idea. You didn't come to Hart, so I assumed you opted out."

"I never would have taken the position even if it had been offered. Everything I love is here," Tyler said.

"Well, that is certainly apparent," Colton said. "But still. I had no idea."

Tyler somehow felt closer to Colton knowing his brother actually cared enough to be upset at what their father had done. Tyler was starting to believe that he had no idea who his brother really was. He had a ton of questions for Colton, but now was not the time. Rita obviously didn't know about Colton's suspicions about their father, so he didn't press any of the matters.

"I have a meeting," Rita said. "In person. I'm hitting the shower."

"I'll join you." Colton grinned, to which Rita turned with a smirk and hurried to the shower.

Ew. But adorable. Tyler watched them go. He had never truly been jealous of Colton—they were just too different. And their father had always preferred Colton, since Colton was quite a bit like him. Tyler was softer, maybe more like his mother, and Ethan Hart did not respect soft. Tyler didn't care. He tolerated his mandatory visits to New York, but after a while his dad had figured out that Tyler would not change, and simply gave up.

Tyler had actually felt sorry for Colton, even when he bullied him. But right now, as he watched his brother look at Rita with a softness he'd never seen before and he watched Rita look at Colton with nothing but love, he found that he was jealous of Colton for the very first time ever.

It had nothing to do with the fact that Colton had Rita, the woman Tyler had dated in the past. It had everything to do with the love that they so obviously shared. It was the real deal.

That was what he wanted.

Chapter Twenty-Three

Saira

After a very full day at the clinic—and a snake as a patient—Saira walked to her car dreaming of a glass of wine on that gorgeous sofa of Tyler's and enjoying the view. Maybe she could convince him to grab some sushi. She could just picture them both on that sofa, looking at the view, maybe holding hands. Maybe leaning into each other. Maybe Tyler would lean down and kiss her neck…

No. Nope. Stop.

Saira shook her head as if she could shake that image from her mind. She got in her car and focused on answering a few school/work-related texts and emails. It must have worked, because she nearly jumped out of her skin when someone knocked on her window. It was Aneel.

She opened the window. "What the hell are you doing?" she yelled at him.

"I could ask you the same thing. Do you know how unsafe it is to sit in your car and be on your phone?" Aneel lectured her.

"Are you kidding me right now?" she nearly screeched. "Why are you here?"

"Can I get in?" he asked.

She sighed deeply and unlocked the door. Aneel jumped into the passenger seat.

"What?" She didn't even bother to try to hide her annoyance. Her heart was still pounding away.

"You're avoiding me."

"No one ever said you were dumb. Well, not to your face at least." She pulled into traffic.

"You seem pissed."

She gave him a thumbs-up.

"You're pissed at *me*?" He shook his head. "That's rich, considering that you're the one sneaking around behind my back."

"I wasn't sneaking."

"You weren't forthright."

"I do not remember you giving me the play by play on your dating life with Karina."

"This is Tyler! When did you even start having feelings for him? What was the instigator of you two dating? Was it when we were fighting and he took you in?"

Saira and Aneel had had an argument over her seeing their father. No surprise, Aneel had not wanted her to see their father and tried to lay down the law. Saira had been curious about their dad, and pissed at her brother, so she went to Tyler's.

Saira had buzzed Tyler's building in the middle of the night, her anger at Aneel a rock in her chest. Tyler let her in, no questions asked. Upon seeing him, the tears had started to flow and Tyler wrapped his arms around her and held her while she sobbed her fury into him. He asked no questions, said not one word.

Saira had felt safe in that moment. Heard, even though she hadn't spoken. And when she confided in him, Tyler listened quietly while she paced and raged.

"You want to stay here for a while?" That was all he said.

The three weeks she spent with Tyler were the first time she had been without her brother for any length of time. She missed Aneel but she had been so very tired of arguing with him over her life.

It was also the first time she and Tyler had spent any length of time together without Aneel. Tyler had been supportive and understanding and fun. Saira had thoroughly enjoyed her time with him.

There had been a moment a few days after she had begun staying there.

She had been ranting about Aneel wanting to control everything in her life—which was true.

"I mean come on. This is our dad! I know he stayed away longer than he should have, and I'm told he was horrible to Mom, but he came back now. How will we ever know his side if we shut him out? Bhaiya can do what he wants, but I'm going to see him. Maybe I get hurt, but I guess that'll be on me, then."

She had prepped herself for Tyler to take Aneel's side. To say something like "he's just looking out for you" or "he wants to be sure you don't get hurt."

Instead Tyler had looked at her with something close to admiration. He had taken a beat and looked her in the eye. She still remembered the sensation of those intense blue eyes focused on her, seeing her. "You do whatever you feel is right. If your dad hurts you, I'll be here." He had smiled softly. "This shoulder—" he pointed to his left shoulder "—is always available to you."

She had been so taken aback by his response she hadn't known what to say. She just sat there and basked in his blue-eyed gaze.

"Well maybe this shoulder." He grinned and pointed to his right shoulder. "In case the left one gets dislocated." He had chuckled and the spell was broken.

But Saira had felt something more than just gratitude toward an old friend in that moment.

"Yes." It wasn't a lie.

"That was barely six months ago! And now you're engaged? In six months?"

"I've known him my whole life." That kiss from the morning played again in her head. It had been playing in her head all day. Hence her daydreams, she supposed. "You met Karina eight months ago and you're married."

"Why didn't you say anything?" Aneel asked again, ignoring her comment.

She pulled up to his restaurant. "Because of this. Because I knew you would do this, so I kept it to myself and I made Tyler do the same."

Aneel stared at her.

"What's the big deal anyway? I mean, you know Tyler. He's part of our family already."

He just shook his head at her and got out of the car.

She watched him go in and felt a pang of regret. Maybe she should tell him the truth. He would understand her telling a lie to help Tyler. They didn't usually fight like this, and she didn't like it. But she was tired of him feeling entitled to make decisions about her life. She remembered what Tyler had said last night.

No. Aneel would have to come around.

Saira entered the condo to find only the light from the sunset coming in. No furry blur running to greet her. No lights on. No sign of anyone in the house. Her heart started to pound a bit in her chest.

She inhaled. No, everything was fine. But where was everyone? She glanced at the breakfast bar. There were dishes in the sink, and a cutting board was out with a knife and unchopped tomato. Had they left in a hurry?

Her palms started to sweat. A part of her noted that everything could have a perfectly normal explanation. And even if there had been an emergency, it would behoove her to stay calm.

There was no note, no text from Tyler—she assumed he had Kiara. Was Kiara okay? Was that why no one was home, because they took Kiara to the hospital? Or had Tyler gone to the hospital? Was something wrong with him?

Her breath became shallow. She couldn't breathe. How could she help Tyler if she couldn't breathe? She leaned on the breakfast bar to hold her up.

The pounding in her chest came faster and harder. Was she having a heart attack? What was happening? Where was everyone?

The door behind her clicked open. "Hey! You're home."

Tyler!

Saira spun and jumped into Tyler's arms, squeezing him tight.

"Hey, hey, what's going on?" Concern colored his voice as he dropped the bag in his hands and encircled his arms around her. He smelled of his soap and sunshine. His T-shirt was soft and she leaned into him, drinking up the comfort that was Tyler like he was water in a desert.

"I came home, and no one was here. I thought something had happened to Kiara or you. Or both of you." She was whining like a child, but she did not care.

"Whoa. You're shaking." He held her tight. She was aware of Kiara at their feet. "We're fine." He spoke softly into her ear. "Kiara and I went for a walk, made some friends, picked up dinner." He did not pull back from her. "You sound like you're having trouble breathing."

She nodded.

Tyler pulled back, keeping one hand rested on her as he calmly took her into the kitchen and got a small paper bag from a drawer. She started to breathe into it, and he led her over to the sofa and had her sit. Kiara jumped into her lap and curled up. Tyler stayed next to her, his hand still holding hers.

When her heart rate calmed, and she could breathe, she put down the bag and looked at him, feeling sheepish. "Sorry, I don't know what got into me."

"Looked like a mild panic attack." He said this as if he were talking about allergies. "How many have you had since the wedding?"

She was getting them a few times a week now, a bit more often than before the wedding. Kiara helped keep them manageable. If she told Tyler the truth, he might tell Aneel, argument or not. "I'm okay. Really. It's just panic attacks. They go away."

"All the time, then?" he said softly.

"Once a week." She did not need him hovering over her.

"So at least two to three times a week?" He raised an eyebrow at her.

She pursed her lips and stared at him.

"Okay." He stood and returned with water for her.

"You're not going to freak out?" she asked, taking the water. It was cool and refreshing and she instantly felt like her old self.

"No. But I think you should consider seeing someone for these." He sat down next to her so their knees were touching. She wanted to melt right back into him.

"I'm fine. I have Kiara, don't I?"

"Is that why you got a dog? Because of these attacks?" Tyler narrowed his eyes at her.

Saira shrugged. "She helps with all that."

"Sai, I really think—"

"Ty. Are you going to tell Bhaiya?" She needed to know, because if he was going to report all her happenings to Aneel, she needed to find somewhere else to stay. Tonight.

Tyler furrowed his brow, seemingly offended. "No. Of course not." He leaned closer to her. "He's my best friend, but I am not his spy."

What was Saira to him? The question was on the tip of her tongue, but she somehow managed to not blurt it out. She was afraid of the answer.

"I saw him today," she said, mostly to change the subject. She saw him sigh and hesitate before taking her lead.

"You told him the truth?"

"No. Of course not. He just wanted details about our relationship and got pissed because he didn't like the details I was giving him."

"Like what?"

"Like when did I start having feelings for you, et cetera" She looked away, suddenly having difficulty meeting his eyes.

Tyler froze for a second. If she hadn't known him so well, she might have missed it. "What else did he say?"

"Nothing. Just that he thought six months of *dating* was too fast for us to get engaged."

"What did you say?" Tyler seemed amused.

"I told him he knew Karina for less than that when he proposed and that you and I have actually known each other all our lives."

Tyler grinned. "No way to clap back to that."

She smiled. "He seemed irritated about it."

"Where did you get the six months from?"

"I told him things changed between us when I stayed here last September." She felt heat rising to her face and looked away.

"We had fun those few weeks." Tyler chuckled.

"It was all right." She smirked at him with a small eye roll.

Tyler shook his head. "You loved it."

Those weeks had been just her and Tyler. She had seen him in a different light. She had seen the man in him, rather than just the boy she had grown up with. She suspected that he had shown her a part of himself that even Aneel did not get to see. She had felt closer to him and loved it.

Maybe she developed new feelings for him, but she couldn't be sure. He was Tyler, after all. Tyler who she loved and had grown up with.

Tyler, who she now acknowledged had the most fantastic lips, in whose arms she found real comfort, who she had known her whole life, but was only now getting to really know. She flushed thinking about that kiss and she longed to repeat it.

Instead she squeezed his hand. "What did you bring for dinner?"

Chapter Twenty-Four

Tyler

"**O**ur favorite." He stood quickly and nearly ran for the bag. The way she had just looked at him, there was no doubt she had been thinking about that kiss from the morning. He was desperate to ask her what she thought about it, but he was afraid of what she would say.

"Sushi! From Sushi Queen." Her face lit up.

They had a favorite place. Just the two of them. The idea made him feel a bit giddy. "You got it." He took out the sushi and laid it out on the coffee table so they could put on a movie or something.

"About that kiss—this morning," Saira started and he nearly dropped the food.

"Yes." Did he sound nonchalant? Because that was what he was going for.

"It was nothing, right?" She was looking in his direction but avoiding his eyes.

Was she asking or telling him? He couldn't tell. Not that it mattered. He'd never be able to have her. She could have anyone she wanted; the idea of her wanting him was…well, it wasn't even an idea. "Of course. Just for show." There. He had managed nonchalant. "Colton was standing right there. So it worked."

She seemed to sag a bit—maybe in relief? And she nodded. "Of course. Made it look good to Colton."

He handed her chopsticks, and she mixed the wasabi and

soy sauce in her little bowl. Then she made a second mixture in his bowl, this one with less wasabi, and slid it over to him.

"You know how much wasabi I like?" He was slightly dumbfounded that she paid that kind of attention to him.

She frowned. "Of course. We eat sushi like three times a week. I pay attention."

It was pathetic that he grinned like a teenager and the little voice in his head was ecstatically jumping up and down singing, *She pays attention!* But he couldn't help it.

"Speaking of Colton. He thinks something is up with our dad." He dipped his spicy tuna into his mixture.

"What do you mean?" she said around her first bite.

"He overheard a heated conversation between our dad and some guy. The other guy was upset over the way Dad had handled his DUI or something of that nature." Tyler shrugged. "He hadn't told Rita, so he stopped talking about it when she came in."

"Are you surprised? Your dad walks that ethics line pretty tight."

Saira wasn't wrong.

"True." It's probably nothing. Except that Colton seemed upset by this. "I'm going to check in on my mom tomorrow. Want to come?"

"I'll be late at the clinic. And we're not really a couple. You don't have to include me in everything." She half smiled.

"We may not be a couple." He tried to keep his voice neutral, so as not to reveal his disappointment at this idea. "But we are family."

Saira stopped chewing mid-bite, but her expression was indiscernable. She nodded. "We are family."

"We're having an engagement party." Tracy Hart's voice left no room for debate. Tyler had stopped by his mother's place as he usually did a couple times a week, to check on her. He knew

Aneel stopped in a couple times a week as well. As did Saira, even though she had opted out of coming today.

His mother didn't really need him "checking in" on her. Her social/work schedule was as busy, often even busier, than his, but he liked seeing her. And besides, she made the best crab cakes in Maryland, hands down. He had tried many times to duplicate them, but was unsuccessful. Even Aneel, the chef, couldn't recreate them exactly. Tyler suspected his mom was holding back about some key ingredient.

When he got there, the aroma of crab cakes soothed him until he saw that Colton was already there.

"Ah! Both of my boys are here." She smirked. "It's true what they say, cook it and they will come."

Tyler hugged his mother, whose head barely made it to his shoulders. "Of course, Ma. You think I come for the company?" He lithely dodged his well-earned swat, laughing as he helped himself to a beer from her fridge.

Colton looked up from his beer, his gaze flicking between the two of them. His brother shifted in his seat, looking, of all things…out of place. Tyler recognized that look, because he wore it every time he went to New York. There was something else in Colton's face though that Tyler had not seen before. Longing. "You let him get away with all that, Mom?" Colton said with a smirk.

"I am ashamed to say that I do." She laughed. "What can I say? I'm a big softy when it comes to my boys."

Colton grinned, but Tyler saw pain flicker in his eyes. His interactions with Mom were slightly different from Tyler's. Colton didn't joke as much, likely because he didn't know how to. They hadn't spent nearly as much time together, so they weren't as close.

They were better than Tyler's interactions with their father, however. Tyler's interactions with Ethan Hart were formal at best. Every line tagged with "sir." Tyler had tried sarcastic remarks, one-liners, they had all fallen flat, with his father staring him down with the same green eyes he had given to Colton. Ethan Hart respected ruthlessness over kindness, something Tyler had never mastered. So Tyler had stopped trying to impress his father. He did his duty and that was all.

Tyler attacked the crab cakes with true gusto, thoroughly enjoying his mother's cooking.

"Colton. You should come down here more often for these crab cakes alone," Tyler said.

"Mom sends them to me and I freeze them," Colton said.

Tyler looked at his brother. "Yeah, okay. But it's not the same, is it?"

Colton grinned. "It is not."

Their mom started a trip down memory lane that included many happy memories of the three of them together. Tyler had forgotten how much he had enjoyed being together when they were children. He had forgotten that there was a time when he and Colton simply had fun as brothers.

It was then, when Tyler was relaxed with a full belly and a couple beers and happy memories, that his mother brought up the engagement party.

"It's really not necessary," Colton started.

"He's right, Mom. So unnecessary," Tyler said, trying to hide his panic.

"Nonsense. Neither one of you has any idea when your weddings will be, and I want to celebrate. I'm a mom and I can celebrate my children if I want. It would be wonderful for you and your respective fiancées to attend."

Tyler rolled his eyes. His mom, the comedian.

"You haven't even purchased the ring yet." His mother pointed a finger at him. "How that woman said yes to you without a ring…"

"That woman is Saira, who you basically raised," Tyler said.

"And you are damn lucky to have her." She paused. "I'm still unclear as to how all of that happened without me finding out that you were dating, but I'll let it slide for now. In fact," she said as she sipped at her own beer, "if I were busy with an engagement party, I won't have time to ask uncomfortable questions."

Tyler sighed. There was no changing her mind when she got like this. He risked a glance at Colton and saw the same resigned expression on his face. There was now going to be an engagement party. For his fake engagement.

Saira was going to love this.

Chapter Twenty-Five

Saira

"No." This was completely nonnegotiable. She loved Tracy Auntie, but playing along with an engagement party for their fake engagement was too much. Way too much.

Tyler sighed. "You can try to say no, but it's happening."

"Seriously, Tyler?" She was nearly whining, she knew it, but this couldn't happen. Not now. She had graduation and boards. What was she saying? This couldn't happen because it wasn't real.

"Yes, seriously. You know how she gets."

"Let's break up." The words were out of her mouth before she really thought about them, but the more she thought about them, the more they made sense. She started to smile as the idea took form.

"What?"

"It's perfect." She stood and paced while she spoke. "We'll say you found someone else and now I'm heartbroken, but I'll be fine. But I can't forgive you and we're calling off our engagement."

"Why do I have to be the bad guy? Why can't you find someone else?" Tyler asked.

She looked at Tyler. Honestly. "I'm not going to be the bad guy. Your mom will kill me."

"She'll kill me for hurting you," Tyler said. "And that is a literal fact."

He wasn't wrong. The three of them knew Saira was her favorite.

Neither of them brought up what Aneel's reaction might be.

"Fine. Let's make it mutual, then. We realized that we were better as friends. We're too close like this and we really have no spark."

She met his eyes as the memory of the spark they shared returned to her like a thunderbolt.

"Okay." She started pacing again. She could feel Tyler's eyes tracking her as she moved. "We need a plan. It should take about a week. We can't just walk out there and announce we're over. It has to be believable."

Tyler shook his head. "A week is too fast. Let's make it two."

Saira narrowed her eyes, considering. "You're right. We can have little arguments and then blow up at the end." She stopped and grinned at him. "Easy-peasy. Besides, it'll give me two weeks to find my own place. We can't exactly be sharing a room if we're broken up. I haven't had any luck so far. But I'll put Lin and Lora on it. They'll find something."

"You can stay as long as you need to find a proper place. Brokenhearted or not, I would never make you move out if you didn't have anywhere to go. You'll have a job soon enough and then you'll get a nice place that welcomes Kiara."

He was right; she had never known Tyler to put his needs in front of hers, ever. That's just not who he was. None of the people who knew them would question that she still lived here, if there was no other option. She nodded and grinned at him.

"You're going to miss being engaged to me." She smirked, putting on the sass, as it occurred to her that she might miss being engaged to him. However fake it might be.

"Ha! Not as much as you'll miss being engaged to me." He paused. "I am going to like having my whole bed back though." He chuckled.

She threw a pillow at him. He caught the pillow and studied her, his blue eyes intense on her for a moment. "I'm in. But I'm telling you that while it might work to keep the engagement party from happening, it sounds too good to be true."

Saira should have taken his words to heart.

Chapter Twenty-Six

Tyler

"Tyler. I hope you don't mind, but Rita and I are going to need to be in Baltimore for a bit longer. You've been great so far, and I hate to impose…" Colton was rambling a bit, as if he were nervous to ask this of Tyler.

Tyler put a halt to it. "Colton. You're my brother. Stay as long as you need."

"Yeah?" He seemed unduly happy about this.

"Of course. We shared a womb and everything." Tyler grinned. "What's a condo?"

Colton rolled his eyes. "I just… Thanks."

"You just…?"

"I guess I just never thought you liked having me here. It felt like you tolerated it until I left," Colton said, eyeing Tyler for the truth.

"You're very perceptive," Tyler said, a smirk on his face.

Colton didn't flinch. "Tell it like it is. Don't hold back."

Tyler sighed and softened. "We're family. You can stay however long you like, even if it irritates me." He paused. "Even if you irritate me."

"I don't understand."

Tyler nodded. "I know. That's the difference between you and me."

"Well, how about I cook tonight?" Colton offered.

"Sure." Tyler grinned. "Let's see what you got."

Tyler discovered later that night—among the aromas of onion and garlic being sautéed with spices, and a quality white wine Colton had specifically paired with this meal—that what Colton had was an amazing ability to cook.

"Where did you learn how to do this?" Tyler asked as he looked at Saira and bugged his eyes out in disbelief. She shrugged and shook her head as she stuffed her mouth with fish like she'd never eaten.

Colton shrugged. "I used to help Mom in the kitchen when I would come down."

"I helped Mom too," Tyler said.

"Not when I was there," Colton said softly.

"Well, I am very impressed," Saira piped up in between bites. "I never would have thought it."

"What do you mean?" Colton eyed her as he added another small salmon fillet and vegetables to her plate.

"I mean you seemed the type to hire a chef or do takeout or go out to fancy restaurants." Saira was honest, no doubt about it.

"I was. For a long time." Colton nodded as he shared a small smile with Rita.

Saira leaned into it. "What? What am I missing?"

"Well, my cooking is one of the reasons that she agreed to go out with me." Colton was nearly blushing. Tyler stared in disbelief.

"Really?" Saira continued, turning her attention to Rita. "Tell me all about it."

"Not much to tell, really." Rita sipped her wine and leaned on the counter, watching Colton as if he were the only man on earth. "He would bring leftovers from the night before to the break room and share with me. Our companies are in the same building. His cooking was *sooo* good." She glanced at Saira and they shared some kind of look. "I thought if he could cook this well, I almost didn't care what else he could do."

Colton grunted and Rita pursed her lips. "I said *almost*. Anyway, one night he offered to cook dinner for me at his place, and that was that." Rita shared another look with Saira and whispered something that had both women laughing. She gave a sly smile and clasped her hand in Colton's.

"I cooked so I would have leftovers to share at work. A stomach is not only the way to a man's heart. Works for women too." Colton grinned at Rita.

"I do love to eat," Rita said, still focused on Colton.

Rita was completely entranced by him. Tyler was in awe.

"That's lovely," Saira said. "I wish Tyler would cook more. Takeout gets tiring after a while. And he's a great cook."

"Oh," Tyler said. "I had no idea. I'm happy to cook more. Maybe Colton over here can share recipes."

Saira shot him a quick glare.

Oh, right. They were supposed to start bickering so that their breakup would make sense.

"Actually though, I don't know how you expect me to cook more when I have this awful schedule and now someone has to care for Kiara," Tyler said. The words even tasted bad on his tongue.

"Well, I didn't hear any objections when I told you I wanted to bring a dog home." Saira's response was immediate.

"I thought you would be taking on the bulk of the Kiara burden, seeing as how you're the veterinarian," Tyler shot back, glancing at Colton for support. Instead, Colton's eyes were narrowed at him.

"I'm still in school! I have exams and boards and the whole thing." Saira stiffened and grabbed his arm. She looked pale and clammy.

Tyler's heart thudded in his chest as Saira gasped for breath. "Colton." He commanded. "Grab me a paper bag. Drawer next to the silverware." Tyler barked out.

Colton was up in an instant, the paper bag in Tyler's hands

in seconds. He held it over her mouth as she breathed into it. He met her eyes. *Again?*

Her brown eyes answered him with some fear, even though she shrugged and continued breathing into the bag. After a few minutes, the fear left her eyes, and her body relaxed as her breathing regulated.

"Are you all right?" asked Rita, true concern in her eyes.

Saira nodded. "Just a mild panic attack." She side-eyed Tyler. "It comes on when I think about graduation." She laughed. But everyone in the room knew it was forced.

Colton met her eyes and nodded at her before looking at Tyler.

Tyler's heart thudded in his chest. Colton was wondering if Tyler even deserved Saira. Tyler wondered the same thing.

"You were great!" Saira whispered as they readied for bed a few hours later. "I mean I almost believed you for a second. *Burden of Kiara*, ha!"

"Saira." He pulled back the covers as they both climbed into bed. They were so used to sharing this room now it didn't seem to faze her. Tyler however was more aware than ever of her every move. "You had another panic attack."

She turned her gaze away from him as she applied lotion to her hands. The scent of honeysuckle wafted toward him. "No big deal. It's just because of thinking about graduation and waiting on the boards scores. It's stressful, but it'll all be over soon."

"The attacks are getting more frequent. Didn't you say your dad had panic attacks along with his depression?"

"I'm not like him," Saira snapped at him. Subject closed.

Tyler watched her slip into bed. She protested too harshly. The subject was anything but closed.

Chapter Twenty-Seven

Saira

"Tyler. Wake up." The sun was just rising, early rays of pink and orange poking through their blinds.

He groaned and turned toward her, his eyes still closed. Saira had to admit she was rather starting to enjoy waking up with Tyler next to her. She was a light sleeper and woke up a couple times every night. She found it reassuring to find Tyler next to her in the bed. She fell back asleep almost instantly every time to the soothing sound of his breathing.

Not to mention he looked amazing with his hair sleep-tousled, eyes closed. He was so warm she had to hold herself back from cuddling into him.

Whoa! There would be no cuddling. This was Tyler Hart. Her brother's best friend and her…her…person she grew up with. She knew him when he was a skinny teenager and a scrawny kid, and he had seen her throw a fit over the wrong mint chocolate chip ice cream. (Honestly, if it doesn't have chocolate chunks, why even bother?)

"Tyler," she whispered as she nudged his biceps. His very hard biceps. He might not be built like Colton, but Tyler Hart had some muscles. She nudged him again. "Tyler!"

He moaned and wrapped his arm around her, pulling her close to him. "Saira," he whispered, his voice content. And deliciously gravelly.

He was warm and strong and being in his arms felt safe. Not

to mention, the sound of his gravelly morning voice had stirred something in her.

Wait, what?

Before she could process what he had just done—in his sleep—and how she had responded, he woke properly. His eyes widened at her proximity, and he removed his arms from her as if he'd been burned. "Saira. What...?"

He scrambled backward toward the edge of the bed, stopping just short of falling off.

Saira gathered herself from the sensation of being thrown from his arms and sat up. "I was trying to wake you up to plan our morning argument."

Tyler stared at her, bewildered—but then he nodded. "Right." He paused. "Did I...did I...?"

"You hugged me. That's all. You were still asleep." He had held her like he was dreaming about her. *Was* he dreaming about her? What was the dream? "People do weird things in their sleep."

"Do they?"

"It's a fact." She needed to change the subject. She could not dwell on the idea of Tyler dreaming about her. "So I was thinking we would argue about the dog."

"You can't expect me to take the dog out when I need to be at the clinic in twenty minutes!" Saira barked at Tyler as she left their bedroom, Kiara trailing behind.

"I have in-person meetings today," Tyler insisted as he followed her out. "I told you this."

"I can't remember everything. It's not on the calendar." Saira stood her ground. She looked around and sure enough Rita was getting her morning coffee.

"Regardless. I'm late. You're going to have to deal." Saira felt the choke in his voice as he said these words to her. He pulled down both of their to-go mugs, but at a quick flick of the eyes from Saira, only poured his own coffee into a to-go cup with a soft, "Good morning, Rita."

"Tyler!" Saira demanded in a tone she imagined one would use when frustrated with their own partner.

"Gotta go!" Tyler left the apartment, coffee in hand.

He really did have in-person meetings today, but they didn't start for an hour. This just seemed like a good opportunity to have another "argument."

"I can't believe it." Saira huffed for Rita's benefit. She still had an hour as well. She looked around. "He used to pour my coffee too," she said softly.

"So unlike Tyler." Rita sipped her coffee, brow furrowed, staring at the door Tyler had just left from. Saira remembered that Rita had once dated Tyler for a whole year. He must have doted on her, because that was how Tyler loved. A wave of jealousy crashed into her. In that moment she wanted nothing more than for Rita to think that Tyler loved *her*, Saira, more than anyone or anything in the world. That Tyler was 100 percent irrevocably, undeniably *hers*.

"He's usually so doting and caring, and literally would do anything for me," Saira said.

Rita looked at her and Saira's jealousy was sated with the wistful look she gave her. "That is undeniably true."

"What is?" Colton's voice came from behind them.

"That Tyler would do anything for Saira," Rita said as her eyes lit up at the sight of Colton.

"Except maybe walk the dog when I'm running late. So I guess that's still on me." She grabbed Kiara's leash and ran out the door. She must have taken their role playing too seriously, because what the hell was that? She wanted Tyler to be *hers*? No, she didn't.

"Do I?" she asked Kiara as they went down in the elevator.

Kiara just looked at her with what she could swear were raised eyebrows.

By the time they hit the warm spring air, Saira's head had cleared and she was feeling much more herself.

Of course she did not want Tyler to be *hers*. The idea that he would even entertain those feelings for her or that she could feel that way for him was laughable.

She looked at Kiara as they walked. "Ridiculous, right?"

Kiara responded by squatting for a poop.

Chapter Twenty-Eight

Tyler

Tyler rushed out the door, knowing he did not have meetings for another hour. He was…discombobulated. That was the only word that really came to mind. Waking up to find Saira in his arms had been wonderful and dangerous all at the same time. He must have reached for her in his sleep; that was the only explanation. He really should go back to the sofa.

She had gone along with it though, hadn't she? When obviously there was no one to see. She had been snuggled up to him, even if it was only for a few seconds. Huh. Was he really going to fantasize about Saira having feelings for him when he knew it couldn't work? Aneel was showing no signs of coming around and Saira might not want her brother dictating her life, but she loved him and wanted him in it, so she would never stay in a relationship her brother disapproved of.

He shook his head. No good would come from dwelling on the idea of them really being together.

He slowed his pace. The morning was warm and pleasant. He still had an hour before his first meeting. Arguing with Saira— even fake arguing was taxing. His heart rate was accelerated, and his mood was crap.

He texted her, over the top?

Her response was immediate. No. Rita seems worried. She added a thumbs-up emoji.

That was good, right? He was getting confused as to what

was the desired outcome. He was enjoying being engaged to Saira. That's how pathetic he was—he enjoyed being even *fake* engaged to the woman he loved.

He really needed to get a life. Maybe he should call Jackie? But he had to admit that nothing about the beautiful and intelligent Jackie excited him—even though there was nothing wrong with her except that she was not Saira. He stowed away his to-go cup and ducked into a coffee shop a couple blocks from his building. Might as well have breakfast before that first call.

He was settling in with his coffee and breakfast sandwich and laptop, when a familiar man approached him.

"Tyler, correct?" The man had a slight accent and a very friendly voice.

Tyler swallowed his coffee and extended his hand to Saira's father. Aneel's father. Huh. "Yes, sir. Yogesh Rawal, right?" He really did resemble Aneel.

The man smiled and nodded.

"Please join me," Tyler said.

"I don't want to intrude." He nodded at Tyler's laptop, which sat open on the table.

Tyler smiled and closed it. "I'd much rather chat than answer emails." Tyler motioned toward the empty seat. "Please."

Yogesh Rawal smiled and sat down with his coffee. "So, you are the young man who stole Saira's heart."

He wished. "Yes, sir. I supposed that is correct."

"What do you do?"

"I'm a lawyer. In fact, I come from a long line of lawyers. My dad, my brother. My mother is a social worker..." He trailed off. "You get the picture."

Saira's father fixed him in his gaze, his voice soft but firm, holding a hint of regret. "I suppose I long since wrote off my right to question you or threaten you with bodily harm if you hurt her, but that doesn't mean the protective feelings of a father aren't still there."

Tyler started to smile, but then caught the hardness behind the older man's brown eyes and his smile died. It was similar to the hardness in Aneel's eyes when he was angry—a sight he experienced quite often these days. "Of course. Understood."

"I assume Aneel has given his approval along with similar warnings?"

"To be honest, no." Aneel had not yet reached out at all since he had made it clear that Tyler had no business marrying Saira. "Warnings, yes. Approval, no."

Yogesh's eyebrows raised in surprise. "That does not bode well for your future together."

Tyler pressed his lips together. "It does not." Good thing there was no "future."

"Do you know Aneel well?"

Tyler paused as he assessed this man. He might be Aneel and Saira's father, but he really had no idea about their lives once he divorced their mother. "We…uh…well, we grew up together. Aneel is a brother to me. Our mothers were best friends. Both single moms, trying to make ends meet and raise their children."

Sadness came over the older man. "I regret that more than anything. That I never reached out to my children when I was able."

"Able, sir?"

He shook his head and waved a hand. "Long and complicated story. I do not make a good impression in it, that's for sure. Tell me about yourself."

"There isn't that much to tell. My parents divorced when I was little, my brother grew up with my dad and I stayed with my mom. Aneel and Saira became my family. Their mother was a second mother to me." Even after all these years, tears prickled behind his eyes, thinking of Malti Auntie. He blinked them back. What would she say about all this?

Yogesh Uncle studied him for a minute. "You really love my daughter?"

Tyler sipped his coffee before answering. "Your son is more of a true brother to me than my own biological brother. Aneel has gotten me in and out of more scrapes than I can count." Tyler shook his head and chuckled. "His support and influence, along with my mom's, is the reason I am who I am today." Tyler paused and looked Yogesh in the eyes. "But your daughter… Saira…is the air that I breathe. Without her in my life, I have nothing. I would do anything for her." Even fake break up with her.

Saira's father had tears in his eyes. He nodded at Tyler. "See to it that you never forget that."

Chapter Twenty-Nine

Saira

Saira thought it best they wait a day or two before having another "argument." They couldn't have timed it better, because she woke in the morning knowing it was a cinnamon-bun day. Sure, she tried to eat healthy, but every so often she *needed* a cinnamon bun. And it had to be from this specific bakery. Tyler usually bought half a dozen and froze them, so she had them on hand when she needed one.

Today was one of those days. She knew that Tyler had a stash of them in the back of the freezer, as well as a couple in the pantry. She took those and hid them in the closet in their room.

Saira waited for Rita to come and pour coffee. She then made a big show of desperately looking for something in the kitchen.

"Hey. What are you looking for?" Rita asked.

She managed to look sheepish as she responded. "Every so often, I get a craving for these cinnamon buns Tyler gets from the bakery a few blocks away. Today is a cinnamon-bun day but I don't see any. Though now that I'm looking, I also don't see eggs, fruit." She looked around. "Bread."

Tyler came out of the room. Saira questioned him, on cue, using her super sweet voice that meant there was trouble. "Hey, did you not get groceries?"

"I did not, because I thought you were going." Tyler added an edge to his voice that was quite rarely heard.

"When would I go? I'm at the clinic until after the stores

close most days." She forced the sense of entitlement into her voice that was necessary for this argument.

"I have had meetings like crazy because of this new project, not to mention the paperwork. I haven't gotten off the phone long enough to go to the bathroom, let alone the store." Now Tyler was irritated. Anyone who heard would not doubt it.

"We don't even have the cinnamon buns!" Saira raised her voice. She could have sworn she saw him flinch. He took personal pride in making sure her cinnamon buns were available when she wanted them, even though her want for them was on an unpredictable schedule. "And we're low on dog food."

"I thought you were getting the dog food," Tyler said.

"Yes, when I get the groceries. Do I have to run everything around here? Can't you see we are low on bread, eggs, et cetera, and just get them?" She sounded like a spoiled brat, and she was making him out to be lazy.

His eyes widened and he clenched his jaw.

A pit grew in her stomach as she imagined she was really hurting him. This was harder than she thought.

"Tell you what," Rita interjected, "I have some time today, I'll get the groceries." She looked from one to the other warily. "It's the least I could do since we have been here longer than anticipated."

"That would be lovely," Saira said, glaring at Tyler with what she hoped was an accusatory face.

"No problem," Rita said cheerily. "You know, Colton and I simply make a schedule ahead of time, or we touch base each day on how our schedules are for the next couple days. Helps with the basic stuff like figuring out who'll handle buying groceries."

"Something to keep in mind—" said Tyler, pinning Saira with a look of such pure annoyance she sort of thought it was real "—should we be moving forward."

Saira gave him a thumbs-up behind Rita's back. Perfect.

They had to start hinting at the idea that they may not be able to keep this up.

Rita stopped in her tracks. "Oh, these are simple squabbles, with easy solutions."

Saira shrugged one shoulder before leaving the apartment. "Whatever."

Saira got to school just in time to slide into the seat Lin had saved for her. Lin furrowed her brow in question but Saira just shook her head.

Her day was so busy at the clinic she barely had time to chat with Lin, who kept throwing her odd looks all day long. Lin caught up with her in the lounge at the end of the day.

In typical Lin style, she wasted no time. "You're engaged? To Hot Tyler? And you never said anything? What is happening?" Her dark eyes were curious, but Saira could see that she had hurt Lin by not telling her.

"How did you hear about that?" Saira asked.

"Your sister-in-law cooks for us twice a week." Lin widened her eyes and stared at her friend.

"Okay, yes, I am engaged to Tyler," she admitted. She didn't want to put Lin in the position of having to maintain a lie with Karina. Better to tell her the same story everyone else was getting. "But we're having second thoughts." Yes, this was the way to go. They'd be broken up in a week or so anyway.

Lin stared at her. "Why didn't you say anything? You never even told me you were dating."

"Right…because Karina cooks for you and we didn't want my brother to know, so I had to be careful who I told." She looked sheepish. Normally she would have told Lin everything. Every detail. Even now, a part of her wanted to tell Lin that Hot Tyler—yes, that was the most accurate name for him—had looked at her this morning like he wanted nothing more than to keep her in bed. Possibly do anything but sleep. And that she had been there for it. The slightest sign from Tyler and she would have been willing putty in his hands. She'd had to keep talking to prevent any such thing.

If that wasn't the craziest thought she'd ever had.

"But engaged?" Lin shook her head.

"I truly am sorry I didn't tell you," Saira said. "It just happened so fast."

"Hot Tyler?" Lin's eyes widened and she smiled. "Tell me everything. I want to know how it started. All of it. You're buying drinks and spilling."

"I'm buying drinks?"

"Yes." Lin led them to their local hangout and ordered two old-fashioneds. "Start talking."

Saira shot Tyler a quick text that she was with Lin, and could he take Kiara out, please? It almost *was* like they were together.

"So, I guess it started when I lived with him for a few weeks last year when Aneel and I were fighting." She studied Lin's face.

Lin sipped her drink. "Makes sense."

Good! "Well, so I had my own room but we shared the rest of the place."

Lin leaned in. Saira sipped her drink; it was slightly sweet and strong and warmed her on the way down. "Yes?"

"But then I noticed little things like he always had my favorite cinnamon buns in the freezer so they'd be available whenever I wanted them. He made my favorite foods and stocked my favorite wine. And my favorite hot sauce." He always seemed to know what her favorite hot sauce was even though it changed all the time. "He…uh, always had a to-go cup of coffee for me to take to class." She grinned at the memory, realizing she had stopped him from doing that just this morning, to keep their "argument" believable. "We spent hours talking."

"Didn't you do that growing up?" Lin asked.

"Not really. He and Aneel are closer. We all hung out and

did fun things together, but Tyler and I never really talked, like just the two of us. Well, except for that time I got dumped after college."

"That guy, Dhruv?" Lin rolled her eyes.

She nodded. "Even then, he was more focused on me rather than opening up as much himself…" Tyler had done a lot for her and continued to do so. Huh.

"Hello… You're drifting away." Lin snapped her fingers.

"Yeah. So. One night, we cooked together. Tyler's a great cook and I can hold my own as well. I don't even remember what we ate. I just remember being in complete harmony together. We moved in the kitchen like we'd been cooking together forever. It was fluid and comfortable. And he did that thing, where he rolls up his shirt sleeves." She grinned. Tyler did have fantastic forearms.

She remembered that night clearly. She hadn't felt like she was with her childhood friend, Tyler. She had felt like she was hanging out with a man who was kind and thoughtful and considerate. And she had absolutely noticed how attractive he was. Had she been attracted to him then? They had talked about anything and everything. There had been laughter and good food and a comfort she hadn't felt with any other man, even Dhruv, the man she had thought she would marry.

"We ate and cleaned up and then he somehow bumped into me. We just looked at each other, and we knew." She smiled. That really had happened. She had ignored the moment, she realized, so she wouldn't have to deal with the fact that she might be attracted to him. And being attracted to Tyler Hart was not in her game plan.

"You've been with him for six months? Like you've *been* together?" Lin's eyes widened.

Saira snapped out of her daze. "Yep. Yes. That's what I said." They had not gone to bed together, but there had been an… electricity between them that was hard to ignore. Yet ignore it was exactly what they had done, even when it had existed almost as a presence in the room. Just like whatever was hanging between them now.

Lin downed her drink. "Damn, girl. Okay fine. You are forgiven. Lora is going to have a cow. But what do you mean you're having second thoughts? Look at you. I've never seen such complete contentment vibe off you this way." Lin fished out the cherry from the glass. "Doesn't make sense. Sure, relationships have issues, but that's part of life."

"I'll keep that in mind." She paid the bill and grabbed her stuff. "I need to get moving. Still have charting to get through at home."

"See you tomorrow." Lin raised her empty glass to her.

"Love to Lora."

"Always."

Chapter Thirty

"**Y**ou got a minute?" Colton poked his head into Tyler's room.

Tyler held up five fingers and nodded. He finished his call and found Colton.

"What's up?" Tyler was still frazzled from his argument with Saira this morning. Fake or not, it sucked. He had returned at lunch to finish out his calls at home.

"I have someone looking into Dad's past with the mystery guy. They got his name and my paralegal did some covert research for me. Turns out it's a guy who hit someone in a DUI. Now, according to Maryland law, the max the guy can get is ten years in prison."

Tyler narrowed his eyes. "For killing someone?"

Colton pressed his lips together. "Yes. This was not the man's first DUI charge, so the prosecutor was going for the full sentence."

"They never give out the full sentence."

Colton nodded. "The man served six years."

Tyler looked at his brother. "So, Dad got him six years instead of ten. That's the job, right?" Five seemed too low, quite frankly.

Colton nodded in agreement. "Absolutely, for better or worse." His brow was creased in thought, his mouth pressed together.

"What?"

His brother shrugged. "I don't know. Something is missing. Why was the man upset? *Was* he upset, or did I misunderstand something?" He shook his head. "I don't know."

"Colton, why are you so caught up in this? Why does it matter?" Tyler glanced at his screen. Ten minutes before his next meeting.

"Because there is a possibility that Dad did something unethical, and I need to know what it was." Colton sounded sad. "He's tough and kind of scary, but I look up to him, you know?"

Tyler nodded. "Me too. I mean he's our dad, right?"

"I always wanted to be like him, you know? Or at least I thought I did." Colton shook his head.

"Rita opened your eyes?"

"Rita helped me deal with what I saw when I opened my eyes." Colton paused. He leaned back against the counter. His shoulders were uncharacteristically hunched over, his arms folded across his chest. He looked defeated. "The more I work with Dad, the more I question what he does. He toes the line between what's right and wrong, not always in favor of the client. He's ruthless—a bully even—and I was turning out just like him." He sighed. "I don't want to be that guy."

He straightened and fixed Tyler with an almost desperate look. "I'm sorry to dump all this on you, but you're literally the only person who would understand."

"You're not dumping on me. Brothers talk." Tyler nodded, not knowing how to react to this show of trust and vulnerability from Colton.

"That's also why we're still in Baltimore. I just can't go in person to the office right now." He paused. "To be honest, I may not be going back to Hart Law at all. Rita and I are thinking about opening our own little firm in New York." He shrugged. "It would be nice to be my own boss. Serve the underserved, do some good."

"That sounds…more like Mom than Dad," Tyler said on a chuckle.

"If you weren't dedicated to Baltimore, I'd ask you to join us. We might be great together, you know?"

Tyler stared at Colton. "You serious?" There had been a time when all Tyler would have wanted was this kind of recognition from Colton. "Wow. Thanks for thinking of me. But everything I love is here."

"Totally get it," Colton said. "The door is always open to you."

"And you. You're welcome to stay however long."

"You sure? Us being here seems to be causing a bit of strain. Rita told me about the arguments…"

"You're fine, really." Tyler grinned at his brother. "Things with Saira and me have nothing to do with you." *HA!*

"Well, you be sure to let me know if we're cramping your style. We could always stay with Mom or get a hotel room or something. You've been in love with that woman for years. I'd hate to see things go sour because of houseguests." He smirked at him.

Tyler watched as Colton returned to his room to continue working.

Huh.

Hours later, Colton and Rita were out to dinner when Saira returned from clinic. Tyler placed a cinnamon bun on a plate and placed it in front of her. She grinned sheepishly.

"Sorry," he said softly.

"I'm the one who hid them," she said, dropping her things to pick up a very excited Kiara. "On purpose."

"I hate the arguing." He shuddered. "I know it's fake, but…"

Saira sat down and took a bite of the cinnamon roll before she spoke. She closed her eyes and groaned. "I hate arguing, but this is the best damn cinnamon roll. You need to have some."

She broke off a piece with her fingers and held it out to him. "The ratio of cinnamon to sugar to bread is perfect and the whole thing is so light it just melts in your mouth," she said.

He opened his mouth and she fed him with her hand. His lips grazed the tips of her fingers as the flavor of the cinnamon roll hit his tongue. Her eyes flicked to his.

"It really is amazing," he said softly. Her hand was suspended in front of him, and he had the thought that he could lick the excess cinnamon from her fingers. He was toying with this thought when the door buzzer went off.

They both started and seemed to come back to themselves. "I'll get that." Tyler stood and pushed the button. "Hello?"

"Hey, it's us—Lin and Lora—and we brought your favorite Afghani food."

"Um, yeah. Come on up." He widened his eyes at Saira.

Saira stood and walked around to the sink to wash her hands. She grinned. "So, Lin found out from Karina that we're engaged…"

Tyler sighed and rolled his eyes. He opened the door just as Lin and Lora walked up, carrying insulated bags. "Hey! How's it going?" Tyler peeked around them. "Where's Andrew?"

"He's with his favorite sitter," Lora said as they entered. "Where's the little monster?"

"You mean the Beast?" Tyler asked as relieved her of the large bag and kissed her cheek.

"Kiara is—" A ball of black fur zoomed up, tail wagging at Lora, who grinned and bent down to pick up Kiara. "Looks like someone taught you manners," she cooed.

"It was Tyler, if you can believe that." Saira smirked at him.

He met her gaze, the memory of her fingers in his mouth still lingering in the air between them. She hugged both women. "What's with the surprise food?"

"We're celebrating you two, of course!" Lin said. "It's not every day that one of my best friends gets secretly engaged to a guy she was secretly dating without telling me." Lin and Lora hugged them both. Then Lin pulled a bottle from one of the bags. "Let's celebrate!" she said as she opened the wine.

"Here's to one of the cutest couples ever. It's about time. Love you." Lin's eyes were wet. They all clinked glasses and sipped.

"Let's get to this food. It smells amazing!" Tyler said, pulling out plates while Lora unpacked the food.

"What do you mean, it's about time?" Saira asked.

Lin and Lora shared a look and a small eye roll. "You two were meant to be. Anyone could see that."

Saira gulped at her drink. Tyler avoided looking at her.

The four of them sat down around the small coffee table. Saira sat in the plush white chair, Tyler on the floor next to her, and Lin and Lora on the sofa. Lin looked between the two of them. "So, we never got to hear your proposal story."

Tyler glanced at Saira who looked at him, her face frozen in a smile that told him she had not considered this question. "Oh…well." He cleared his throat and glanced around. "It was… well…" Truth was, he had given this some thought, in that he had fantasized about this very thing. "Well, as you know, I haven't gotten the ring yet, so the proposal was quite spontaneous." He glanced at Saira. She was watching him with curiosity, waiting to see what he'd say.

"Saira had been quite stressed out about graduation, and the boards and the new job." He glanced at Lin. "As you know."

Lin nodded. "Not to mention, she was staying in that dump of a studio apartment." Lin rolled her eyes at Saira.

"Hey. That was my dump." Saira pouted, but she seemed more amused than irritated.

Tyler grinned at her. Right now Saira was curled up in that chair, Kiara in her lap, curly wisps of hair rebelling against her cruel ponytail, still in her scrubs, with that look on her face, and she had never looked so beautiful. Tyler caught his breath.

"Anyway. I thought a pet might help. So I went to the pound

to find a dog for her, and Kiara more or less latched herself to me. I couldn't resist, so I brought her home. Well, I actually took her straight to Saira's place." Tyler paused. He would have done this had she really been his.

"He showed up with this completely adorable, heart-stealing puppy," Saira said softly, as if envisioning it herself.

Lin frowned. "All this time, you never said Hot Tyler got you Kiara."

Saira smiled at Lin, an eyebrow raised. "We weren't ready to say anything—you know how Aneel can be. Besides—" she narrowed her eyes at her friend "—I recall a certain couple secretly having a baby."

"Kiara was meant to be a gift," Tyler said. "But once Saira held her, I knew that was the moment." He made eye contact with Saira. "I knew that I loved Saira more than anything, and that I had for a very long time. I was completely sure that I wanted to spend my life with her." Her brown eyes softened, and Tyler was aware of only her. He took her hand. "So I got down on one knee, apologized for not having a ring and asked her to marry me." He brought her hand to his lips and gently kissed her hand. "The happiest moment of my whole life was when she said yes." He paused. "We brought Kiara here that very night."

"She had destroyed my apartment, and my landlord kicked me out," Saira said. "We had no choice."

Lin looked at her with a side grin. "Well, that's what you get for leaving her unsupervised while you…celebrated your engagement."

Saira giggled and threw a pillow at her friend. But she did not let go of Tyler's hand. "Shut up."

"That is the cutest proposal ever," Lora said, wiping her eyes. "You two are clearly meant to be." She held up her phone. "Okay. Get close, we need a picture."

Saira rolled her eyes. "Seriously?"

"Just do it," Lora commanded. Saira stood and went over to Tyler.

"Sit in his lap," Lin said. "It'll be a cute picture."

Tyler looked up and gave her a small grin with just the tiniest little shrug. He patted his legs. She sat gingerly on his knee.

"Oh, my god!" Lora exclaimed. "Sit. In. His. Lap."

Saira did not look at him as he put his arms around her and pulled her into his lap. He left one arm around her waist and used the other to pull her legs perpendicular to his. Which meant her their faces were quite close together.

She placed her hand on his chest and looked at him as his heart thudded against her palm. Her face was not quite an inch from his and her floral lotion scent surrounded him. He might have been able to resist, except in the next second her gaze drifted to his mouth.

All rational thought left his brain as he simply reacted. The next moment, his mouth was on hers, in a kiss that was anything but chaste. She tasted like cinnamon and spices and he only wanted more. He registered that she kissed him back with equal fervor, as if she were drinking him in.

It was Lin and Lora's laughter that pulled him out of it. He pulled back, glancing at Saira, whose eyes were still closed. "Sorry," he said sheepishly.

Saira's eyes popped open. "No that…was…"

"You two are adorable." Lin grinned at them.

Saira popped off his lap in an instant. "We should get dessert going."

Tyler's heart sank and he stood. Whatever had just happened, Saira was not happy about it. "Let me," Tyler said. He passed Saira without a glance and went to the kitchen.

Chapter Thirty-One

Saira

That was some story he had come up with on the fly. That was some kiss. She had no idea what had come over her. Sitting in Tyler's lap and feeling his heartbeat had let loose something in her that she now realized had been building for quite some time. No sooner had she glanced at his mouth than he was making her wish come true with what had to have been one of the most amazing kisses she'd ever experienced.

She was still dazed from it. She needed Lin and Lora to stay because there was no telling what she might do next if she was left alone with Tyler. Between the cinnamon roll in his mouth, and his mouth on hers, she was literally just a rush of hormones. But giving in wasn't an option. She couldn't just have sex with him, even if the thought of being in his bed *for real* made her want to shove her friends out the door.

Tyler wasn't really hers. And the idea that she might want him to really be hers was laughable. Ludicrous. Completely preposterous.

Saira watched him in the kitchen. He must have gone for a run, because his hair was curling slightly at the edges, like it did when he didn't have the time to tame it. He was wearing a T-shirt from a 5K they had done together to raise money for an animal shelter. He rinsed the dishes while Lin and Lora told stories about their son, and his love for the Avengers.

Saira grinned. Aneel had always loved the Avengers. In fact, so did Veer, Karina's son.

"He's adorable," Tyler said as Lora held up her phone to show off pictures of Andrew. "I hope our children are as amazing as Andrew."

Saira snapped her head to him. He was talking about their future children now?

"I mean, when and if—no rush," Tyler corrected himself.

"Oh, you two will make wonderful parents," Lora insisted. "When you're ready."

Saira just smiled at him. Potential children with Tyler should have been putting her into a panic attack. But the very opposite seemed to be happening. The thought of children with Tyler was comforting, soothing even. Something to be anticipated.

"Kiara will guide them to mischief, I'm sure," Saira said, laughing. She caught Tyler's eye and warmth flooded her body. He looked at her over Lora's shoulder, his gaze intimate, like there was no one else in the room. Like Lora wasn't even talking to him.

Like he really was in love with her.

"We should get going. The sitter," Lin said, catching Lora's eye. "Plus, early morning." She nodded at Saira.

"Of course. Thanks for the surprise." Saira loved her friends.

Lin and Lora left, and Saira stretched and yawned as she picked up Kiara's leash. She started to slip on shoes to take Kiara out.

"I got her," Tyler said. "You get to bed."

Saira looked up at him and saw the same Tyler she had known all her life. Kind and thoughtful. But when she looked at him now, she also saw the man he'd become when she wasn't looking. Strong and steady and handsome as f— She flushed as her body responded to the memory of the kiss. She handed him the leash, his fingers grazed hers and electricity flooded through her, as if she were nothing but a conduit for his energy.

Saira needed a shower. A very cold one.

She hopped in the shower and that seemed to do the trick. She was dressed in her sleep T-shirt and shorts and in bed scrolling on her phone. She was feeling calmer than she had a few minutes before.

She certainly wasn't waiting for him.

Tyler walked Kiara and cleared his head before returning to his apartment. What was that kiss? Amazing? Yes! But Saira had kept her distance from him afterward, which sent a very clear message. They should just ignore it. This whole faking thing would be over in a few days. Real feelings for Saira were never going to work. He was wise to let them go.

And what was he doing mentioning children? Kiara finished her business, but Tyler kept her out for a bit longer. He needed Saira to be asleep when he returned.

He tiptoed into his bedroom so as not to wake her. He needn't have bothered.

"Hey," she called from the bed where she was likely doom-scrolling.

"Hey." He grinned at her. "I thought you had an early day tomorrow—I figured you'd already be asleep."

She shrugged, her focus on him. "That was some story," she said, not shifting her gaze.

His heart thudded against his rib cage so hard he was certain she could hear it. "Oh, well, I figured it made sense." He shrugged and went into the safety of his walk-in closet.

"Nice touch saying that you had feelings for me for a long time," she called from the bed. She cleared her throat. "And the kiss was an added bonus."

"Bonus?"

"Yes. Made it more believable," she replied.

He closed his eyes. "Yes. I thought it made the whole thing more…real, you know?"

"Except that we're trying to break up right now," Saira said.

"Well, yes. But they needed a good proposal story." He popped his head out. "And what's a proposal story without a little kiss, right?" He went back in the closet and changed into his sleeping shorts.

"How did you come up with it?"

Her voice startled him from behind and he knocked his head on the wall.

"What are you doing back here? I'm trying to change." He squinted at her. Her curly hair was tousled, and she was in the white T-shirt and pink shorts that she slept in. In other words, she looked…hot and sexy and very, very kissable. So basically everything he should not be thinking about right now.

"Sorry. How did you come up with the story?" she asked again.

He made the mistake of making eye contact. He knew when she saw something in his face, because her eyes widened. He turned away. "I do have an imagination. And Kiara was there. And anyone who knows you knows the way to your heart is a puppy."

"That is true." She seemed to be considering something. "Okay." Her voice sounded farther away, so he thought that she had headed back to bed. He turned to go to the bathroom and bumped into her.

He closed his eyes. "I thought you went to bed." His body grazed hers so closely he could feel the heat coming off her. Honestly, this was pure torture.

"I came back."

"Obviously." He could not step back without being obvious, and she wasn't moving. "What?" He looked down at her. Her skin was silken bronze and this close he could see the deep brown of her eyes.

He tried not to look, but he couldn't help dropping his gaze to her mouth. Lush full lips that he'd only just started to taste. He shifted his gaze back to her hair. Not much better. The curls nearly begged for his fingers to run through it.

"Just for the record, I like diamonds too," she said, looking up at him.

He swallowed. "Noted." His voice came out in a low growl. He cleared his throat. "I'll be sure to tell your future *real* fiancé to show up with a diamond."

"Right." She still looked up at him, her voice small. She stepped back. "I need to sleep."

"Good."

"Okay. I'm getting back in bed," she said as she backed up.

"I'm going to shower."

"Great."

"Good."

Tyler took his time in the shower so Saira would fall asleep before he got to bed. Thankfully, the lights were out by the time he emerged. She was facing the other direction, and her breathing was even.

He let out a sigh of relief and carefully climbed into bed, being sure to leave space between them.

Then he lay there in the dark, willing sleep to come.

Chapter Thirty-Two

Saira

Saira really did have an early day. She woke early, thoroughly exhausted from lying next to Tyler and trying not to think about his kisses, or his fingers, or the fact that he was laying right next to her. Sleep had not come until the wee hours of the morning. She had lain there next to Tyler, pretending to sleep while denying the fact that she was starting to feel something for him that she had not expected.

As she brushed her teeth, she tried to come up with an argument for them to have this morning. Maybe something more her fault since she seemed to be making him the bad guy quite a bit.

She hopped into the shower, still struggling to come up with an idea. She was toweling off when it happened.

Her chest tightened. Her breath came short. She was having a panic attack. Where was Kiara? She needed Kiara. Her hands were clammy. The walls were too close. There was no space in the bathroom. She was frozen to her spot, unable to walk. She somehow grabbed the plush robe that Tyler had gotten her and held it close, unable to even get it on as she slid down the wall to the floor.

Where was Kiara? Kiara was her answer to this, her protection. This would pass if Kiara were here. She opened her mouth but only a whisper came out. "Kiara."

Her hands shook, then her body. Now she was gulping at air.

Where was the oxygen? "Kiara." More loudly this time. This had to pass. It would pass. "Kiara."

It was hardly five seconds before Tyler was in the bathroom. His face immediately filled with concern.

"Saira. What happened? Did you fall?" He knelt close to her and his normally bright blue eyes were darker, his brow furrowed, hair tousled. "You're shivering." He reached for the robe and managed to get it on her as best he could while she still sat.

She shook her head. "Kiara," she gasped.

"Kiara, come," he called out without moving his gaze from Saira's. Within seconds, the puppy was padding into the bathroom.

He nodded and started to stand. "Okay. I'll get the paper bag."

She shook her head and reached out to grab his hand. "No. no. Don't leave me here alone." Her voice was a whimper. Kiara climbed into her lap, but still her heart raced, fear engulfed her, filling from the inside out and she continued to shake.

She stroked Kiara and a spark of calm came over her.

Tyler knelt in front of her. "Look at me."

She did, her hand still brushing over Kiara's fur.

"Breathe deep. With me." He inhaled slowly, and she tried to copy him. "Then let it out. Slow."

She did.

"Again."

She followed his lead and continued to stroke Kiara, and her heart rate decreased back to normal. She stopped sweating, and her breathing evened out.

"Better?" Tyler's face was contorted with concern, but he smiled at her.

"Yes." She nodded, the fear slowly dissipating like a fog rolling back. She was mortified that she'd had yet another panic attack around him and she was also currently mostly naked with a dog in her lap.

Tyler stood and offered his hand. She clutched the robe closed and took it as she stood. She wobbled, but Tyler caught her around her waist, the robe partly opening. He snapped his eyes to hers, a flush coming over him.

"I better get ready for school," she said, not quite meeting his eyes, pulling the robe closed even as she felt heat rushing to her face. "You better not have looked."

"Wouldn't dream of it." Something in his voice made her snap her head to him. He flushed as if guilty and she felt oddly certain in that moment that he had imagined her naked before. Surprisingly, she did not mind. "You need to brush your teeth."

He shook his head and chuckled. "On it." He moved to the sink. "You're welcome."

She looked him in the eye in the mirror. "Thanks."

She wasn't in denial. She knew her panic attacks were getting worse and more frequent. Google told her that happened during stressful times in life. This was a very stressful time in her life.

Google had also told her that many people had panic attacks of varying degrees. And not everyone required therapy. She would be able to handle these attacks, Google said, using various techniques. One of them was to have a pet. Check. Also to identify if this was a stressful time in your life. Check.

She was advised to seek counseling if she had any of the following symptoms: overwhelming sadness—no; adjusting your daily schedule around your fears—hardly. She was fine.

As soon as she graduated and got her boards scores, the frequency of these episodes would decrease, and she would be fine. She was sure of it.

Chapter Thirty-Three

Tyler

Sleep had never really found him last night. He had tossed and turned, in and out of sleep, unable to get Saira out of his mind. It hadn't helped that she was sleeping next to him.

So. Close.

He had heard the shower turn on and then off, so when she called for Kiara, he thought she simply wanted to greet the puppy. Kiara, for her part, had not moved. When Saira called out twice more, urgency and fear in her voice, he was up in an instant.

His heart thudded in his chest at the sight of Saira shaking on the floor in the bathroom, terror in her eyes and face.

He glanced at her now, confidently packing her bag, curly hair trapped in its tight ponytail, scrubs and sneakers. The cutest veterinarian ever. He would have a houseful of pets if she were their doctor. He considered the possibility of men doing just that, and a sudden fury came over him. He shook his head. What the hell?

At least there was no sign of her panic attack from this morning.

He handed her coffee to-go cup. "You okay?"

"Don't do that."

"Do what?"

"Baby me because I had a little panic attack."

"I am not babying you. I'm showing concern."

"Well, don't. I'm fine."

"I know you got Kiara to help, but maybe you need something…more?" He grinned at her. "Like therapy?"

"Not necessary. I've got it handled." She headed for the door.

"Sai…"

"I am fine," she said, and then she was gone.

Tyler stared at the door for minute after she left. A large part of him wanted to make her get help. But he knew enough that if she did not want help, it wouldn't matter how many therapists she saw—and that was only if he could get her to agree to go at all. No, she needed to seek it out for herself if therapy was really going to help.

His phone buzzed. *Mom.* He picked up. "Hey, Mom."

"Tyler, I was considering hiring Amar and Divya as the caterers for the engagement party. We can have it at that swanky hotel in town, Lulu's Boutique Hotel. I have an appointment with the owner, Reena, today at three. I'm going to try and see if she can squeeze us in in a few weeks."

"Mom. This is not really necessary—"

"It is, and it's happening. All I need you to do is get that ring for Saira."

Crap.

"Mom—"

"I'm not listening to protests. Just get her a ring in time for this party."

He was screwed. They needed to break up and soon.

Tyler had no idea where Saira was. Clinic closed at 6:00 p.m. and it was close to 8:00 p.m. now. It wasn't like her to not text or call to let him know where she was. Mostly because if she was late, she liked to know that he was around for Kiara.

Which he was, but how did she know that?

"She's never this late," Tyler said for the tenth time in what must have been five minutes. He saw Colton and Rita exchange a look. "I'm just saying, she usually shoots out a text." His leg pumped under the table.

By the time he heard the door unlock and Saira entered, he had worked himself up. Colton and Rita were cleaning up after dinner.

"There you are," Tyler exclaimed, relief and anger vying for dominance.

"Here I am," Saira said sweetly as she entered. She bent down as Kiara raced over to greet her.

"Where were you?" As soon as he said it, he knew it was the wrong thing. But at the moment he did not care.

"What's it to you?" she asked, defensive.

"You didn't text or call. I had no idea where you were. Clinic is over at six, it's eight now."

"If you must know, I had drinks with Lin. And I did." She pulled out her phone and looked at it. "Oh. I typed out the text and forgot to hit Send." She giggled. "Sorry."

"Sorry? That's it?" Tyler glared at her. "You always text if for no other reason than to be sure Kiara is cared for. I thought something happened to you."

"I don't know what else to say, Tyler. I thought I texted. I didn't hit Send. I apologized." She sounded irritated now, and her voice became raised. "And clearly Kiara is cared for, so I think we're all good here. What the hell is your problem, anyway?"

"My problem is that I didn't know where you were!" He widened his eyes and cut them to Colton and Rita, silently signaling to her. Now that they'd gotten started, why waste an argument?

Sai followed his eyes. "Well, you need to get over yourself. I am certainly not going to answer to you about my whereabouts. Don't you trust me?"

"This has nothing to do with trust."

"Because if you don't trust me, then what are we even doing here?" Saira spat back.

Good.

"What the hell does that mean?" Despite the fact that he knew they were acting, his stomach filled with dread. As if Sai was really getting ready to break up with him.

Even though they weren't really together.

"That means that I believe the basis of a relationship is trust, and since you don't have any, maybe we should not be together. I mean how much of a commitment are you making if you still haven't even gotten the ring?" Saira glared at him.

She was good.

"That's how you feel?" Tyler narrowed his eyes at her.

"That's how I feel!" She was vehement.

"Then I guess there's no reason to even get a ring, is there?" Tyler shot at her.

"No, there is not." Saira stomped toward the bedroom. Tyler followed. She grabbed a pillow and a blanket. "I'll take the sofa."

"*I'll* take the sofa." He grabbed his own pillow and a blanket and stormed from the room.

He wasn't going to let her sleep on the sofa. He turned to find Colton and Rita staring at him.

"She'll come around." Rita was soothing him.

"No, she won't. And I'm fine with it." He tossed his pillow on the sofa. "Good night."

Chapter Thirty-Four

Saira

Well, that had worked out quite neatly. A real argument, lengthened into a doozy that really did feel like solid ground for them to break up. Tyler had quite chivalrously taken the sofa, so she had the bed to herself.

Thank god. She was exhausted. It was tiring fighting with your best friend/fake fiancé.

She changed and plopped herself right into the middle of his very comfortable giant bed.

And then proceeded to toss and turn. It was lonely in this huge bed. She had gotten used to Tyler's warm presence beside her, the steady evenness of his breathing. Well, she'd just have to get over being used to it, since it wasn't like he would always be in her bed. The thought of him *being in her bed* sent heat pulsing through her.

Lin was right. Relationships had ups and downs—but wait, she wasn't in a real relationship with Tyler. This farce was over now, so they could go back to normal. Whatever that was.

She cursed when her alarm went off, because naturally, she hadn't really slept at all. It was because boards scores were due in a few days, she told herself. It had nothing to do with her thoughts of Tyler and wishing he were in the bed with her.

She dragged herself from the comfort of the bed and trudged to the bathroom. She missed her toothbrush with the toothpaste and got toothpaste all over the counter. She managed to get some onto her toothbrush to brush her teeth. It was going be a double-coffee day. Just as she was finishing up, Tyler stumbled in looking as bad as she felt.

"All of my sofas suck. Why did I even buy them?" Tyler grumbled as he shuffled in. He was shirtless and seemed completely unaware of it. Saira had to force herself not to stare at him. Every part of his chest and legs was cut with what she imagined to be very hard, very strong muscle. At present, his shorts seemed to be barely hanging on.

"You, uh…well…probably did not think you were going to be sleeping on them." She tamed her wild curls into a ponytail to wash her face. She touched her scar as a matter of habit and found Tyler watching her in the mirror. "Hey, how come my cleanser is almost gone?" she exclaimed.

Tyler widened his eyes in mock innocence while he finished brushing his teeth. He shrugged and rinsed. "Maybe someone realized how good it was and has been using it?"

She narrowed her eyes and shook her head at him. "Fine. But the next bottle is on you."

"Actually, we'll probably need two bottles." His gaze rested heavy on her.

She nodded, not looking away. They would not be sharing a bathroom much longer. "Yes. I suppose so." She paused. "Nice argument last night."

He shrugged and flicked imaginary lint from his very muscular, very bare shoulder. "Thank you." He smirked at her for a second, his features quickly softening as he continued to look at her. "Though I was concerned for real that you hadn't texted. You're usually so good about that."

She inhaled. "You're right. I get it. I was with Lin, and I totally thought I hit Send…"

He broke into a huge smile that somehow made her heart thud. "Next time I'll be calmer. And I'll just call you."

"Next time I'll make sure that I hit Send."

Silence grew between them as they both realized that there likely would not be a next time.

"Sai?"

"Yes?" She was surprised at the expectancy in her voice.

"I need the shower."

"Right." She inhaled. "Of course. I'll put on coffee, and we will continue the fight."

"Absolutely." He grinned and a part of her melted a little. Lin was right. Hot Tyler was *H.O.T.* She tried to move around Tyler to exit the bathroom, but he moved at the same time, and they collided. She was right. Very hard. His muscles. Were very. Hard. She tried to sidestep, and he matched her move.

Tyler put his hands on her arms and held her steady. "I'll walk around." He swallowed hard. She noted that his gaze had dropped as well, and she became very aware of the fact that she had no bra on, and that it was chilly in the bathroom.

Tyler walked past her and she made her way to the closet to put on a bra and her running clothes. Her things were already mixed in with his, and her heart grew heavy as she realized that she would have to separate all that as well.

She went out to the kitchen to make coffee. As if the scent of coffee were a siren call, Colton and Rita emerged from their room. They eyed her carefully before pulling out eggs and vegetables for breakfast. Saira decided the easiest thing was to lean into it. Her engagement to Tyler would be over sooner rather than later.

That was the goal, right?

"Good morning, Saira," Colton said, pouring two mugs of coffee.

"If you say so," she quipped. It was way easier to be flippant with Colton than Rita. Luckily, Rita didn't say anything. Too bad, she was starting to like Rita.

She waited until Tyler came out from getting dressed, shooting him a glare and huffing and leaving for her run. She hoped Tyler played his part.

She returned, sweaty yet exhilarated to an empty apartment and a text on her phone from Tyler. Stayed frigid. He added a winky emoji.

Great. Maybe they were almost done with this charade. The thought did not fill her with the relief she had been expecting. She texted him back. I'll be late again. Meeting my dad. She let her finger hover for a second over the backspace to delete the last three words and then decided against it. But we can pretend I didn't tell you that.

His response was almost immediate with a thumbs-up emoji.

She showered and dressed for clinic, gathering Kiara with her for a day at the clinic. Saira absolutely loved this clinic. Five exam rooms and an operating room, capable and caring staff, and state-of-the-art equipment. Many veterinary interns cycled through here over the years, but not all were offered positions. Saira was the first one in a few years. It was all contingent on her passing the boards. If she passed, she had a job at this amazing clinic. If she did not—well, she did not want to think about what that would mean.

The day was busy and challenging, but Kiara did wonderfully. She was the perfect ambassador for the clinic, welcoming the animals as if she ran the place.

Saira met her dad at a pet-friendly brewery, not too far from the clinic.

"Hey." She sat down across from her dad. After a long day at work, Kiara simply curled into a donut and fell asleep on her lap. This little motion brought Saira so much joy.

"Hi!" He smiled at her. Up until now, he had always worn a suit and tie. She had assumed he came from work. Today he was in a long-sleeve shirt and jeans. All very high-end, mind you, but practically slumming it.

There was a level of comfort between them that had grown without her noticing. She no longer had butterflies in her belly in anticipation of seeing him. She didn't necessarily look forward to their meetings with anticipation, but not being apprehensive seemed a step in the right direction. Simply the fact that she was okay referring to him as "Dad" was a new high point in their relationship.

They talked about her school, her impending job. They even laughed a little. "So, I ran into Tyler a few days ago at a coffee shop. We chatted for a bit."

Saira's heart pounded. Because Tyler and her dad had chatted, or because Tyler's name was mentioned? Hard to tell. "Oh, that's great."

"You are a very lucky young woman. That man loves you desperately."

She furrowed her brow. "Does he?"

"Well, of course he does. You are getting married, are you not?"

She nodded. "Right." She shrugged, trying to be nonchalant. "What exactly did he say that made you so certain of his love for me? Because Bhaiya still has doubts."

"He said that you were the very air that he breathed."

Saira stared at her dad. She didn't think he was making up what Tyler had said, but that wasn't the same as believing he actually meant it. Because if she believed that Tyler had meant that, then…then nothing. She and Tyler could not happen.

Her father grinned and patted her hand. "He is the real deal." He glanced at his watch. "Our time is up."

She stood. She needed to get out of here. "Next time?"

He nodded, a huge smile on his face. "Next time."

Saira and Kiara walked home. Saira needed time to digest what her father had just told her. Tyler must have simply been playing his part well. It couldn't be true. But what if it was? The thought exhilarated and terrified her all at the same time. The idea that Tyler had real feelings for her warmed her, even though she felt like it should terrify her. Her and Tyler? Together? No. It would never work. Look at how Bhaiya was reacting. No. Tyler was simply playing his part with her father. That made the most sense. And soon, their breakup would be official, and neither of them would have to pretend anymore.

A couple blocks from the condo, a pit formed in Saira's stomach at the argument she had yet to have with Tyler, no matter how fake. She wasn't scared of the argument itself, but what it might mean.

Chapter Thirty-Five

Tyler

Today was the breakup day. He had a pit in his stomach, which made absolutely no sense, since he and Saira weren't really together. Strangely enough, he had felt more "together" with her in the last couple weeks of putting their breakup into motion than he ever had before.

If he had thought he was in love with Saira before, it was nothing compared to how he felt about her now, after really getting to know her as a person. He had fallen in love with the feisty young woman who worked hard and was fiercely protective of anyone who was dear to her.

He was currently completely and utterly lost to the strong beautiful woman who loved the people she considered her family but would not sacrifice her dreams to them. She was sweet and funny and thoughtful and tough, and she always had to have the last word, all at the same time. As much as he was dreading this "breakup fight," he would not trade the past couple weeks of really *seeing* Saira Rawal for the amazing person that she was.

Not to mention that all of that came in what he thought was the most beautiful package. She had curves for miles, and he was willing to bet her skin was softer than silk. Her eyes had fixed him into place more than once, not to mention her luscious mouth that was as likely to be snarky as it was to be kind. He found it hard to breathe sometimes, just seeing her in her scrubs.

Going back to "normal" would be anything but pleasant.

Now that he had really seen her and come to love all of her, even the parts that irritated him, he had no idea how he was going to function without her. How was he going to go back to accepting Saira as simply his friend that he grew up with?

Tyler was certain that if they had really been together, he would never have missed having her cinnamon buns; he would have gladly purchased groceries and cooked for her every day of his life. They might bicker about whose turn it was to take out Kiara, but that would only be so that he could warm her up properly when she returned from the cold. He would never put his work over hers; they would always be the team that they were today.

The team that was scheming to end the fake engagement that they had only started so he wouldn't look like a loser in front of his brother.

Saira entered the bedroom while he stared at his computer from the bed.

"How was the jungle today?" he asked.

"Probably better than the animals you deal with." She smirked.

"Can't argue that."

"But we have to argue, don't we?"

"Well, that is the plan," he said on a deep sigh. "I know how you feel about a plan."

She smiled and sat down next to him on the bed, letting out a deep breath. "I just don't really feel like arguing with you today. I hate the fighting—even the fake fighting."

"Me too." He squeezed her hand. "One last one and we're free. We can be ourselves again."

She grinned. "That is true." She looked at him and squeezed his hand back but left her hand in his. "Back to our old selves."

"Are they here yet?"

"Bhaiya and Karina are on the way. So is your mom. Colton and Rita are prepping dinner." She widened her eyes at this, because Colton's cooking was on a whole new level. "I convinced the family we were going to discuss plans for the engagement party."

Tyler's phone buzzed at the same time as Saira's. They didn't move. He knew without looking that the families were here. He continued to look at her. She was watching him, her eyes soft. He could say something right now. Tell her that he really truly loved her. That this did not have to be a farce.

Then what?

He knew the answer. Then nothing. It would be laughable to believe that she might have feelings for him after watching him grow up. Even if she did, the fact that Aneel did not approve would weigh on her. On both of them.

"Showtime," she said softly.

"This is so exciting. I'm so glad we're doing this." His mom's voice drifted back to them.

"Whatever you're making, Colton, it smells amazing." Karina's voice carried back to them as well.

"Well, come on in," Rita was saying. "I'll get drinks. Tyler and Saira just finished for the day. They should be out shortly."

Saira looked at him and nodded. *Now.* He squeezed her hand.

"Honestly, Tyler." She had raised her voice, but he saw pain in her eyes. "It's like you don't even care about what I have to do."

"That's not true," he countered, raising his voice. "I'm *busy*. And you should have texted that you were going to be late."

"No. I am not going to answer to some man." She opened the door as if she were walking to the kitchen.

"Some man? Is that who I am to you?" *Who was he to her, for real?*

"That's not what I said." She took a few steps.

"Yes, it is."

Saira stopped and turned to face him. She raised an eyebrow

at him and smirked so quickly where no one else could see. She was admiring the level of pettiness that they had dropped to.

Tyler had to dig down deep into a memory of his parents arguing to figure out what to say. "You simply have no appreciation of what I do around here."

"I could say the same for you. I can't do this, Tyler. I know my mom made sacrifices for a man and that did not work out for anyone. I'm not going to fall into that trap." She took another couple steps and turned back to him. "Maybe this was a mistake."

"What was a mistake?" Tyler made sure his voice carried.

"Getting engaged. I don't think we should be together," Saira said, a hint of sadness in her voice. Damn she was good.

"Well, I certainly do not want to be with you if you don't want to be with me." Tyler made sure to throw the words at her.

"What are you saying, Tyler?"

"I'm saying the same thing you are. This is too hard. It shouldn't be this hard," Tyler said. He softened his voice.

"It is way too hard," Saira agreed. Her voice had come down to a normal level, so it sounded like they were being reasonable, and not simply saying things in anger.

They glanced down the small hallway to see their family watching them, aghast.

"Sorry." Saira dropped her head for a moment and glanced at Tyler as if considering her words. "Well," Saira said, putting her chin up and walking all the way to the living room, "since you've heard everything, I guess you already know that Tyler and I are breaking up. It's just not going to work," Saira told him and the room.

"We're sorry to have put you through this, but maybe we jumped the gun." He looked at Saira.

"We absolutely jumped the gun," Saira agreed.

"But your arguments were about basic stuff," Rita said.

"What do you mean?" Tracy asked.

"Like who takes the dog out, who buys groceries—just normal couple bickering," Rita said. "That's not reason enough to break up."

His mother narrowed her eyes at the both of them. "This doesn't really make sense."

"Agreed." This coming from Karina.

Aneel said nothing. He seemed to be fuming.

"We just can't do this anymore," Saira said softly. It was true. They were tired of all the pretending.

"You need counseling." Colton spoke softly from behind everyone.

Saira turned to him in horror. "What?"

Colton put his hands on Rita's shoulders. "We've been going about once every two weeks. It's been incredible." He pulled her close and they gazed at each other lovingly.

Made sense. No wonder Colton wasn't acting like a bully anymore.

"He's right," Rita agreed, beaming. "It has worked wonders for each of us individually as well as together."

"I think we're fine as we are—we just don't work as a couple," Tyler said. "We'll go back to the way we were and all will be well."

"No," his mother said, her blue eyes flaring. "You're going to therapy. Couples or separate—pick one. But we can't let you give up on each other."

"It's not necessary," Saira insisted.

"Are you saying that you don't love each other?" His mom pushed.

He glanced at Sai and she at him. Neither of them of them opened their mouths.

"Tracy Auntie is right. Give it try," Karina said. "It's clear you two love each other."

"Therapy will help," Colton said.

Tyler's heart pounded in his chest. Because it was sounding like all the people closest to them really believed that Saira loved him. Was it possible they were right? He wasn't sure. But next to him, Sai had frozen.

"It's not necessary. We will be fine," Saira insisted.

"Let them do whatever they want." Aneel finally spoke, his voice full of challenge. He folded his arms across his chest as he passed his gaze over Saira, landing on Tyler with narrowed eyes. "They seem to know what's best."

What the hell was his problem? Anger boiled in Tyler so hot he almost agreed to counseling just to spite Aneel.

"Fine." Saira spoke up.

Tyler snapped his head to her. "What?"

"We'll go to counseling," Saira nearly barked as she glared at her brother. Clearly, she'd had the same thought as him. Aneel's face was expressionless.

Tyler widened his eyes at her.

She pressed her lips together in determination.

They were going to therapy.

Chapter Thirty-Six

Saira

"That brother of mine is the most irritating man on the planet. How Karina fell for him is beyond me." Saira paced by the window in their room. When did she start thinking of this as their room, and not Tyler's room?

"Well, the two of you are a bit odd when it comes to the other," Tyler said. He was surprisingly calm, considering the whole thing had just backfired, and Saira had agreed to *couples therapy*! They had even sat through a major planning session for the engagement party. Everyone was solidly convinced that Saira and Tyler would "fix" things in therapy, so the party planning was still going ahead. "Remember when you tracked his phone and we went to Karina's house at two in the morning?"

"That was different. We didn't like Karina then," Saira defended herself. "And he never stays out that late."

"Well, the way Aneel keeps glaring at me, I half expect him to challenge me to a duel." Tyler stood and went to the closet to change.

"Okay. So, we'll just fake therapy." She knelt on the bed while Tyler changed.

He popped his head out. "Are you out of your mind, Sai?"

She really did love the way he called her Sai. "What do you mean?"

"We're not faking therapy. We're not faking anything anymore. It's too much. We're coming clean," Tyler said from inside the closet.

The idea of coming clean was too much for her. Things had gone too far. If they confessed, Bhaiya would never trust her, never let her be an adult. "At this point, they will be so mad at how we lied to them we almost have to keep going."

"To what end, Sai? We're still breaking up. We're still going to go back to the way it used to be."

But did they have to? She didn't want that. Maybe she had at the beginning. But now? What if the feelings she was having for Tyler were real? Was there a possibility that he felt the same way? She opened her mouth to say the words. He was still in the closet; it'd be easier this way. What was she going to say? *Hey, Tyler. I might have feelings for you, but I definitely love seeing you half naked.*

Um. NO.

Hey. I have feelings for you.

No.

Tyler, I definitely feel something for you, and I don't want to go back to how it was before. I'm not sure what the feelings are— Stop.

If she wasn't sure of her feelings, what was she going to confess and why? If Tyler didn't feel the same way, she'd be making things even more awkward. And how could she ever find out if he felt the same way when she couldn't even describe what it was that she felt?

Nope. Better to just keep her mouth shut for now. But if they kept up the ruse, that might give her time to figure out how she felt.

"Coming clean will only make them mad at us. So, we fake our engagement for a bit longer," she called out.

Their phones dinged. Tyler came out of the closet in his sleep shorts and yet another race T-shirt. This one was a 10K he had run a few years ago. She and Bhaiya had gotten up at the crack of dawn to be with him at the start line.

"You PR'd in that race, didn't you?" she said, pointing to the shirt.

"I did. It was a new personal record for me." He looked at her, his brow furrowed. "You remember that?"

"I remember waking up before the sun to see you off."

He held his phone up. "Names of therapists," he said, defeated. "From my mom. She'll know if we go or not. And as a bonus, she has decided to postpone the engagement party for a month for us."

"Wait, what do you mean when you say she'll know? Would the doctor tell her? Doesn't that violate patient-doctor privacy?"

"Well, Mom can't ask, and the doctor can't really tell her, but there are ways to get around that." He shook his head at her. "It seems like you're right and we can't get out of this." He inhaled. "I'll make some appointments tomorrow."

Chapter Thirty-Seven

Tyler

Tyler was able to set up some initial appointments over the next two weeks, once he mentioned who his mother was. He really did not know how this was all going to turn out. Maybe they could hit a few a sessions and then say they were a hopeless case and needed to break up.

In any case, he met Sai in the waiting room of the first therapist. Dr. Lucy Wright, LMFT. Reviews said she was heart-felt and understanding and had helped many couples resolve deep issues and lead more loving lives.

Okay.

Tyler sat down in the chair next to Sai in the tiny waiting room. The carpet was a worn-in brown. There were the two chairs that they occupied as well as a bench along the far wall. The customary periodicals were hanging in a magazine rack. Tissue boxes were scattered throughout the small space. She looked up at him, putting her phone away. "I signed in for us."

He nodded, almost afraid to speak because he felt watched. He looked around and realized that he was indeed being watched by the very young-looking receptionist with a Goth vibe. Her gaze upon him was intent, though he couldn't tell if it was because she was checking him out or plotting his death.

Sai leaned into him and whispered, "Someone has a crush." He could hear the smirk in her voice. Her breath on his ear was intimate, and he chided himself for enjoying it.

"Could be a crush on you. She's looking at both of us," he whispered back.

She flicked her gaze in the receptionist's direction. "Nope. Most definitely a Tyler groupie," she whispered again.

He rolled his eyes at her and pulled out his phone. Better to doomscroll than make eye contact with what appeared to be a fifteen-year-old girl.

A door opened and a couple walked out. The woman was smiling, the man's eyes were red-rimmed, and he grabbed a tissue on his way out.

"Saira Rawal and Tyler Hart." The young receptionist nodded in their direction, her voice monotone. She didn't stand, simply jutting her chin toward a different door.

A petite woman with a tight blond bun and a flowing floral dress greeted them as they entered. "Hello. I'm Dr. Wright. Please sit anywhere."

Tyler sat on a sofa to the side of the small room, and Saira sat beside him.

"Hm," Dr. Wright said as she nodded at them. She was older than them, closer to his mother's age.

"What?" asked Sai.

"Nothing, at all," said Dr. Wright, though her cheery demeanor seemed forced. Maybe the other couple drained her? She sat opposite them in a chair, with a small table between them. "So, tell me why you're here."

They looked at each other. Saira spoke. "Well, we were on the verge of ending our engagement, and our family suggested couples therapy before we called it quits."

Dr. Wright nodded and turned toward Tyler. "How about you?"

"What she said." Tyler nodded his agreement.

"Do you have any thoughts about this that are your own?" Dr. Wright asked.

"No." Tyler pressed his mouth tight. "I agree with her."

"Uh-huh." She turned to Saira. "So, you are Indian?"

"Yes. My parents came here from India." Saira narrowed her eyes.

"And you, Tyler? What is your background?"

"Oh, well. My great-grandparents are of European background."

Dr. Wright nodded. She looked at them for a moment. "So, I believe that your issues stem from your cultural backgrounds. Saira comes from a traditionally conservative culture and you, Tyler, have lost touch with your culture completely."

Tyler and Saira stared at her in disbelief. A total of four minutes had passed.

Tyler spoke first. "You think our issues are because she is Indian and I am not?"

Dr. Wright smiled at him, as if pleased he had caught on so fast. "Yes."

"We've literally been here for four minutes. You asked us each one question, and we haven't described our problems at all other than to say we have them," Tyler said.

Dr. Wright smiled as if he were complimenting her. "I am very good. As I'm sure you found in the reviews."

Saira stood and Tyler stood with her. "Thank you, Dr. Wright," he said, and they walked out. Saira grabbed his hand, but didn't look at him. He stayed focused on leaving the building. It wasn't until they had reached the safety of the street that they risked glancing at each other. And then immediately burst into laughter.

"I don't know why I'm laughing. I feel like I should be insulted," Saira said as she gathered her breath.

"Me too," Tyler agreed. "But it's too ridiculous." He caught his breath. "Let's get dinner. Mom has Kiara."

Sai caught her laughter and nodded at him. "That sounds amazing." Sai led the way toward their favorite sushi place that was on the next block. Tyler threaded his fingers with hers as if it were the most natural thing to do.

Saira squeezed his hand and smiled as they laughed about their session. "Too bad though. Her receptionist—"

"Is a child. She cannot even be eighteen," Tyler finished.

"Well, she's old enough to know what she likes." Saira drew her gaze up and down Tyler.

He smirked at her. "Jealous?"

"As if."

Tyler might really like going to therapy.

Chapter Thirty-Eight

Saira

Saira was still laughing to herself about that first therapy session when she met up with her dad the next day for lunch. She felt lighter than she had in a while, though she tried to deny that had anything to do with the rest of the evening, during which she and Tyler enjoyed sushi and then walked along the harbor the way they all used to when they were teenagers.

"Hey," her father said as he sat down. "What's so funny?"

She shook her head. "Tyler and I are trying couples therapy, and the first therapist basically took one look at us and decided our trouble is our respective cultures." She shook her head.

"You and Tyler are in couples therapy?" He leaned in, interested.

"Well, not yet. Still looking for a good fit with a therapist, you know?"

Her dad nodded. "I am familiar. Spent quite a bit of time in therapy myself."

She nodded. He had said as much on many occasions.

"I went to get help with my panic attacks—and with my depression. I needed to find coping methods that didn't involve alcohol."

"Did the therapy help?"

"Yes. But you didn't answer. Why are you and Tyler in couples therapy?"

Before she could come up with a proper lie, she caught sight of Tyler, Colton in tow. "Well speak of the devil, here he is," Saira said as she waved them over. Tyler looked pretty amazing today in his suit. He must have had a day at the office. The suit was a shade of blue that complemented his eyes and was perfectly cut to fit his body.

Tyler and Colton came over. "Dad, you know Tyler. This is his brother, Colton. Colton, this is my father—Yogesh Rawal."

Yogesh stood and shook each of their hands. "Nice to meet you, Colton."

"Nice to meet you, Mr. Rawal." Colton stared at the man's face.

Weird. Though her father was giving Colton the same appraising look. "You look very familiar to me. Can't place it, but I will."

"Tyler and I just stopped over to grab some takeout. Didn't mean to interrupt," Colton said.

"No interruption. I enjoy getting to know people in Saira's life," her dad said with a small chuckle. "You're welcome to join us."

Saira shot Tyler a small glare to signal that he should find an excuse to say no.

"Nice seeing you again." Tyler nodded. "But we both have working lunches today. Maybe another time." Tyler bent down and kissed her cheek as if it were the most natural thing to do. "I'll see you tonight," he whispered, his breath sending a current down that side of her body. He waved at her father as he and Colton went to grab their takeout.

Saira literally floated when Tyler kissed her cheek.

Her dad waved and sat back down. "If I didn't know better, I'd think your fiancé is trying to avoid me."

"Not true." She watched Tyler as he and Colton walked away. He simply wouldn't be her fiancé for much longer. The relief that should follow that thought was now replaced with dread.

That was weird.

"So, do you plan to stay at General Pawspital?" he asked.

"As long as I pass my boards, that's the place to be. Good money, good hours." She shrugged. "It's very coveted."

"But what about progress? Is there room to grow, or to own?" This seemed like a very parent-like question to ask, and it made her smile.

"To be honest, I do not know. There does seem to be a turn-over rate of about five to seven years," she answered.

"Something to keep in mind." He shrugged.

"As long as I can see the patients. Because it's not usually the patients that stress you out. It's the owners." She shook her head. "Humans will drive you up a wall." She chuckled.

"I can understand that. People are complicated. Animals are simple, am I right?"

"You most certainly are," Saira agreed.

"Listen, I don't know what's going on with you and Tyler. You didn't ask my opinion. But here it is. It is clear that he loves you and that you love him. If it takes therapy, it's worth it. Don't give up on him."

"Tyler." Colton met his eyes, once they reached the apartment. There was concern in his eyes and in his voice. "That was Saira's dad?"

"Yes. They've just recently started reconnecting—"

"Tyler. That's him."

"That's who?" Though Tyler was starting to guess who.

"That's the guy that dad was talking to. The one who was upset with him. He recognized me because—"

"You look like Dad," Tyler finished. "But how do you know?"

"I peeked into the room, remember? I saw him and I heard him. That's him. And my paralegal got his name, remember?"

Tyler stared at his brother. "This better not be—"

"Tyler, I'm not that bully you grew up with. I have changed.

I'd rather this have nothing to do with you or people you love, but I'm telling you the truth." Colton looked at him, his green eyes filled with desperation that Tyler understood what he was saying.

Tyler believed him. The pain in Colton's face was too real to doubt him. Whatever had happened in the past, Colton was making a genuine attempt at making amends. He wouldn't have said anything about Saira's father unless he was absolutely sure.

Tyler nodded. "Okay. Let's find out what the hell happened back then. But not a word to anyone—not Mom, not Rita not Sai."

"You sure you don't want to give Saira a heads-up?"

"Not until we know what we're dealing with." He wasn't about to take Saira's dad away from her until they knew for sure what was going on. Not when it had taken this long for things to come even this far between them.

Colton nodded. "I'll have my paralegal take a look. I'll let you know what I come up with."

Chapter Thirty-Nine

Saira

Tyler had made a few more appointments with other therapists so they could find one they liked—or at least one that actually did more than a five-minute assessment based on basically nothing.

It was an exercise with an odd ending for sure, but Saira found herself looking forward to what therapist #2 was going to be like. She waited outside the building in the cool spring evening. She saw Tyler before he saw her.

He had removed his tie, unbuttoned the top button, but still wore his suit jacket. His stride defined grace and confidence but didn't cut a path. Instead Tyler navigated strollers, small children and dogs with enough agility that it appeared he had always known they were there. He smiled and nodded at people, his hair flopping around in the breeze as he did so. He carried no bag, his arms hung loosely at his sides, ready to help a fallen child or wave at some known (or possibly unknown) person. As he got closer, she noticed other people noticing Tyler.

He turned heads, that man. And he very clearly was oblivious to it. He ran his fingers through his hair and glanced at his phone as he approached her.

"Hey." He leaned down to kiss her cheek again—this had become their new way of greeting one another. "You okay?"

"Yeah. I'm good." She nearly sighed from his kiss but caught herself. "Let's get some therapy."

"Yeah," he said with a forced smile.

Saira looked at him, concerned. "Is everything okay? You seem a little on edge."

"Everything's fine," he insisted, though his smile got even more strained. "It's just… It's Colton. He's really worried about this whole thing with our dad. But don't worry, we'll figure it all out."

"Any leads?" she asked.

He shook his head. Was it her imagination or did he look away from her?

"How are things going with your work?" he asked. "Everything good with the clinic?"

"Well, my dad did mention that I might want to think about advancement possibilities at General Pawspital—wherever I work in general," she shared.

"I agree. There's plenty out there, and you're one of the best."

"You don't know that." Saira waved him off.

He stopped dead in his tracks and lay his hand on her arm. "I do know that. I've seen you in action. Not only at school but growing up. You were made to be a vet. Don't doubt that."

Saira was taken aback by Tyler's obvious passion on this subject. "Yes. Okay. Of course you're right."

They reached the door of Dr. Tim Sharpy, LMFT. Saira looked at Tyler and smirked. "Take two." She inhaled and opened the door.

The space was small but modern. A quite attractive receptionist sat at the desk, greeting them with a smile. She was slightly older than the young girl in Dr. Wright's office.

"Saira Rawal and Tyler Hart." They checked in.

"Have a seat. He'll be out in a minute," she said pleasantly.

"Well, at least this receptionist isn't checking us out," Saira whispered.

He chuckled softly near her ear, his tousled hair brushing her forehead. It was nice, being this close to him. They sat next to each other on a small bench. There was a fake plant to her right.

"What's with the fake plant, do you think?" She leaned toward Tyler, taking in his slightly musky scent from being outside mixed with that Dove soap.

"Fake beauty," he answered.

Within a few minutes a man a few years older than them came through a door and summoned them in. Saira sat down on the sofa and motioned for Tyler to join her.

"Huh. You sat down where she told you to sit," Dr. Sharpy commented.

Tyler looked up at Dr. Sharpy. "She just patted the seat next to her."

"And you obeyed," the doctor said. He turned to Saira. "You're a vet, right?'

"Well almost." Saira smiled at him.

"Do you expect everyone to obey you?" he asked

Saira was taken aback. "I don't expect—"

"I mean it was clear that you intended to dictate where Mr. Hart sat, even coming into this room. I can only imagine what else you dictate in his life."

"She doesn't dictate anything," Tyler said, a clear edge in his voice.

"Are you certain? Or are you so used to it you can't tell the difference? You seem to be getting upset, Mr. Hart."

Tyler stood, clearly agitated, which was saying something, given how easygoing he was. "Come on, Sai."

Saira stood and took Tyler's outstretched hand.

"Oh." Dr. Sharpy looked at her. "Do you just do whatever he tells you?"

"Run," she whispered.

She and Tyler walked as quickly as possible out into the reception area, down the elevator and out the door. Tyler led the way and she followed, not letting go of his hand. She was quite enjoying this hand-holding business. Tyler was fuming and led them to a bar. They ordered food and drinks before he was able to speak.

"The nerve of that guy to talk about you like that," Tyler said as the waiter set down their beers.

Saira shook her head. "I'm good, really."

"I think we're done with this whole therapy thing," Tyler said, taking a pull of his beer.

"How about one more? You've already made the appointment. Besides, three sounds like we gave it chance, you know? The family will have to let us break up then."

Tyler did not look like he thought this was a good idea, but he shrugged. "I suppose so, since you expect me to obey you anyway." A small grin curved his lips.

Saira chuckled. "That's a good boy!"

He raised his beer and clinked her bottle. "You know it."

Chapter Forty

Tyler

"How's the therapy going?" Colton asked. It was just the two of them for dinner tonight. Saira was meeting her dad and Rita was meeting some law school friends. It was Tyler's turn to cook.

"Still looking for the decent therapist—the first two we saw were awful." Tyler shrugged as he chopped vegetables. He shook the small pan that was roasting his spices. Aneel had taught him a basic tandoori spice and he was going to try it on salmon tonight.

"Yeah. I know how that goes." Colton poured them some white wine.

"Yeah?" Tyler turned to his brother.

"I wasn't lying. Rita and I have been in therapy. But I did go on my own as well." Colton was frank and unabashed about sharing this.

"You did?" Tyler asked, removing the spices from the heat.

He shrugged. "I was feeling lost. So I went."

"You do seem…different."

"I am. I was a bully, because I thought that was what power looked like." He shook his head. "That is simply not the case." Colton sipped the wine.

Tyler chuckled. "Well, for what it's worth, this is a much-preferred version."

"Glad to hear it." Colton paused. "I know I was not the best brother to you growing up, but I plan on changing that."

"I've noticed."

"Yet, you're still skeptical."

"Do you blame me?"

"No. Not really." Colton chuckled. "But whether you believe me or not, I do want what's best for you, and we both know that's Saira. You've been in love with her for years. But she doesn't know that, does she?"

Tyler became completely engrossed in putting the spices in the blender and blending them up.

Colton laughed. "It's fine. I'm not meddling. I just don't know why you haven't told her. It's obvious to everyone how she feels about you." Colton paused. "Be honest with her, be honest with Aneel."

"Colton I—" Wait, did he say *how she feels*? How did she feel? What did everyone see?

Colton held up a hand. "I'm just saying that putting everything out there is best."

"It's not real." The words left Tyler's mouth before he could think.

"What's not real?"

"The engagement. The whole thing," Tyler confessed. "I'm sorry. Saira announced it when you got here, because you were with Rita, and she was afraid I would look like a loser to you… Then it got out of hand."

Colton paused. "I never ever thought you were a loser."

"You were always one-upping me."

"Yeah. I had to keep up. I couldn't look like the loser twin whose brother was amazing at everything when I was not," Colton said.

"You were trying to keep up with me?" Tyler's eyes widened. "And wait, you thought I was amazing?"

"Of course. You got your job *without* the help of our father.

Everything you have is because you worked for it. Even my football days—Dad had a hand in. What did you think?"

"I thought you were just trying to always be better than me."

Colton shook his head at Tyler. "We are quite the pair, aren't we?"

Tyler started laughing. "We are ridiculous. All this time…"

Colton joined in. "Agreed."

Tyler gathered himself as he seasoned the fish and put it in the oven. He picked up his wineglass and held it up. "Here's to being real brothers."

"I'll drink to that." Colton clinked Tyler's glass and they both drank.

"So, what are we going to do about Saira?" Colton asked.

"What do you mean?"

"Listen. Therapy got you an extension on your fake breakup or whatever you're doing. But I still think you should tell her, Tyler. Tell her how you really feel. You may be surprised by what she says." Colton was insistent.

"Are you saying you believe she has feelings for me?"

"Ty— I don't know her. I know you. Stop holding back."

"I don't want to lose her. Or Aneel. They're all I've ever had."

"You've got to take the risk. You can't pine for her your whole life. Someone will fall for her and have the courage to tell her. Are you going to watch her love someone else without even trying?"

Tyler was suddenly imagining Saira on her wedding day, Saira with a baby, Saira with a grown-up Kiara…all with another man. A pit hollowed out in his stomach. He looked at his brother. "Oh, shit."

Colton nodded. "Exactly. What's the worst that could happen if you're honest with her? She may not return your feelings, but at least you can move forward then."

"I don't know if I'm ready to take that chance," Tyler confessed.

"It can take time to find the right therapist, you know?" Colton said. "Take your time. But Mom is doing this engagement party. If you aren't really together, you have to tell her."

"Mom will be so mad."

"No kidding."

The oven timer dinged. Time was up.

Tyler walked the few blocks to therapist number three's office and waited for Saira, who had texted she would be late. Colton's words from the night before continued to echo in his head. Tyler was enjoying this time with Sai, no matter that Colton knew the truth. Colton had assured him that he had not told anyone, even Rita. And he had no intention of saying anything.

"Hey." Sai came up from behind him.

"You okay?" Tyler turned to face her. She was beautiful, small curls popping out from her ponytail.

"Just a long day, some uncooperative patients and some demanding owners, you know?" She sighed, her eyes watery, and her voice caught. "Had to put a dog down today."

"Sai." He pulled her close and wrapped his arms around her. "I'm so sorry." She melted into him, and he felt her crying. "Why don't we cancel this and reschedule for another day?"

"No." She pulled back, wiping her eyes. "I'll be fine. We're here. Let's just do it."

Tyler studied her for a moment. She looked defeated. "Seriously, Sai—"

"Don't tell me what to do, Ty. You know I hate that." She gave him a half smile.

Tyler chuckled low and shook his head. Sai had been saying those words for as long as he could remember. Being the youngest in their little trio, she was frequently subjected to either him or Aneel attempting to call the shots—what game to play, what movie to watch, etc. She lost it one day at the ripe age of seven when Aneel had said they would watch *Finding Nemo* again.

"No." Saira had said. "We're watching Brother Bear.*"*

"We want to watch Finding Nemo.*" Aneel and Tyler had insisted.*

"I'm watching Brother Bear.*" She had inserted the DVD and sat down on the sofa. "Stop telling me what to do."*

"Wouldn't dream of it, *Brother Bear*." Tyler opened the door to the building and waved Sai through. He took her hand as they approached the elevator.

"Who is it today?" she asked as she threaded her fingers with his.

"Dr. Maya Port. She specializes in emotionally focused couples therapy." Tyler sighed, still skeptical.

Sai simply nodded. They entered the office to find an older receptionist in a modest waiting room. They checked in and took a seat. No fake plant. Just a painting of the ocean and a few chairs.

In a matter of minutes, a woman in a sleek dark ponytail, wearing dark slacks and a cream blouse came out and introduced herself as Dr. Maya Port.

"You can call me Maya, Dr. Maya, Dr. Port. Whatever makes you comfortable." She led the way into her office, and Tyler and Saira took seats on the sofa next to each other.

"So, you're an attorney." She nodded at Tyler.

"That's correct."

"And you're a veterinarian." She nodded at Saira.

Saira did not respond. Next to him, Saira's grip on his hand intensified. Her breathing started to get shallow. He turned to see beads of sweat on her upper lip, her eyes wide with fear.

"Sai? Saira?" he said softly. "I'm here."

She didn't respond.

"Saira. It's Tyler. Look at me." He continued to speak in a firm soft voice.

She turned her head to him.

He nodded and smiled. "Inhale with me."

She tried. She started shaking.

"Again. Sweetheart. Inhale." Tyler inhaled. Saira looked pale, her eyes were wide, her hands were clammy and beads of perspiration were building on her upper lip. It was clear this attack was worse than the one in the bathroom a couple weeks ago.

She inhaled.

"Exhale."

She exhaled.

Tyler kept this up, talking softly to her, not leaving her side, not even looking around. After about ten minutes, which felt like an eternity, Saira was breathing more easily, the worst of the panic attack seemingly over. It was then that he remembered they were in a therapist's office.

"Oh," he said, turning to Dr. Maya. "She gets panic attacks sometimes."

Dr. Maya smiled kindly and nodded. "I see that. You both handled that beautifully. It's clear you have a very supportive and patient relationship."

"Thank you?" Tyler had expected some kind of reprimand.

"Saira?" Dr. Maya asked. "How are you feeling now?"

Saira nodded. "Better."

Dr. Maya paused and looked from Tyler to Maya.

Here it comes. Tyler braced himself to grab Saira and bolt.

"Might I suggest that in addition to the couples counseling you have expressed interest in, Saira considers a therapist for herself, to help with her anxiety and panic?"

Silence filled the room.

Tyler had not expected anything rational here today, but that certainly was rational. But it was Saira's call.

"No. I'm okay. I manage the attacks just fine. They really only happen when I'm stressed and today was a particularly rough day. We'll just take a few sessions of couples therapy, thanks," Saira said as if she were ordering fast food.

Dr. Maya nodded. "Of course. But if you change your mind, my partner specializes in—"

"I'm good."

Tyler furrowed his brow. He knew Saira valued her ability to take care of things, but he disagreed with this decision. Regardless. It was hers to make.

Chapter Forty-One

Saira

"So now, you're in couples therapy with Tyler?" Lin asked. They were in the small break room at the clinic having a quick snack while waiting for their patients to show.

Saira looked away. "Yep, seems that way."

"Well, good for you. Lora and I did a few sessions as well."

"Really?" Saira was genuinely shocked. Lin and Lora were completely in love. "But you two are perfect for each other."

"Well, yes." Lin flushed. "But relationships are hard. It's nice to get some guidance. Helps navigate some of the rocky stuff, you know?"

Saira shrugged.

Lin shook her head at her, popping the last piece of a protein bar into her mouth. "Asking for help does not make you weak. The help actually makes you stronger. Just be honest about your feelings with yourself and with Tyler—and with your therapist. This is a good thing."

"Hey, Doctors, the patients are ready for you." Camille, the assistant, peeked her head into the break room.

Lin raised her eyebrows at Saira before she left room. "Honesty is hard. It was really hard for me, but Lora is worth it. So, I put my fears aside and went for it. And I have never been happier."

Saira and Tyler had decided they would spend two sessions with Dr. Maya, fighting with each other, which would satisfy the family that they had at least tried. Then they would be free to break up. It was a good plan and had every reason to succeed.

Except that Saira was having second thoughts about breaking up with Tyler.

Lin had said to be honest.

She flicked her gaze at him as they sat side by side facing Dr. Maya. He was focused on the doctor, a small smile on his face. He really did have a fabulous mouth. The memory of that mouth on hers haunted her day and night. Saira followed his gaze. Dr. Maya was quite attractive, with her olive skin and sleek straight black hair that was currently swept up in a high ponytail.

Saira shifted in her seat.

"So, what brings you here?" asked Dr. Maya.

"We had an appointment," Saira retorted. Maybe a bit too aggressively.

Dr. Maya smiled indulgently.

Saira continued, "We've been arguing a lot lately and thinking that this relationship may not be for us."

"Tyler?"

"I disagree. I think *she's* been arguing a lot lately."

"Okay. Let's get back to the arguing at another point. Can you tell me about how you got together?"

"Sure," Saira said. She'd recycle the story she told Lin. But Tyler started speaking before she had a chance.

"We've known each other all our lives. Up until recently, I'd always just thought of her as Aneel's little sister, Saira. We grew up together." Tyler shrugged.

"What changed?"

Saira turned to face him.

"Well. It sort of crept up on me. One day, she was a little girl, the next she was a beautiful young woman being dumped by a man she thought loved her."

Dhruv. He was talking about that night?

Dr. Maya nodded for him to continue. He remained focused on her.

"Saira called me when this guy, who she had planned on marrying, suddenly decided he did not love her. We stayed up the whole night, talking, drinking." He cut his eyes to her, then back to the doctor.

"Her heart was broken, and I found myself not only angry at the man who had hurt her, but jealous that he'd had her affections, when he most certainly had not deserved them. It was the first time I acknowledged that my feelings for Saira might be something more than what I had allowed them to be."

"Did you tell her?"

Tyler shifted in his seat and cleared his throat. "Um. Well, no. At the time, she was heartbroken. It didn't seem like it was the right moment at all."

"How about now? How do you feel about her now?"

Tyler was silent for a beat. "I love her. I mean I am in love with her. There's nothing I want more in the world than to be hers, to be by her side." He paused. "I'll be honest with you, Dr. Maya. I love her even when we are fighting. I have always loved her fighting spirit. So maybe I love her a little extra when we're fighting." He gave a half smile and a one-shouldered shrug. "The thing about Sai is that she won't fight unless it's worth her while. When she fights with me, it's like I'm worth her while."

Saira just stared at his profile, her heart in her throat. Was he telling the truth?

"What does she do or say when you tell her this?" Dr. Maya asked.

"I don't know," Tyler said as he turned to face her, his blue eyes melting into hers.

What she saw there made her heart thud. His eyes, his mouth, his face…he was naked. There was nothing hiding how he was feeling in that moment.

"I haven't ever told her until now."

Saira's heart thudded in her chest. She broke into a sweat. Tyler Hart was in love with her.

She looked at Dr. Maya. "I'm sorry. This was a mistake." She stood and ran.

Chapter Forty-Two

Tyler

Tyler had no idea where Saira was. By the time he gathered himself and got up and ran after her, there was no sign of her red coat anywhere. He ran after her a few blocks in each direction, but no Sai. He had walked home, a pit in his stomach, hoping she would be waiting for him there. But she wasn't.

Colton's advice to be honest was either the most amazing or the worst he'd ever received. He'd gotten the opening, so he had gone with it. And Sai had just bolted out the door.

He had taken the chance, and it might have backfired. His heart was heavy and possibly broken. He needed to explain. But explain what? That he was madly in love with her and had been for quite some time? That sharing that bed with her the past few weeks had been nothing short of the sweetest kind of torture and he would endure it if it meant he was near her?

Pathetic.

He tried calling her, pinging her phone. But nothing. He lay on the bed still fully dressed with Kiara next to him. By now, he was convinced that telling her about his feelings was the worst mistake he'd ever made. The one time he listened to Colton. He sighed and went to the family room. Maybe she was at Lin's. Or even Aneel's.

Either way, it was clear she needed to be away from him. He stood in the dark, staring out at the water, the only light coming from the partial moon and the few streetlights. Colton was right about one thing. At least now he knew where he stood with her. He had spilled his heart, and she ran.

Pretty self-explanatory.

Maybe now he'd really be able to move on from her. Maybe he would join Colton and Rita in New York. If he was going to get over Saira in any real way, moving to New York might be the solution.

He leaned forward, allowing his forehead to touch the window. The glass was cool, and his breath fogged it up. Who was he kidding? A part of him was destroyed when she ran out of that office. He was finding it hard to stay standing.

"Tyler."

He froze at the sound of her voice, unable to move or turn around. He felt rather than heard her move closer to him until she was standing next to him. He finally lifted his head from the window and turned his body to face her.

The tight curls of her hair framed her beautiful face. There was just enough light to see clarity in her brown eyes. "Sai."

She reached up and touched the side of his face. Her fingers were featherlight as she traced his jawline. "Do you remember when I broke my arm on the monkey bars?" she asked.

"Did you hear what I said in Dr. Maya's office?"

She ignored his question. "Do you remember?"

"Of course." Tyler nodded, confused, but going along anyway. "You used to spend the whole recess on them."

"When the cast came off, I wanted nothing more than to return to my beloved monkey bars," she said softly. "Aneel lectured me at the doctor's office. Mom simply warned me not to injure myself again." She grinned. "I got on those monkey bars as soon as the recess bell rang."

Tyler nodded. He remembered it clearly. Aneel was pissed that she was being so reckless, but he couldn't control her, so he had simply shrugged and gone off with the other boys.

"You came with me, even though you were like eleven."

"Twelve."

Her hand had slid from his face, trailed his jawline then his neck and was now on his chest, resting over his thudding heart. Every place she touched left a trail of fire.

"I heard the other boys teasing you for coming on the monkey bars while they wanted to play kickball."

"I got teased a lot." He shrugged. "I didn't care."

"But you didn't climb the monkey bars." Her gaze never left his. "I remember, because I thought it was weird. I mean why would anyone stand in the middle of monkey bars and do nothing? Especially when they could be playing kickball."

Tyler swallowed but did not answer.

She smiled at him and stepped yet closer. "I just figured it out. You stood in the middle of the monkey bars that whole recess…in case I fell. You were there to catch me if I needed you." She grinned. "My whole life, my brother tried to keep me from falling by restricting what I was allowed to do. But you… You just made sure you were there to catch me. Still do."

"You're a force, Sai. You do what you want. It's one of the many things I…love about you," he said softly, trying to read her eyes in the dim light. "I don't want to stop you. But if you fall…" He shrugged.

"You'll catch me," she whispered, her voice low and husky. "Always."

Saira moved her mouth to within millimeters of his lips. "That is why I love you." She kissed him. Her lips were on his in a kiss so demanding only Saira could give it. He opened for her and pulled her close. The only thing separating their bodies were the clothes they wore.

He should probably be sensible and pull back. Insist that they discuss what he had said this afternoon. Find out where she had been all this time.

He should.

But he wouldn't. She had said she loved him.

That was enough.

More than enough.

He was already lost in her kiss, in her arms. She stepped back long enough to take off her shirt. She then got to work unbuttoning his, while he put his mouth on whatever part of her, he could reach. His fingers threaded in her hair. He had brushed her hair many times as they grew up, but he'd never felt it like this, silk covering his hands, soft, inviting.

His shirt dispensed with, her mouth was on his again. He pulled her close, he needed to feel her skin on his. He kissed her face, her neck, shoulders. He slowly worked his way down to kneeling and passed his mouth over her breasts and relished in the soft moan that followed a hitch of her breath. He drew his tongue down her naked belly. He tugged on her scrub bottoms and looked up at her.

Her eyes were dark with desire as she smirked at him and nodded.

He removed them and pulled her down to kneel with him. She reached for the button on his pants. He gently moved her hands away. "Not yet," he whispered into her mouth.

She arched into him.

"Keep doing that, Sai, and this will be over pretty fast." He smiled, but he wasn't joking. He had wanted her for too long, and he felt like he was already on the edge.

She smirked and pulled him down on top of her. She kept her hands on his pants and arched into him again.

"Sai." Her name was a groan in his throat.

This time when she went to remove his pants, he took her hands and held them over her head. He was rewarded with her writhing beneath him, that smirk still on her beautiful face.

"Let's take our time," he whispered to her as he removed her remaining clothing with his mouth.

Sai woke a few hours later curled up on top of Tyler. They were still in the family room, never having made it to the bed.

Not yet, anyway. She lifted her head to look at Tyler. He was handsome even in sleep.

After fleeing the therapist's office, she'd walked around for hours. She had ended up at the vet school. She thought about everything she had been through with Tyler. She'd had no idea how long he had really loved her. Maybe he hadn't even known. What she did know was that she had all these feelings, and she knew they were love. It was completely different from what she had felt with Dhruv. This was light. This was joy and strength.

This was Tyler.

He opened his eyes and smiled when he saw her. He sighed. "You're here. I thought I was dreaming."

"Not a chance," she said. Hot Tyler might be the perfect name for him. Certainly, right now with his hair mussed from her fingers, not a lick of clothing on and the way he focused those blue eyes on her, he made her feel cherished and cared for and loved.

"Want to go to the bed?" he asked.

She sat up and shook her head at him, need already pulsing through her body. "Absolutely not."

He pulled her down to him, and with that gravelly voice Saira had only just heard tonight for the first time, he said, "I was hoping you would say that."

Chapter Forty-Three

Tyler

"Well, I guess we don't have to cancel the engagement party," Tyler said with Saira still in his arms.

"If that is your idea of proposing to me, Tyler Hart, you have another think coming." Saira turned around in the bed to face him. At some point they had made it to the bedroom.

Tyler laughed. "You are awake."

"I am." She laughed. "How come you never told me that you had these feelings for me all this time?"

"How would I say that? Even faking, look what happened. Aneel is beyond pissed."

"We should come clean to Aneel," Saira said.

She was right.

"What are we going to say?"

"We're going to say that we were faking to impress Colton, but then I fell for you, and lucky me, you already loved me," she said. "Or we could just say that therapy works." She giggled.

"Let's just enjoy this right now. We can worry about the family later."

"I knew I loved you for a reason." Saira gently pushed him back and straddled him. "Because that is the best idea you have had so far, Tyler Hart."

Chapter Forty-Four

Saira

Tracy Auntie brought more food out to the four of them. Saira usually enjoyed family dinner at Tracy Auntie's. It was only twice a month, but it was Auntie's way of being sure she got her whole family together. Tracy Auntie was a fabulous cook. But more than that, having family dinner here reminded Saira that she had a family, even after her mother was gone. That she and Bhaiya were not alone in the world. Delicious aromas of fried pakora and crab cakes floated around the house. The meal was always a hodgepodge of whatever they had requested. This time, Tyler had wanted pakora and she had actually requested the crab cakes.

Saira glanced at Tyler. He was tense. She turned to Bhaiya, who looked equally tense. Karina Bhabhi caught her eye, then rolled her own eyes and shook her head.

Saira really liked her. She hadn't been a fan in the beginning, but once she got to know the real Karina, she realized that Aneel couldn't have picked a better partner.

Meanwhile, her generally happy, go-with-the-flow brother was being grumpier than ever. Aneel and her now real fiancé were going out of their way to ignore each other.

No problem. She would talk to Karina Bhabhi.

"Where's Veer today, Bhabhi?" Saira asked as she dipped her potato pakora into cilantro chutney.

"He spent the weekend with Chirag. They need some father-son time alone, you know?" Karina said as she too dipped her pakora and took a bite.

"Speaking of fathers," Tracy Auntie said. "I noticed Yogesh Rawal's name on the engagement party list."

Bhaiya froze.

"Yes, I added it." Saira stated this firmly—almost defiantly.

"No. He doesn't get to come," Aneel said.

"That is not up to you," Saira snapped at him.

"He was never a dad to us. He doesn't need to be there." Bhaiya was being an ass again.

"He is our father. And I am building a relationship with him. I would like to invite him," Saira said, turning to Tracy Auntie.

"I'm afraid that I have to agree with Aneel to some degree on this one. Your mother would not have wanted him to attend." Tracy Auntie was at least attempting a diplomatic voice, but her views were clear.

"Tracy Auntie." Saira spoke softly now. "I know you loved my mom and that you were best friends, but my mom is not here, and she hasn't been for a long time. So, we really have no idea what she might or might not have wanted. And I want him to come."

"Tyler, what are your thoughts?" Tracy Auntie looked to him.

"This is Saira's call. She wants her father there, he's there." Tyler grinned at her. Under the table, he let his leg rest against hers.

"Humph," Bhaiya grunted. "Big surprise. You let Saira do whatever she wants."

"For the record, I don't *let* Saira do anything." Tyler narrowed his eyes at Aneel. "She's a grown woman if you haven't noticed. She does what she wants."

"Whether or not it's good for her, apparently," Aneel said.

"Okay. I've had enough." Saira stood. "Bhaiya. I love you, but whatever you've been doing these past few weeks is completely ridiculous. I am in love with Tyler. And he is in love with me. We are engaged. And our father will be invited to the celebration. You do not have to like any of this, but you do have to stop treating me like a child and you have to stop treating Tyler like you think he's not good enough for me."

At this, Aneel snapped his head to Tyler and furrowed his brow. "I never said—"

Tyler glared back at Aneel. His words came from deep down. "You didn't have to. I got the message loud and clear."

Saira had never heard Tyler talk to Aneel this way. In his voice, she could hear so much anger, so much hurt.

Aneel set his jaw, but he looked stricken.

"Saira, Yogesh might have changed, but I just don't think—" Tracy Auntie started.

"You don't think people deserve a second chance? He was suffering from depression and serious panic attacks. That's why he drank. He's sober now and he goes to therapy. He appears to be calm and he genuinely is interested in me and my life."

Tracy Auntie stared at her as if she were having a struggle of conscience. Saira had seen this look a few times before. Tracy Auntie was mentally having a conversation with Saira's mother, imagining what her best friend would have said.

Tracy Auntie finally sighed, resigned. "Very well. If that is what you want."

Saira grinned. "It is."

Aneel said nothing. He simply went back to eating, every so often throwing furtive glances at Tyler.

Tyler, for his part, ignored him.

Saira shook her head. They just needed to get through this dinner. Her phone buzzed. Lin.

Boards scores are up.

"Boards scores are up," Saira said. The table went silent. Tyler's hand was immediately at her back.

She logged onto the site on her phone and pulled up her NAVLE score. The goal was 425. She nearly dropped her phone as she read the number: 421.

How could that be? She had the highest grade point in the class. She worked hard and studied hard. Her hands shook. Everyone was watching her, waiting for her answer.

Her hands shook so hard she dropped her phone. She started sweating and it became hard to breathe.

Tyler was kneeling in front of her in an instant. "Saira. Breathe with me."

She shook her head at him. Tears burned at her eyes. She'd failed. She was a failure.

"Saira." Tyler's voice was steady. "Look at me." He brought his face closer to hers. "I love you."

She looked at him.

He put a smile on his face. "That's great. Breathe. Inhale." He inhaled. She copied him.

"Exhale."

She copied him again.

He nodded.

The room shrank to only her and Tyler. She inhaled and exhaled with him until her breathing became normal. Her heart rate calmed down.

Tyler stayed steady.

"I love you," she finally said. Tears ran down her cheeks. "But I failed." She sobbed and collapsed into his arms. "I failed."

Chapter Forty-Five

Tyler

Tyler wrapped Saira's arms around his neck and put one hand under her knees, then he picked her up as he stood. She continued to sob. The look in her eyes had told him everything.

"I...failed. I'm a failure," she sobbed.

"You are not a failure," he murmured to her as he sat down on his mother's sofa, Saira in his lap. "It was one test."

"I can't get licensed," she cried.

"We'll figure it out." His heart broke to hear her like this. She was the most capable person he knew.

He had no idea how long they sat like that. He let her cry until she fell asleep. At some point, Aneel and Karina cleaned up and left, promising to check in the next day. Aneel had rested his hand on Tyler's shoulder before leaving.

His mother made up her guest room for them. Tyler carried Saira upstairs and tucked her into bed before crawling in next to her, spooning her close to him.

The next morning, when he woke, Saira was still sleeping. He made coffee and logged into his computer, sitting in bed next to her. Lin texted him.

She never responded last night. Just checking in with you.

Tyler: She's still asleep. Can you let the clinic know?

Lin: Will do.

Saira finally stirred close to noon. "Tyler?" She called out his name, her eyes not quite open.

"Here." He reached out and squeezed her shoulder.

"Where are we?"

"We are in my childhood bedroom," he said softly.

Saira opened her eyes and looked around. "Oh...yeah." A feeble smile fell across her face. "I remember." She turned all the way so she was facing him. "Why are we here?"

"You fell asleep on the sofa."

She nodded. Her face darkened as the evening came back to her. "I failed the boards." She spoke this matter-of-factly.

"Yes, you did," Tyler said softly.

"I can't take them again for a whole year."

Tyler nodded. He had done some research this morning.

"I have no job."

"Well, you need to talk to the clinic. They can hire you as an assistant until you retake the boards. Plus, there are classes that help you prepare—"

"You know I had a panic attack during the exam," she said softly.

"I did not know that."

"I mean not a full blown—not like the bathroom. I just froze up and it was hard to focus..." She shook her head. "What if that happens again?"

"What if it doesn't?"

"What did my brother say?"

"He didn't say anything. He helped Mom clean up, then he and Karina left."

"Did he seem disappointed?"

"No. He looked worried because you were crying."

She nodded. "Is he still mad at you?"

"No idea. I'm still mad at *him*, but that is not your concern." He grinned at her. "Want to play hooky today?"

"You have to get me the proper mint chocolate ice cream,"

she said, all serious. "With chunks of chocolate. None of this shredded chocolate business."

"Whatever you want. Let's go home."

She smiled at him. A genuine smile. "I like that."

"What?"

"That we have a home together."

He leaned over and kissed her. Mostly because he could. He kissed her for all the times he'd wanted to kiss her but hadn't. "Wherever you are, that's home. Let's go."

They went home. He got her favorite ice cream while she talked to Lin. She called out sick from work and settled in front of the TV. She and Tyler watched rom-coms and thrillers and ate ice cream out of the carton and cuddled with Kiara. Saira cried every so often.

Tyler was happy to be there for her.

"I'll go in tomorrow and see about work," Saira said as they prepared for bed that night.

"They would be unwise to not take you," he said.

She smiled small and nodded, cuddling up to him, and they fell asleep in each other's arms.

Chapter Forty-Six

Saira

Saira opened her eyes the next morning with every intention of attacking the day like she always had. This was not her first setback. She and Aneel had had their share of challenges over the years. She always met them head-on.

Tyler was already gone. He had some very early meetings since he had played hooky with her yesterday.

She sat up in bed and was overcome with a feeling of dread. She forced herself to get to the bathroom.

She managed to brush her teeth, but then she felt so exhausted that she thought maybe she should just lay down for a few minutes before showering. She could go for a run tomorrow. She climbed back into bed.

"Saira. Saira, honey?" Tyler's voice came to her from very far away. She opened her eyes.

"Tyler?" Her voice was croaky. "What time is it?"

"It's dinnertime."

"Oh, no. I never made it to work." She tried to sit up. But it took too much energy.

Tyler nodded, his eyes narrowed. "You feeling okay? Shivers, sore throat?" He lay his wrist against her forehead.

"No. I'm okay. Just tired." She sniffed the air and wrinkled her nose. "What's that smell?"

"Kiara." Tyler shrugged.

"Oh, I never took Kiara out? Shoot." This time she sat up

in bed. "I'll clean it. I'm so sorry, Tyler." Tears burned behind her eyes again.

"Don't worry. I already took care of it. Lin texted. She was worried about you."

"I'm okay. Just really tired."

Tyler nodded. "Okay. Want some food? You haven't eaten."

Her stomach growled. "Sure."

"I'll make you something." Tyler left.

She watched him go. Her heart filled with love for him. She got out of bed and washed up. Tyler brought her dinner in bed.

"I'll go in tomorrow," she said as she ate the burger he had made.

"Sounds like a plan," Tyler agreed.

Tyler cleaned up and they got ready for bed. Saira undressed for the shower as Tyler entered the bathroom. He froze in the doorway as he looked at her, and her body heated. She missed him. The strength of him, the security she felt when she was with him.

"*Beautiful* does not even begin to describe you," he said softly.

She grinned. "Want to join me?"

Tyler was at her side in one step. "I thought you would never ask."

"Oh, I'm asking," she said as she took his mouth with hers and melted into the most delicious oblivion. This was what she needed to get out of her head.

They made love soft and slow as they bathed each other. It was everything Saira needed. She felt cherished and wanted and loved. Her body was sated and limp when Tyler finally dried her off and carried her to the bed.

They lay next to each other like they had so many times before, talking softly.

"So, graduation next week," he reminded her. "So proud

of you. Everyone is excited to come and see your hard work pay off."

Saira just stared at him in the dark. She had completely forgotten that graduation was next week. How could she go when she had failed her boards? She was suddenly overcome with exhaustion again.

"I'm tired, Ty."

"Okay." He wrapped his arms around her, and she cuddled close to him, putting all thoughts of boards scores and graduation out of her mind.

"Sai? Saira." Tyler's voice was so far away. "Saira. Let's get up and get you to work."

She moaned. She didn't want to face the world today. It was too much. "I need another day, Ty."

"You need get up, Sai."

"Just one more day."

She didn't hear anything more, so fell back into sweet sleep. She didn't go the next day either. She just kept sleeping.

"She's been sleeping for like four days." Tyler pressed his mouth into a line as he spoke into the phone. "She eats when I feed her, but other than that, she's in bed. I didn't know who else to call. I've been taking Kiara to my mom's."

"No problem," Lin said. "I'll come over after work and drag her out."

"That would be great. Thanks, Lin."

Tyler looked at Saira still in bed. Hopefully Lin could do something to get her out of this funk.

Chapter Forty-Seven

Saira

"Hey!" Lin looked completely fabulous in her jean skirt and halter top. Saira sat up in bed.

"Hey. What are you doing here?" Her voice was groggy, and her stomach growled. How long had she been asleep?

"Well, someone who loves you a ton said you were feeling a bit sad. So, I thought I'd come over and cheer you up."

Saira managed a smile. "He's the best," she admitted. "What did you have in mind?"

"Get dressed and I'll just surprise you."

Saira got out of bed and hit the shower. This was what she needed, some girl time, where she didn't need to think about her future. The future was too...daunting. That's why she was avoiding it. But a night out, blow off some steam. That would set her right.

When was the last time she had showered? The water felt good on her skin, washing everything off. She scrubbed and washed her hair. She picked out an outfit similar to Lin's and even put on makeup.

She felt better already.

She walked out to find Lin and Tyler chatting at the island. Tyler had bags under his eyes, his hair was disheveled, but he was as handsome as ever. Saira went over and wrapped her arms around him.

"I'm sorry I worried you. I promise that I'm feeling better

now. You look exhausted from taking care of me. Please get some rest. I'm fine now." She smiled at him. She really did feel better. All she'd needed was the little push in the butt that he gave her by calling Lin.

"You sure?" Even his voice was scratchy.

"Drink some turmeric water and go to bed. I'll be fine," Saira insisted.

Tyler hugged her tight. "Okay. Have fun."

"I'm ready when you are," she announced to Lin.

Tyler's smile widened and reached his eyes. Damn but that man was handsome. He planted a kiss on her that made her re-think going out.

"Mmm," Tyler said as he pulled back. "Maybe you stay home."

"Nope." Lin came over and separated them. "You can have sex later. I'm taking my girl out." With that, she took Saira by the hand and whisked her out the door. "Don't wait up, Hot Tyler."

Saira squealed with laughter. "Lin. You did not just call him—"

"I did." Lin giggled as they waited for the elevator. She threw her arm around Saira as they entered the elevator. "What's going on? Where have you been?"

"The scores, Lin. I failed."

Lin nodded. "Tyler said." They hooked elbows and walked arm in arm to the street, Saira following Lin's lead. The air was warm and a bit sticky, but that was Maryland. "You have options. But you need to talk to people. Retaking the boards is not the end of the world."

Saira nodded. Of course, Lin was right.

"We're going dancing," Lin announced. "There's a bar close by that does salsa dancing on Thursday nights."

"Is it Thursday?" Saira asked

"Yes, it is," Lin said.

Saira could not help but get caught up in Lin's energy. They ordered margaritas and danced and laughed. All the while, Lin helped her come up with a plan for her future.

Between the margaritas (which were plentiful) and the dancing, Saira was feeling much better as they stumbled out into the night.

Though Lin did not appear to be stumbling at all. How many margaritas had Saira had? Enough to not really care about failing the boards, or even missing work for the last few days. She was happy.

"I feel sooo much better," she said to Lin.

"I can see that," Lin said as she held Saira by the shoulders. Saira stumbled and Lin caught her.

"Heels are too high," giggled Saira.

"Of course they are, sweetie. Let's get you home. Just a few more blocks," Lin said, throwing Saira's arm around her shoulders.

"Home? Nooooo. Let's go more dancing! Makes me happy," Saira said.

"We can go again tomorrow night," Lin said. "We have to work tomorrow."

Saira broke free of Lin's hold. "No fun!" she pouted. She was happy now; she should go dancing now. She took a few steps backward.

"Saira!" Lin called out too late. "Look out."

Saira did not see the woman with her dog on the leash. The woman tried to get out of the way, but the dog did not move fast enough, and Saira tripped over the dog.

A yelp of pain reached her as she landed hard on the sidewalk, having accidentally kicked the dog on her way down.

She had hurt the poor animal. "Oh, my god. I'm so sorry. I'm so sorry."

"Maybe you should watch where you're going," the woman barked at her as she picked up her dog.

"I can take a look at her. I'm a vet," Saira said softly from the ground.

"I'm not letting you anywhere near her," the woman shouted.

"I'm a vet as well," said Lin in her doctor voice. "Allow me?"

The woman allowed Lin to take a look. "Just a small cut. Should be fine. If you notice anything else, this is the address of the clinic. No charge." Lin handed the woman a card.

The woman seemed placated for the moment and, with a glare at Saira, went on her way. Saira was beside herself. She had hurt an innocent animal. Tears fell down her face. Lin helped her stand.

"I hurt that poor puppy. What is the matter with me?" Saira asked Lin.

"You're drunk, hon. And you tried to walk backward," Lin explained. "Here's the building. Let's get you to Tyler."

"Hot Tyler," Saira said. "I'm so sorry, Lin. Don't hate me."

"I could never hate you. We're good." Lin hugged her and guided her to the building.

Tyler was still awake when Lin brought her home.

"I tripped over a puppy and hurt it, Tyler." Saira's remorse felt overwhelming. How could she have done that?

She heard Lin mumble something about too many margaritas before saying good-night.

The margs were starting to wear off as Tyler undressed her for bed. "Tyler?" She started crying. "I hurt an innocent little puppy and I failed the boards. Maybe I shouldn't be a vet."

Tyler pulled her close. "You hurt the puppy because you weren't paying attention and you had too many margaritas. You failed the boards because of panic. Neither of those mean you're a bad person or a bad vet. Get some sleep. We'll come up with a plan in the morning."

Saira nodded as Tyler handed her Advil and water.

Chapter Forty-Eight

Tyler

"How's Saira doing?" Colton asked a week later.

Even though they shared the condo, Saira had been staying in their room so much that Colton truly had no way to know how she was other than to ask. "Better. She's going to retake the boards next year. She's at work right now."

Both of their phones buzzed at the same time. Mom. They shared a glance before opening the text.

Hope you are both ready for the engagement party!

Tyler glanced at Colton, and they shook their heads. They responded that yes, they were ready.

How's our girl? his mom texted.

Fine, Mom, much better.

It's what he'd been telling everyone, but something nagged at him. Saira wasn't fine, though he couldn't put his finger on exactly what was wrong.

"Aneel is on his way," Tyler told Colton.

Colton had texted that he had some information about Yogesh Rawal that his children deserved to know. He was indeed the man that had come to see their father a few months ago. Colton had thought it fair to speak with Aneel and Saira about this. But with Saira currently reeling from her boards fail, they had kept her out of it.

Tyler knew he would pay for this later, but it was the best option he could think of for now. The door buzzer sounded.

"Come on up, Aneel," Tyler said.

In minutes, Aneel was in the apartment.

"Oh, hey, Colton." Aneel nodded his greeting.

"Aneel."

"Where is my sister?" Aneel asked.

"Saira is at work."

"She's feeling better, then? Glad to hear it."

"I do have some information for you, however. About Yogesh Rawal," Colton said. "I thought you might want to hear it."

"Yogesh Rawal? As in my father?" Aneel's voice became more agitated.

"Yes," Tyler said softly. "It's why I asked you to come over."

Aneel pressed his mouth tight and said nothing.

"Well, it appears that Mr. Rawal has a history of DUIs from back in the day."

"My dad was a drunk. No surprise there," Aneel said.

"On one particular night, his drinking got exceptionally out of hand," Colton continued.

"What do you mean?" Aneel asked.

Colton looked at both of them, his face grim. "Mr. Rawal hit another car. The driver was badly injured and eventually died a week later as a result of those injuries."

"He did what?" Tyler asked. Anger like Tyler had never felt rose up inside him. Saira could never know this. It would destroy her.

"There's more." Colton remained grim. Aneel said nothing.

What more could there possibly be?

"Saira was in the car. She was three years old at the time." Colton paused. "It's in the police report. Saira sustained a gash to the head, and nothing more. Somehow, even in his inebriated state, he had managed to put her in the car seat. It saved her life."

Tyler was going to vomit. Saira had a scar just at her hairline that she said she'd always had—he knew she didn't remember how she got it.

"Mr. Rawal was sentenced to six years in prison for vehicular manslaughter." Colton paused and his gaze fell on Aneel. "There was another document in the file. While Mr. Rawal was in prison, he signed over his parental rights to your mother. Basically, that means he has no rights or responsibility to you or Saira as his children."

Aneel clenched his jaw. "He made sure that he owed us nothing."

"Well…" Colton paused. "Not exactly. That's why he was in the office talking to our father." Colton nodded at Tyler. "Because Dad was also handling an account for him. Mr. Rawal put aside money in a trust that you and Saira have access to when Saira turns thirty. Mr. Rawal wanted to give the money to you both right away, rather than wait. He was buoyed by the fact that Saira was willing to see him and wanted both of you to have the money now. He said that he gave up his rights to you so he would never put either of you in harm's way again. But he opened the account so he could still *provide* for you."

Aneel collapsed onto the sofa. "My memory of that time is really vague. I never wanted to think about it. But I remember Saira coming home with a bandage." Aneel gestured at his head. "Mom was out of her mind with worry that night. Dad was gone and so was Saira. She called Tracy Auntie and you and your mom came over while she tried to track his phone, but that wasn't working. I was maybe nine so I understood what was happening, but I couldn't do anything. I think she got a call because she left in a huge rush."

Aneel shook his head. "That man is nothing but trouble."

He looked at Tyler. "I told you and I told Saira too. Wait until she hears this, then she'll know who Yogesh Rawal really is."

"Saira is not hearing this," Tyler said softly and firmly. There was no leeway here.

"Are you out of your mind? Saira needs to know the truth," Aneel said.

"No. Right now she's getting closer to him. To the man who changed his life. What do you think will happen to her if she finds out her father is responsible for the death of another person, and she was in the car that night, that he caused her scar?"

"I think she'll wise up, that's what," Aneel said. "And stay clear of him."

"All this time, Aneel, all you have ever done is try to keep her in Bubble Wrap." Tyler raised his voice. "And the one time that the Bubble Wrap might be a good thing, might actually protect her from serious harm, you want to do away with it?"

"Right back at you. You are always encouraging her take risks, to face the world's challenges. This is information that might be hard for her to hear but it's important for her to know. And you won't tell her? Doesn't she have the right to decide for herself if she wants to know?"

"No. I won't put her in that position. Because I love her. Not that that means anything to you."

Aneel's eyes widened. "What does that mean?"

"Seriously? That means that you have not been supportive of this relationship since we told you about it. You don't think that I am good enough for your sister," Tyler shouted.

"I never said those words," Aneel shot back.

"If you breathe a word of this to Saira, you and I are finished. Am I clear?" Tyler narrowed his eyes at the man he loved like a brother. Regardless of his feelings for Aneel, he wouldn't let anyone hurt Saira.

"That's right, Tyler. Run. When it gets too hard, just run and avoid it. Isn't that what you did all these years with Colton and your father? They were too much for you, so you avoided them. Now you don't like what I have to say, so you're done here."

"Get out." Tyler softened his voice. He was ready to rage at Aneel, but he couldn't do that to Saira's brother.

He had meant what he'd said before. He would burn down the world for her.

Chapter Forty-Nine

Saira

Saira left work exhausted. It wasn't the first time she'd been this tired, but this felt different. She just wanted to crawl into bed and sleep for days; she was so tired. There was something she was supposed to do today, but she couldn't remember what it was. She kind of felt like a glass of wine would help, but she remembered how she felt when she overdrank last week with Lin. She had fallen and hurt a puppy, and could have injured herself. So there would be none of that today.

Especially when she was simply too tired to do anything, including get herself that drink.

But what was she supposed to do today? *Meet somebody,* she thought.

Tyler kept suggesting that she go to therapy. But that seemed over the top, too dramatic. She was fine. So she slept for a few days after getting devastating information. But failing the boards was a big deal. She had one incident of drinking too much, but people make mistakes. She would be fine. She just needed some more sleep.

She went home and took off her scrubs and fell asleep in the bed in her underwear. Whatever it was she'd forgotten to do, it could wait. She just needed a little nap.

"Tyler? This is Yogesh Rawal."

"Oh, yes." *Speak of the devil.* "What…what can I do for you?"

"I was supposed to meet Saira for a painting class today, and she never showed."

Tyler's heart thudded in his chest. He had come into the office, since Saira had been at the clinic today. She'd been going all week. Tyler felt it was a good sign that she was feeling better. He had continued to gently suggest therapy to her, but she had waved it off.

"I'm fine. Don't be going all Aneel on me now." She had smirked at him like she always did. She had then proceeded to undress him in the kitchen.

"Saira. Colton and Rita could come home any minute." Tyler had warned, though he had made no move to stop her.

"That's the thrill," she had said, removing her own clothes. "I want you right now, right here."

"Whatever you want."

"She is not answering her phone. It's not like her." Yogesh Uncle was clearly concerned.

Tyler wondered if anyone had mentioned Saira's boards scores to him. "Okay, hold on, I'll just track her phone." Tyler pulled up the find-my-phone app. "Did she tell you about her boards scores?"

"Um. No. I haven't seen her in a while. We registered for this class weeks ago."

"She will need to repeat the board exam," Tyler said. The app loaded. Her phone was at home.

"Oh, I'm sorry to hear that." Yogesh Uncle sounded more concerned than sorry.

"Her phone is at my place." Tyler stood and gathered his laptop and files. "I'll be there in fifteen minutes. I'll let you know if she's there or if she went out and left her phone."

"Do you mind if I meet you there? I would like to see her for myself."

"Of course." Yogesh Uncle had done some horrible things in

his past, but Tyler would not keep him from his daughter when Saira clearly wanted him in her life.

Tyler raced home to find Uncle waiting outside his building. Tyler nodded his greeting and Yogesh Uncle followed him into the elevator.

"How did she take failing her boards?" he asked.

"She was upset," Tyler said.

"That's it?" Yogesh Uncle looked surprised.

"She slept for four days, straight—right up until I called her best friend Lin. Lin took her out dancing. Saira got drunk." He shook his head. "It's not like her. She's really not a party girl, you know."

Yogesh Uncle nodded but said nothing. They entered the apartment. It was dark. Tyler went to his room and found Saira fast asleep. He came out. "She's asleep."

"She needs to be in therapy," Yogesh said.

Tyler nodded. "I agree, but I can't force her."

Yogesh Uncle nodded. "That is true. She will only get better if she realizes she needs it."

Tyler stared at this man and tried to reconcile him with the man Aneel and Saira grew up with. With the man who got into a car drunk with his three-year-old daughter and hit another car.

He could not. The man standing before him looked like nothing more than a worried father, a successful businessman.

"Please tell her I'm happy to reschedule."

"Will do."

Yogesh Uncle turned to leave. But then turned back. "I don't know how much she told you, but I have been through this. Depression, alcoholism. For a time, I let it steal my life, because I didn't know how to deal with what was happening to me. I had always been told that men simply *handled things*. I held on to that belief even when I knew I wasn't handling things at all. Even when I was hurting my family. Malti was an amazing woman, and I will never forgive myself for what I put her through." He paused here as if considering something. "Aneel is a happy man on the surface, but underneath all that is an angry man—angry over what I did, leaving my family behind. He has every right to be angry with me, but what bothers me is that that anger will harm him more than it harms me. Though I wish it were the other way around." He paused, tears in his eyes. "Don't let this happen to her. She deserves much better."

Tyler nodded. "I will do everything in my power."

Yogesh Uncle nodded. "She invited me to graduation tomorrow."

"Then you should come," Tyler said.

"See you then." He left.

Tyler was able to coax Saira awake after a few hours to eat something. "You missed paint class with your dad."

Saira put down her food. "I knew I was forgetting something. Was he upset?"

"He was disappointed, but he said he was happy to reschedule and that he'll see you at graduation tomorrow."

She nodded. "Right." She finished her meal and Tyler took her plate to clean up.

"Let's get some sleep. Big day tomorrow," he said. "I'll meet you at the school around five?"

Saira nodded. "Sounds good. Aneel and Bhabhi will be there. Maybe you and my brother can make up?"

"Anything for you." Tyler grinned. His heart ached, because reconciliation with Colton or not, he missed Aneel. He missed his brother.

Tyler walked into the lobby of the main school building exactly at 5:00 p.m. A buzz of excitement filled the air. Graduations were like this. The culmination of hard work so that the graduates could move on to the next phase of life. His mom, Aneel, Karina and Veer were already there. They were dressed in their best, and even little Veer had on a suit. He figured Yogesh Uncle would come and stand in the back away from the family, so as not to cause friction.

The one person who wasn't there was Saira. He imagined she was with the other graduates backstage.

Lin walked over, Lora and Andrew in tow. Tyler gave Lin a huge hug. "Congrats, Doc!" He stepped back and took in her black graduation robe. "You look good!"

"Feels good, not gonna lie," Lin said. "Where's our girl?"

"What do you mean? I thought she was with you, doing her whole graduation thing," Tyler said.

"I haven't seen her yet." Lin shook her head. "I'm sure she's around. We'll catch up later."

Tyler nodded and said hello to Lora and Andrew before they moved along. "I'm going to check backstage," Tyler said.

"I'll go with you," Aneel offered.

Tyler glanced at him and nodded. Saira was not backstage. They asked a young woman to look in the ladies' room, but nothing.

"She's not here," Aneel said.

Tyler shook his head. "Let me track her phone." He did so. "She's at home." He looked at Aneel. "You stay here. I'll go home and get her. There's still an hour before the ceremony starts.

"Do you want me to come with you?" Aneel's voice was gentle and caring. He was clearly concerned about his sister, but he seemed to understand that he may not be welcome by Saira or Tyler. This was the brother Tyler needed—the one who put what was best for his loved ones ahead of his personal feelings.

Tyler pulled him into an embrace. Aneel hugged him back. "I'm good." He suddenly had the urge to confess everything. "After graduation, we need to talk."

Aneel pulled back. "We do."

Tyler nodded. "I'll be back."

Tyler jumped into a cab, his heart in his throat, suddenly wishing Aneel had come with him. No telling what he would find at home.

"Saira. Saira!" he called out to her as soon as he entered the condo. The only light was that of the setting sun. He sprinted to their room.

Saira was beautiful in her blue graduation dress as she sat on the floor with Kiara in her lap.

Chapter Fifty

Saira

"Saira!" Tyler ran to her and knelt in front of her. "Saira."

"Tyler… Tyler, I can't breathe." Tears stained her cheeks and she felt light-headed.

"Okay. Let's take some breaths." He nodded at her. He inhaled and she followed suit.

"I was taking a nap. But I set an alarm," she explained.

He nodded.

"I got up, showered and dressed. But then I started thinking about how could I possibly graduate when I haven't passed the board. Seems weird right?" Saira looked at him.

"They don't have to happen together," he said.

"Anyway. Then I couldn't breathe, and I couldn't find my phone…" Tears welled in her eyes.

"It's okay. All good now." Tyler did not move. "We can go whenever you are ready."

"I'm ready." She stood, put Kiara in her crate and grabbed her gown. "Let's do this."

They made it to the ceremony while they were still calling out the Os. Saira took her seat in the audience.

She looked on stage and saw her teachers and her class-mates, and she felt happy, light. It felt good. She couldn't remember the last time she'd felt this way. Thank goodness Tyler had come to get her.

The dean called her name. "Dr. Saira Rawal." She stood and heard Aneel's whoop of joy as she walked onto the stage and accepted her hard-earned degree.

"That's my wife!" she heard Tyler's voice loud and clear. She laughed. She felt great! She was in love with the most amazing man, and he was in love with her. Their engagement party was tomorrow. She'd fix things with her brother and all would be well.

Everything was going to be okay.

Chapter Fifty-One

Saira

"Saira, honey." Tracy Auntie looked at her, her eyes moist with tears. She held in her hands a delicate flower-print sari in baby blue. Saira had never seen it before. "Your mom gave this to me when she was sick with the instruction for you to wear this to your engagement celebration. It was hers."

Saira stared at Tracy Auntie as tears burned behind her own eyes. Guess it was going to be that kind of day. She stepped forward and hugged Tracy Auntie with all she had. "Thank you. Thank you so much, for everything. Thank you for being a mom to me when mine was gone."

By the time she pulled back, tears were flowing freely down both their cheeks. They wiped their eyes as they laughed at themselves.

"We need some champagne up here," Tracy Auntie called.

As if on cue, Colton entered holding a bottle in one hand and glasses in the other. "You called?" he said as he entered. He was wearing jeans and a T-shirt, so clearly he wasn't ready yet.

Saira wondered if Tyler was ready or not. Auntie had said she had to wait until they got to the party to see each other.

"Thank you," his mother said. "Where is your bride-to-be?"

"She's at the condo, with Tyler. She'll be at the hall on time, don't you worry," Colton assured them as he poured them each a glass of champagne.

"Does wonders for the nerves," said Tracy Auntie as she clinked glasses with Saira and sipped.

"True that," Saira said as she sipped her champagne.

"Scoot now, Colton, so we can get dressed." Tracy Auntie shooed him out.

Colton rolled his eyes, but left.

"All right now," Tracy Auntie said. "Let's get you ready for this party."

Saira knew the basics of draping a sari, so she got started while Tracy Auntie told her stories about her mother. She had heard many of them before, but it was nice to hear them again now. Saira finished her first glass of champagne and Auntie refilled them both.

"I sure do miss your mom, Saira. She was the best friend anyone could ever have. I would have done—and did do—anything for her," Tracy Auntie said.

"Like what?" Saira asked, curious.

"Oh, that's not a conversation for today." She waved her hand and grabbed some safety pins. "Let's pin you up."

Saira held the fabric on her shoulder while Auntie pinned it. Saira's heart ached as she thought of her mother. All the things she missed. The tough life she had. "I miss her too. I wish I had known her better."

"She would have been proud of you. The way you worked in school. The way you handled all those setbacks." Tracy Auntie caught her reflection in the mirror and nodded. "You are very much like her. Resilient. Tough." She smiled.

Tracy Auntie's words hit home. Saira wanted nothing more than to be like her mother. Strong. Capable. Loving. Caring. These were the words that had always been batted about when anyone spoke of her mother. Truthfully, it didn't happen often. But Saira knew it was because her loss was deep for everyone.

"You're also beautiful, like her." Tracy Auntie grinned.

Saira turned to face her. Her surrogate mother. Whom she had been lying to.

"Tracy Auntie, I have something I need to tell you."

"Anything."

Saira sat down and patted the bed next to her. "So, Tyler and I didn't really go to therapy to fix our relationship. We fell in love at therapy."

Tracy Auntie looked at her blankly.

"Let me start over. Colton showed up engaged to Tyler's ex, so I pretended to be engaged to Tyler, so he wouldn't feel like a loser in front of Colton. Then it blew up." Saira paused. Tracy Auntie was simply gawking at her. "But then, I started falling for Tyler for real. In fact, once I realized I was in love with him, I couldn't understand how I hadn't loved him all along. I didn't know what to do with my feelings, so I kept them to myself. Then, while we were meeting with our therapist, Tyler told me how he has loved me for years…and then I knew." She gave a one-armed shrug. "Sorry," she said softly.

Tracy Auntie just stared at her for a moment. Then very suddenly, she burst into laughter. "You…faked…to help Tyler… and then fell for him?" She laughed so hard tears came from her eyes. "You children… You can't make this stuff up!" She wiped her eyes. "I need to go fix my makeup. Go on down. The Uber is on the way."

They both stood. Saira flung herself into Tracy Auntie's arms. "Thanks for not being angry."

Tracy Auntie patted her hair. "It'll take more than that for me to be angry with you."

Chapter Fifty-Two

Tyler

Tyler's mother could not be stopped, so the guest list was close to 150. By the time Tyler and Rita's Uber pulled up, it was clear that most people they'd invited had actually arrived.

Tyler straightened his baby blue and gold sherwani that he was told perfectly matched Saira's sari. Rita was in a beautiful floor-length floral gown and Colton was devastatingly handsome in his tux.

Tyler's palms were sweaty as he exited the Uber and held the door open for Rita. Tyler glanced around, until finally his gaze landed on who he was searching for.

Saira was exquisite in a baby blue floral sari. His heart pounded in his chest, almost as if trying to get to Saira. Focused on reaching Saira, Tyler was forced to navigate the onslaught of guests ready to greet him. He graciously accepted their well-wishes, but he was distracted the whole time. Just when he thought he would not be able to take not being with her for another second, Saira appeared, radiant and beaming by his side.

"I couldn't stay away," she whispered. Someone walked by and put a flute of champagne in each of their hands. They toasted each other and sipped.

"I thought I would never get to you," Tyler whispered. "You look amazing."

She flushed under his attention. "The place looks amazing. Come on." She took his hand as someone refilled her flute.

"I told your mom the truth," Saira confided to Tyler as they walked into the hall.

"What truth?" She held his arm; Tyler wrapped his hand around hers.

"The whole thing. About the fake engagement." Saira raised her eyebrows at him.

Tyler's jaw dropped. "What did she say?"

Saira shook her head. "She couldn't stop laughing."

Tyler let out a laugh of relief. "Seriously?"

Saira nodded. "Seriously." She laughed too.

Tyler took her hand and looked around before leading her away. "Come with me." His stomach was in knots. This was as good a time as any.

"Anywhere you want to take me," Saira said.

They nodded at guests as Tyler led her out of the hall and outside. The day had been warm, but the evening had cooled pleasantly. He led her a block over to the Inner Harbor. The sun setting over the harbor threw an orange-and-pink glow over everything.

"I had a plan for this, but we're going with the flow here," Tyler said.

Saira looked at him, complete trust in her eyes. Whatever he had done to deserve that trust, he wanted to be sure to do for the rest of his life.

"Sai. My love for you was not a lightning strike. It grew strong behind the clouds. It grew and grew until I could no longer deny that I was irreparably and forever bound to you, not only by our past but also by our future together and what it holds for us. As I told someone recently, you are the very air that I breathe. Without you, there is no me. Without you, I am an empty vessel." Tyler slowly got down on one knee, even as his eyes filled. He reached into the sherwani pocket and pulled out the ring. "Asscher cut, 1.2k, the clarity is VVS2 and the color is E. Will you marry me for real?"

Saira stared at the ring. Then she got on her knees in front of him. "Tyler, I fell in love with you when I wasn't looking. I fell in love with you with every laugh, every tear, every conversation in the dark. Yes, I will marry you for real and I will choose you every day."

"Why are you on your knees?" Tyler asked.

"Because you are."

Tyler took her hand, and they stood together. Saira leaned closer and kissed him. "You're easier to kiss in these heels."

"We'll have to keep that in mind," Tyler said as he kissed her back. She melted into him right there as the sun set.

"You going to give me that diamond?" she asked when they parted.

"You kiss me like that and I'll forget my own name." He chuckled as he slid the ring on her finger.

"You got it exactly right."

"I do pay attention." He examined it on her finger. "You make it shine brighter."

Chapter Fifty-Three

Saira

They headed back to the party, in no particular rush to get there. Her hand in Tyler's felt like home. The diamond on her finger caught the light and she sighed.

"We could skip the party," she whispered

"My mom would kill us—but you make it really hard for me to care when you look at me like that." He chuckled.

"Like what?" She widened her eyes in innocence.

"Like you want to rip my clothes off."

Saira flushed as she bumped his shoulder. "You wish."

"Oh, I most certainly do," he whispered close to her ear, sending shivers down her body.

They arrived at the venue quicker than she would have liked. Tyler squeezed her hand. "A few hours and then I'll rip that sari from your body."

She smirked at him. "Promise?"

He kissed her neck in answer. She held back her moan. He opened the door to the hall filled with people eating and drinking and catching up. Saira squeezed Tyler's hand, suddenly feeling anxious.

"What's up?"

"It's a lot of people."

He turned to face her. "I'm right here, okay?"

She nodded as someone handed her a glass of champagne and she drank from it, instantly calming her nerves.

"Have you seen Aneel?" she asked Tyler during a small break in the congratulations.

He shook his head. "I'm sure he's here somewhere."

"I'm tired of fighting him," Saira admitted.

Tyler nodded, but something flitted across his face. "What happened?" she asked.

Tyler shook his head. "Don't worry. It's nothing Aneel and I can't fix."

She narrowed her eyes at him. "You sure?"

"You fix your stuff with him. I'll fix mine."

She grinned. Fair enough. "I need the bathroom. Back in a minute."

Saira made her way to the bathroom. On her way back she heard voices coming from one of the smaller rooms. As she passed the room, the voices sounded familiar. Her brother!

"I thought I texted you not to come." Aneel's voice was angry. Angrier than she had recently heard it.

"She's my daughter. She invited me, and I wanted to be here." Her father.

"You lost your right to be here when you had that accident." Aneel's voice was basically a growl. And what was he talking about? What accident?

"What do you know of it?" Her father sounded gruff, but not without fear.

"I know plenty. What you don't know is that Tyler, Saira's fiancé—and my *brother*, by the way—is also Ethan Hart's son. Tyler has a twin, Colton, who still works with their father. Colton Hart saw you in New York when you went to see Ethan Hart months ago, and what he overheard rubbed him the wrong way, so he did some digging."

"What do you think you found out?" Her father's voice shook, as if he were hiding something.

"Ohh, I don't *think*. I *know*. Colton told us all about what happened that night. You were drunk. And you got into a car. Even worse than that, you took Saira with you. Mom was out of her mind. That is what I remember. She couldn't find you. She couldn't find Saira. Up until that moment, I don't think she thought you would ever do anything to actively harm either me or my sister. That night, everything changed. She called Tyler's mom. And she came over to stay with me. Mom didn't know where you were until she got the call from the police."

"Oh, god." Her father sounded sick.

"Turns out that not only did you take my three-year-old sister on a drunken drive, but you hit somebody."

"Stop. Please stop." Her father's voice thickened as if with tears.

A pit filled her stomach as if she already knew the rest of the story but couldn't bear to hear it. A waiter passed by with glasses of champagne. Saira grabbed one and downed it.

"Stop?" Aneel repeated. "It's too late to stop. The damage is done. That man you hit, he died, didn't he? A week later as a result of those injuries. Saira's scar is from that accident."

Saira touched the scar near her hairline. Her mother, Tracy Auntie… No one had ever told her what that was from. She thought maybe she had been born with it. But no. It had been given to her by the man calling himself her *father*.

"Aneel, please stop. I know what a terrible mistake I made. I changed my life after that day."

"Not before you went to prison. Not before you signed over all your parental rights to Mom so you wouldn't have to deal with us."

"That's not why. I thought it was best for you and Saira that I not be part of your lives. But there's money. That's why I was at Hart Law. I put aside money for you both—"

"We don't want your money," Aneel nearly spat at him. "If it were up to me, I would tell Saira so that she would know once and for all, finally, what kind of man you are. And then she'd stay the hell away from you. But her fiancé? Tyler?" Here, Aneel's voice softened some. "He is a kinder man than me. He wants to keep your ugliness from Saira so she can have a father."

Saira couldn't believe what she'd just heard. She stepped into the room. "What is going on here?"

Both men snapped their heads to her. Her brother pressed his mouth tight into a line. Unapologetic.

Her father—*if you could call him that*—looked at her with watery eyes and opened his mouth.

But Saira didn't want to hear it. She couldn't listen to more lies. How many times had she asked him why he had never come for her? How many? She shook her head at him. "What have you done? This is why you would never tell me why you stayed away, isn't it? It's because you had to stay away. You were forced to stay away because you killed a man. Because you put a baby into a car—your own baby—" Saira's voice cracked. "While you were drunk. I don't know who you are. I don't *want* to know who you are. Leave."

"Saira," her father said. "Please."

Saira was nearly screaming at him as tears poured down her cheeks. "No. No, I don't want to hear it. I want you to leave now. I should have listened when Aneel and Tracy Auntie told me that you did not need to be here, that my mother would not have wanted you here. This is why. This is what I did not know. Leave. Don't call me, don't text me. I want nothing more to do with you."

She didn't turn as he brushed past her to leave. She turned her gaze on her brother. "I'm sorry I didn't listen to you about him. You were right. He's a monster and I don't need that in my life."

Aneel looked at her with sorrow in his face and handed her a handkerchief. She wiped her face with it and turned to leave. Her stomach was in knots, and she was starting to find it hard to breathe. She headed straight for the bar.

"I am one of the brides to be." She forced a playful smile on her face. "You keep my glass full."

"No problem, ma'am," the bartender said. "Congratulations."

Saira had already had a few glasses of champagne. She downed the first one he handed her and held it out for a refill. She needed it to get through the night without a panic attack. "Keep them coming."

The music stopped and Saira turned to see why. *Aww*, Tracy Auntie was giving a speech. Tracy Auntie spoke fondly of both her sons, then about how lovely Rita was. Finally, she came to Saira. Tears filled Tracy Auntie's eyes as she spoke of the special bond she shared with Saira and how she was beyond happy that Saira and Tyler would be married soon.

Somehow, this all seemed amusing to Saira. When Tracy Auntie called all four of them to stand by her, Saira stood between Tyler and Rita and tried very hard not to laugh. But she failed. She laughed so hard she fell over. Which only made her laugh more.

"My brother should be making a speech, but he's too pissed to be happy for me," Saira said and continued laughing.

Tyler helped her up. "Wow, isn't he so strong?" she asked. "Big muscles," she said into the mic.

She had the vague notion of Aneel taking the mic away and Tyler holding her hand and leading her somewhere. *Ohh. Did he have more diamonds for her? That would be so fun.* But then they were in an Uber, and there weren't more diamonds. Saira started to cry.

"I heard Aneel talking to my dad," she sobbed. "I know everything."

Tyler looked at her with such sadness. "You weren't meant to hear that."

"I also heard that you weren't going to tell me." She tried to glare at him, but everything was so swimmy she couldn't bring him into focus.

"I wasn't." Tyler was helping her out of the Uber and up to their condo. She almost made it to the bathroom before she vomited. All over the white carpet. Hah. She was the same as Kiara.

Then everything went black,

Chapter Fifty-Four

Tyler

Tyler picked up Saira and got her cleaned up before removing her sari and putting her to bed. Did he want to rail at Aneel for yelling at Yogesh Uncle without thinking through the consequences? Maybe. Not really. He really just wanted Saira to get better.

He cleaned the carpet, still in his sherwani, praying that Rita and Colton did not arrive soon. He barely noticed when Aneel entered the apartment. Without a word, Aneel grabbed a wet towel and kneeled beside Tyler and helped clean up the mess.

They worked in silence.

Tyler finally sat back and looked at Aneel. "I don't know how to help her. You were right." Tears burned at his eyes, then rolled down his face. "I have no business being with her. I don't know how to fix this."

Aneel slid over next to him. "I was the one who was wrong. I was taken aback at the news that the two of you were together, I never really believed that you weren't good enough for her. I was hurt because I hadn't been in the loop, and I let it consume me. I'm so sorry. You are everything I would ever want for my sister. I was an idiot for not seeing it sooner. Not to mention, I never should have confronted Yogesh Rawal at the party."

Tyler felt some of the weight lift from him, but he too had a confession. "Well, you're going to be pissed now, when I tell you the truth."

Aneel raised an eyebrow. "What's that?"

"That when we first said we were engaged, we really weren't. Sai just wanted to help me save face in front of Colton and Rita, so we faked it. Then it got out of control."

"You faked being in love with her?"

"No." He met Aneel's gaze. "I have been in love with Saira for years."

"You never said anything."

"Of course not." Tyler shook his head. "Look how everyone freaked out."

"So, all this is fake?"

Tyler shook his head. "No. She fell for me too. Don't ask me how or even why. But she did. So, at this point, it's all real." He looked at Aneel. "I just don't know how to fix this."

Aneel and Tyler stood, wiping their hands. Aneel pulled Tyler into an embrace. "We'll figure it out together. We're family. I promise you that. No matter what happens, you're always my brother."

Tyler squeezed Aneel harder. He had his brother back. Now he just had to figure out how to get Saira back.

Chapter Fifty-Five

Saira

Saira woke with the mother of all hangovers the next day. She stayed in bed, while Tyler and Aneel took turns bringing her food and fluid.

"Do I want to know what happened between you two?" Saira asked Tyler.

"We're family, Saira. That's what happened."

That was enough for her. "What happened at the party? I only remember snippets."

Aneel joined them in the bedroom. "Do you remember our dad being there?"

That she remembered clearly. She'd heard the whole story. She touched her scar and nodded. "I had a few glasses to calm me after I heard what dad did," she said quietly.

"You had more than a few. You drank pretty heavily after that," her brother said. There was no accusation in his voice, only sadness. She looked at Tyler. He took her hand, but the grim look on his face did not go away.

"Oh, god."

Aneel nodded and tapped his phone. "Take a look."

What Saira saw on the video put a fresh pit in her stomach, and brought tears to her eyes. The woman she was watching was not just a hot mess. She was a joke. She ruined the party that Tracy Auntie had worked so hard to put together. She made a mockery of everything. That was supposed to be Colton and Rita's celebration as well, but she'd ruined it.

She was a horrible person.

"Oh. God. I'm just like him, aren't I?" She jumped from the bed, and everything tilted. But she stayed standing. "I remember. I threw up all over the carpet. Oh, Tyler, I'm so sorry." As she saw the video, more of the awful details came back to her. "I felt a panic attack coming on after I went off on Dad. So, I told the bartender to keep them coming."

Her brother was looking at her with sorrow in his eyes.

"This is how Dad was, wasn't he?" Tears fell down her face. Her head pounded. "Wasn't he?"

Aneel did not answer.

"He was! I'm right! I'm just like him. He killed someone! And I'm just like him!" Her heart was pounding and she was screaming. Tyler wrapped his arms around her and held her tight. Aneel left the room.

She wanted to melt into the security that was found in Tyler's arms, but she did not deserve it. Not after what she had done, who she had become.

"You're not like him. You're *you*. You can choose whether you're going to be like him or not. It's going to be okay," Tyler murmured to her as he held her tight, and she sobbed. "I'm going to be your husband. It's all I've ever wanted. I love you, Sai. It's going to be all right."

She sobbed as she clung to him. She did love him. She loved him more than life itself. But he was wrong. It wasn't going to be all right. Not the way he thought it would be.

Tyler held her until she quieted and cried herself to sleep. Then he lay there with her in his arms. His kissed her forehead. He would do anything to help her. Anything.

Saira was his whole life.

Whatever she needed, he would do.

Tyler woke hours later. It was dinnertime, so he carefully left the bed to make them something. He heard the shower turn on as he pulled a few ingredients from the fridge. A text came through from Colton.

Rita and I are staying at Mom's for few. Give you and Saira some space.

Tyler texted back his gratitude and pulled out a frying pan. He made them grilled cheese and pulled some tomato soup from his freezer. Aneel kept him well stocked, that was for sure. The sun had set, and the apartment was dark save the droplights in the kitchen.

Saira came out just as he plated the sandwiches and ladled the soup. Her hair was damp, loose curls framed her face, and she was wearing his sweatshirt and sweatpants, which he loved to see.

"Hey you," he said quietly.

She smiled, her eyes red and raw from crying. "Hey you." She sat down at the breakfast bar. He sat with her as she started eating.

"You knew." She said this softly, but the accusation was clear. "You knew my dad killed someone."

"I did."

"You weren't going to tell me." Her voice was firmer now, slightly agitated.

"I wanted you to have a father."

"Not your decision." She raised her eyes to him. Her soft brown eyes were not filled with love, but something else.

"I thought I was protecting you." He kept his voice even.

"You didn't think I could handle it." Her voice cracked as tears swam in her eyes.

"No, that wasn't it."

"Then what was it?" Her words were as watery as her eyes.

"I told you—I wanted you to have your father."

"And you didn't think I could know this and keep him as my father?" She got louder.

"I didn't know what you would do."

"So, you decided for me. Like Aneel." The accusation was crystal.

Tyler opened his mouth to protest, but she wasn't wrong. He had wanted to protect her, and that had led him to make the choice behind her back. "I wanted to protect you," he repeated.

She nodded and swallowed her tears. Or tried to, because they were falling down her cheeks again. "This won't work."

A pit started forming in Tyler's stomach. "What won't work?"

"This." She waved a finger between them.

"What do you mean? We love each other. We can—"

She shook her head. "No. I'm calling Dr. Maya in the morning and getting her recommendation for a therapist."

Relief fell over him. "Perfect. That's a great step."

"And I'm going to move in with Aneel for a bit until I find my own place."

"Why? You can stay here. This is your home," Tyler said, feeling that pit returning.

"No. This can't be my home. Not anymore." She took off the ring and placed it between them.

Tyler's throat tightened. "Don't...don't do that. Put it back on." He could barely get the words out. Tears burned his eyes and prickled his nose, and he did not care one bit. "I screwed up. I should have told you about your dad. It won't happen again. Please, put it back on." He was begging her. He was pathetic. He did not care. He could not imagine his life without her. "Put it back on."

She shook her head. "I will not have you babysitting me when I can't get out of bed, or when I have a panic attack, or get drunk for no reason. I don't want you to have to clean up my vomit because I can't control myself. You would grow to resent me. I won't do to you what my dad did to my mom."

He opened his mouth to protest. She held up her hand to him.

"No. I am just like my dad. I'm a monster and I do not know what is happening to me. You should not have to fix me. Move on, Tyler. You deserve someone as wonderful and amazing as you. There is someone out there who needs and wants and deserves you." She turned to him. "Do me a favor."

"Anything."

"Go to the office tomorrow so I can pack. I won't be able to leave if you're here. And I have to leave."

"No, Sai—"

She looked down at him as he sat and she stood. "You said *anything*."

Chapter Fifty-Six

Saira

Saira had heard, as many have, that sometimes the hardest part of any recovery is that first step. She needed help, so first thing in the morning she made the call to Dr. Maya and got the name of another therapist. Dr. Lali Tam. Dr. Tam could see her as early as tomorrow. Saira took the appointment.

The hardest part wasn't making that call, it was packing her things and leaving the condo that she had thought would be her permanent home. The place she had come to so often seeking solace and always, always getting it. The place that had become a comfort to her. The place where the man she loved lived.

The very hardest part was realizing that Tyler had stayed true to his word when he said he loved her enough to do anything for her.

Because he wasn't home when she left.

She took her things and Kiara and went to her brother's house.

"Hi," she said when Aneel opened the door.

"That was quick," he said.

"I did not want to dawdle."

"Why are you leaving him again?" Aneel asked as he helped get her things up to the room she would be sharing with Veer.

"I can't put him through what Mom went through. I love him too much." Her voice cracked. "And he'll just end up hating me if he's always taking care of whatever mess I've made."

"You're going to therapy though, right?"

"Bhaiya. I'm not going to make him wait around and see what happens to me. We don't know yet if therapy will be able to straighten me out. Things might just end up getting worse instead of better. I don't even have a real job lined up yet, for after I pass the boards."

"I might be able to help with that." He pulled out his phone and tapped.

She narrowed her eyes at him as she put away a few things in the drawers her nephew had cleared for her. "Uh-huh."

Her phone dinged. "Amar and Divya have a dog. Their veterinarian is getting ready to retire. Maybe you can work as a tech for awhile. I just sent you her information."

She opened the contact. "Thanks."

"Are we good?" Her brother looked at her like he was afraid she was still angry with him.

"I don't know, are you going to try and cover me in Bubble Wrap?"

"I'm your older brother. I can't just turn off my protective instincts like that, just because you're all grown."

She raised her eyebrows at him.

"But I'll try." He sighed and smiled.

"Try really hard." She wrapped her arms around her brother. It felt nice to have him back.

"Since you are currently unemployed, you can come and be sous-chef downstairs for Karina."

"My favorite thing to do," she deadpanned. She texted the veterinarian as they went downstairs to set up a meeting. The sooner she made some money, the sooner she could get her own place. She didn't want to really burden her brother either.

She's here.

Aneel texted him when Saira got to his house. He hadn't gone to the office, he had simply gone to a coffee shop to respect her wishes, but the instant he got that text, he wished he hadn't.

He wished he had stayed in the apartment to convince her to stay home. But when he had said he would do anything for her, he had meant it, even if the anything was removing himself from her life.

Colton had joined him this morning.

"You going to keep staring at your phone?" he asked. "She's not going to reach out. You know it."

Tyler nodded and put the phone facedown on the table.

"Tell me about this position in New York in that new practice you're starting with Rita," Tyler said.

"You serious?"

Tyler nodded. "At least let me hear about it. I don't know if I can stay in Baltimore, if Sai is here. It's too hard."

Colton nodded. "Okay. Well, Rita and I found a place in an office building. We aren't doing divorce law, so we won't be stepping on Dad's area at all. We want to be available for regular people who need lawyers, but don't have a ton of money."

"So, there's not a ton of pay." Tyler smirked at Colton.

His brother shook his head. "Not in the beginning, for sure, no. But there will be settlements moving forward. We have a bunch saved up, as I am sure you do. We'd be okay."

Tyler nodded.

"Want to come and take a look?"

The last thing Tyler wanted to do at this moment was leave Baltimore. But it was what needed to happen.

"We can go for a quick overnight, take a look, come back." Colton nodded. "Take your mind off of things."

Chapter Fifty-Seven

Saira

Saira drove in to see the new therapist. Aneel lived a bit out of the city so it was a longer drive, but she wanted to stick with the recommendation. She was in the same building as Dr. Maya. How long ago was it that Tyler had spilled his feelings for her in that fake therapy session? Felt like a lifetime.

She had no idea how to dress for therapy, so she wore her scrubs. She checked in with the receptionist and sat down. The waiting area was pleasant, not drab or intimidatingly modern. Except for the fake tree in the corner.

What was up with that? Tyler would say it was one less thing for the receptionist to tend to. Sai would counter that it must mean the receptionist was lazy. He'd roll his eyes, but he would laugh.

She missed Tyler like she was missing a limb. She wanted him here to hold her hand. To tell her everything would be all right. So she wouldn't feel all alone. So they could giggle about the receptionist together.

She wanted him there because she loved him.

But that would be selfish. That would be about what *she* wanted. Not what was best for Tyler.

Dr. Tam called her in after a minimal wait. Dr. Tam was a petite woman who looked to be about the same age as Saira. Her sleek dark hair hung loose around her face, and she greeted Saira with a warm smile. The office had a floor-to-ceiling window and was well lit and the decor was contemporary without being space age, retaining some warmth.

Saira had gotten a couple other names in case Dr. Tam turned out not to be a great fit, but so far she didn't think she needed them.

"Sit down, please." Dr. Tam's voice was pleasant yet firm.

Saira sat down.

Dr. Tam sat in the chair next to her, as opposed to the across from her at the desk. "So, Saira, is this your first therapy session? I know you said Dr. Maya gave you my name."

"No. That was… Well. This is my first real session to deal with my issues."

"Tell me what brings you here."

Suddenly Saira wasn't so sure this was a good idea. She wanted to get up and leave.

"Just a word or two will be fine—we don't have to get down to the nitty-gritty just yet. Your intake form suggested you've been experiencing panic attacks?" Dr. Tam's voice was kind.

Saira nodded. "Yes."

"How often?"

"Depends on the stress level in my life."

Dr. Tam nodded. "That makes a lot of sense. Do you want to talk about the stress?"

She did not. What if she had a panic attack while telling the doctor?

"Is it about school?"

"Yes."

Dr. Tam waited.

"I failed the boards."

In this way, Saira passed the first hour of therapy. Dr. Tam wanted to see her three times a week for a while. Saira agreed.

Saira returned to her car to find a response to her text to the veterinarian. They would love to see her whenever. Just stop over.

Excited to see the office, Saira punched in the address and

found the clinic easily. It was not far from Aneel's place, so closer to suburbia than the city, but she didn't mind that. The office was a medium-sized clinic. She walked in and introduced herself.

The veterinarian came to see her immediately. "Dr. Drew," Saira said, extending her hand to a woman in her sixties. "Nice to meet you."

"You too, Dr. Rawal."

"Oh, I haven't passed the boards yet."

"But you graduated?"

"Yes."

"You'll take that damn test again and pass no problem. I didn't pass it the first time either."

"You didn't?"

"No. It happens. Listen, I cannot legally employ you as a veterinarian yet. But I can hire you as an assistant. The pay is crap, but it comes with really good health care. You take the test and pass; I'll give you a job here. I'm thinking to retire or cut back soon, and I could use a young doctor to take over."

That was a lot. Saira inhaled and exhaled. But it sounded wonderful. "Okay."

"Yeah?" The doctor seemed as excited as she was.

"Yes. I need the work. I miss clinic."

"When can you start?"

"Tomorrow?" Saira grinned.

Dr. Drew extended her hand. "Done deal."

Saira left the office and got in her car. She immediately tapped Tyler's number without thinking. He picked up on the first ring.

"Saira? Is everything okay?"

The panic in his voice reminded her where things stood between them.

"Uh. Yes. I'm fine. Sorry. Butt dial." She should hang up. What the hell was she doing?

"Saira?" His voice was literally a balm to her soul. Her muscles relaxed; a smile poked at her mouth. Only her heart thudded away. Pounding hard at her chest as if it needed to go to him.

"I got a job," she finally said. The smile made a full and natural appearance.

Tyler's excitement was instant. "That's fantastic! The clinic took you back?"

"No. A smaller office. Just the one doctor right now. She's looking to retire soon. If I pass next year, I'll have a guaranteed full-time vet job. I'll be an assistant in the meantime."

"That's perfect. I'm really very happy for you. We should—" He stopped as if remembering that there was no more *we*. "Well, make sure you do something fun to celebrate," he finished.

Her smile faded, and her heart ached again. "Right." She wanted to tell him about her therapy session. But she didn't. "Well, I'm just sitting here in my car—"

"Unsafe for sure." She could imagine the small smile on Tyler's face, the glint of amusement in those blue eyes. "Take care." The line went dead.

She dropped her phone on the passenger seat and fought tears as she drove back to Aneel's house. She lost and the tears came and then the sobs. Why was she crying? She was the one who ended it. This had been her choice.

By the time Saira pulled into Aneel's driveway, the tears had dried. But job or no job, her heart was heavy. She had a text from Tyler.

It was good to hear your voice.

She answered with a thumbs-up emoji. It was all she could manage right now.

Chapter Fifty-Eight

Tyler

Tyler stared at his phone. He had been thrilled to hear that things were starting to work out for her, but there was so much more he wanted to know. Had she started therapy? Had she had any more panic attacks?

He knew that answers to those questions were no longer his business. This right here was why people did not get involved with their friends. If you lost them, you lost all of them. You didn't even get to keep the parts of them you had before. She and Aneel would go to Aldo's and have celebratory pizza. Karina and Veer would go with them. They would start a new tradition. He wouldn't be invited.

He texted Colton. Let's go to New York. Take a look.

Colton: We can go day after tomorrow.

Tyler: [thumbs up emoji]

Two days later, Tyler, Colton and Rita were on the train to New York.

"I feel like I should come clean," Tyler said to Rita once they were seated on the train. "When you first came to Baltimore, engaged, Saira and I were only pretending to be together. She didn't want me to look ridiculous, since Colton was with an ex of mine." Tyler blurted it all out.

Rita shook her head, looking shocked.

"You know, you never thanked me for that," Colton pointed out.

"Excuse me?" Tyler raised his eyebrows at his brother.

"If it hadn't been for me and Rita, you and Saira would not have been forced together, and you never would have told her how you felt," Colton said, no shortage of smugness on his face.

"She broke up with me."

"But now you know. You took that chance." Rita's voice was gentle. "Tyler, you had feelings for her back when we were together. It's a big part of why I ended things."

"Right now, she's doing what she needs to do for herself." Colton looked at him, all joking gone from his face.

The train screeched to a halt and the three of them entered the city. New York bustled and honked, excitement like an electric current in the air. Colton and Rita came to life in a way that Tyler had not seen in Baltimore.

They chattered nearly nonstop on the Uber ride to the Hart Law offices. Tyler hadn't seen his father in quite some time. It was overdue.

Colton strode onto the floor that housed Hart Law, Rita by his side. Tyler followed behind them, his back straight, chin up. He nodded politely at employees who recognized him.

The offices were all glass walls and windows, save the cubicles in the center that belonged to the team members. They passed their father's receptionist and headed directly for his office.

Tyler walked in beside Colton and Rita and to his surprise, his father's face lit up.

"What's this?" His face filled with a huge smile as he stood. Tyler could not remember his father ever really smiling like this. Ethan Hart was still a handsome man, an older version of Colton in many aspects. "Both my boys at the same time?"

"Dad." Colton extended his hand.

This was more like it. No hugging happened here. Tyler extended his hand as well. "Dad."

His father shook all their hands, then looked at them as if taking them all in. "I heard you were both engaged. Congratulations."

"Well, Dad. It's just them now," Tyler said.

His father shrugged and motioned for them to sit. "What brings you here?"

"Tell me about Yogesh Rawal," Tyler said.

His father's face darkened. "What about him?"

"Just tell us what happened."

Ethan Hart leaned back in his chair. "Fine. Well, your mom and I were separated but I was still working in Baltimore. One day, your mother called me to meet with this man. He was in the hospital, bruised up, drunk—and under arrest, because he had hit another car. And his daughter had been in the back seat." Ethan shifted. "I knew him of course. His wife was your mom's closest friend. So I took the case. There really wasn't much to defend. All the evidence was there, it was obvious what happened, not to mention he wasn't particularly interested in fighting it, especially after the man he hit died a week later. At the time, the max the state could give him was six years. He was happy to take it he was so filled with remorse."

"There's more," Tyler said.

Ethan nodded. "While he was in prison, his wife filed for divorce. But she added a stipulation that he had to give up… sign over his parental rights to her and never come to see them while they were minors. I strongly advised against him accepting this. My experience has been people live to regret this sort of action. Yogesh did not listen. He signed the papers, then had me open a trust for the children that they could have when the youngest turned thirty. She's twenty-seven now, but he came to me a few months ago asking to open it sooner. It's possible, there are just some fees that need to be paid."

Tyler leaned back and looked at Colton. Their dad was legit. No shady deals. He nodded and the three of them stood. Ethan followed suit.

They started to leave, when Ethan spoke again. "The reason I counseled him not to sign over his rights was because your mom and I had already divorced. It was my idea to split you two up. Tracy fought me, but I won. It was the worst decision I ever made. Not only did it mean I lost one of my sons for all intents and purposes, but it meant you lost each other. Seeing you both here today, together, so obviously bonded, warms my icicle heart. But I know I had nothing to do with that and that will haunt me forever."

Tyler stared at his father. On impulse, he went back to his dad and embraced him. "Just move forward. That's what Mom did."

Chapter Fifty-Nine

Saira

Saira made use of the small den on the first floor of Aneel's house to study. The boards review class didn't start for a month, but she didn't want to waste time, and besides, she needed to keep her mind off Tyler.

Aneel had a desk, and a small sofa tucked in there. She was currently on the sofa with Kiara curled up next to her.

"Hey." Aneel leaned in the doorway.

"Hey." She kept working. Aneel would do this a few times a day—check up on her. "I heard from Tyler."

Her heart thudded. "Hm." Maybe if she didn't acknowledge the ache, it would go away.

"He's in New York. Looking at potential office space with Colton and Rita."

She snapped her head up. To hell with ignoring the ache. "He's moving to New York?"

Aneel shrugged. "He hasn't made a decision."

"Seems like he's thinking about it though," Saira said. "Did he talk to his dad?"

Aneel nodded. "Apparently, it went well enough."

"What does that mean? What did he say? How is Tyler doing?" Saira moved closer to her brother, wanting to shake the answers out of him.

"I thought you were over him." Aneel raised an eyebrow.

"That doesn't mean I don't care…about his life."

"Uh-huh." The gleam in her brother's eye was annoying.

"Shut up." She smacked his arm.

"Keep smacking me and you'll have to move out."

"I will be doing so anyway in two weeks." She had found a small place within ten minutes of her new job. She and Kiara could be at work in ten minutes. She scratched Kiara's back.

"We like having you here. Veer loves it," Aneel said for the hundredth time. "You can stay here, until you can afford a better place."

"I could." She looked up at him and nodded. "But I won't. I need to be on my own. I'm fine. I've been going to therapy for the last five weeks and I'm going to continue to go. If I need it, Dr. Tam will put me on meds for the panic and depression. I can't have you constantly eyeing me."

"I've taken care of you all my life."

Saira closed her books and looked up at her brother. "I know. And I appreciate that. I wouldn't even be becoming a doctor without the sacrifices—"

"I'm not talking about all that."

"I know. But I'm saying, you did your job. Your work is done now though. I'll be fine. Use your power for Veer or making babies or whatever."

He gave her a sideways smile.

"Aren't we doing Raksha Bandhan tonight? I'll let you buy me a present." She smirked, but his face went serious.

"Yeah. So, we are doing Raksha Bandhan. I just have one thing I need you to do."

"What's that?" She narrowed her eyes.

"Before I tell you, just know that I went to him. He did not come to me."

"Bhaiya…"

"Our father is coming over for Raksha Bandhan."

Saira stood, anger boiling in her blood. "Are you out of your mind?"

"I am not. Hear me out, before you flip."

She took a few cleansing breaths and picked up Kiara. "Fine. I'm listening."

"I went to him a couple weeks ago, because… I don't know why. I think I wanted to understand better what you might be going through. He has done unforgivable things, and he is not looking to be forgiven for anything. That man's death weighs heavily on him, always will." Aneel paused. "His depression was deep and hidden. He didn't even know he was dealing with depression. He just knew he got these panic attacks, and that drinking alcohol seemed to help him stay in control, at least in the short term. It wasn't until that night that he decided he had to get sober. In doing so, his depression was revealed and he finally sought help. It changed his life."

"Okay, so?"

"So he wants to talk to you."

"About what?"

"I don't know. I met him for coffee a few times. He's seen his AA sponsor recently to help keep him on his path. He's working. And he asked to talk to you. I said I would ask you and see what you wanted."

Saira stared at her brother. "So, you're not making me?"

He shook his head. "As if I could."

"That's true." She stroked Kiara's fur.

"But what could it hurt? Hear him out. After that, ignore him if you want and know that you never have to see him again."

"You're okay with him?"

"I don't know." Aneel shrugged. "But you were right. He's our dad. And I mean, Tyler is speaking with his dad. I figured I could give it a shot too." He sighed. "Besides, I'm tired of carrying all that anger around."

Saira stared at her brother. "Look at you, with all that personal growth." She paused. "Fine. I'll talk to him. He can come to Raksha Bandhan tonight. Because you asked, and you,

Bhaiya, are my hard-core family." For better or worse, Aneel had never left her side. And she knew he never would.

Yogesh showed up on time, and with a guest. Saira had been at his wedding last year, and remembered Deepika Auntie as a warm woman, who clearly loved her father. Saira hung back with Veer and Kiara while Aneel and Karina Bhabhi greeted their guests. To be fair, Karina Bhabhi did most of the greeting.

"This is my son, Veer." Karina Bhabhi nodded at Veer and he put his hands together in namaste and bowed his head in greeting.

Here, Aneel seemed to find his voice. He knelt down so he was at Veer's level and placed an arm around him. "Veer. This is my dad and his wife." He cleared his throat. "I know you call your mom's dad your Dada, but maybe my dad could be your Nanu?"

Saira widened her eyes. Wow. Aneel really was taking some big steps here. Veer looked up at her. "What do you think, Foi?"

"I think you should give him a chance. See what all this Nanu business is about." She shrugged.

This seemed acceptable to Veer. "Nice to meet you, Nanu—" he turned to Deepika Auntie "—and Nani."

Deepika Auntie was taken aback. Her eyes filled with tears, as she knelt down to him. "Well, I am certainly happy that I came prepared." She reached into her oversized bag and produced a figurine of Iron Man.

Veer's eyes lit up and he looked at Aneel, a question in his eyes.

"Yes. You can go add it to the collection." Aneel chuckled. "But what do you say?"

"Thank you, Nani!"

"You are most welcome."

With that, Veer ran off.

Saira stepped forward, still clutching Kiara. "Dad. Auntie. Come in."

They navigated into the family great room where Aneel and Karina had set up some food. Everyone sat down.

Her dad looked at his wife. She squeezed his hand, and he smiled at her. They were happy. They were in love.

"How did you two meet?" Saira asked.

Deepika Auntie answered. "We met at the temple at a Diwali function. He looked quite out of place, but he was so handsome I had to approach."

"Were people trying to set you up, Auntie?"

"They were. I'm divorced and my husband remarried some time ago. All my friends were eager to pair me off. But I was happy on my own. Made my own decisions, did what I wished for once. Then I met your father." She smiled.

Her dad smiled back. "When she approached me at that party, I was aghast. I wasn't looking for any kind of relationship."

"He didn't think he deserved it. Of course I did not know all that in the moment."

"I told her straight up by the end of that night."

"But there was something about him… I had been to therapy after my divorce. But I kept it quiet. Yogesh was upfront, unabashed and told me right away."

"She needed to know who she was pursuing," her father said.

"I was drawn to the frankness with which he approached his treatment. It was refreshing to talk with someone who embraced their healing instead of hiding it from everyone," Deepika Auntie continued. "Anyway. He was unable to scare me off. And here we are."

"Why are you here, Dad?" Saira needed him to cut to the chase.

He looked around.

"You can say whatever you want. Aneel and Bhabhi are my family," Saira said.

"Well, I came here to apologize for not being upfront with you about the circumstances of my divorce from your mother. I don't have any excuse for hiding it from you except that I just wanted to get to know you."

"You gave us up. Turned your back," Saira said.

"For your own good," he said. "When I realized that I had put you in the car that night—" His voice broke and his eyes watered. He swallowed and continued. "I could not forgive myself. I will *never* forgive myself for that. I did not know what my future held past prison. I wanted to make sure that I never harmed you or your brother again. So, when your mother demanded I never see you, I agreed." He paused. "When you and I reunited a few months ago, I had intended on telling you right away. But then Aneel was so angry and it meant so much to me that you were so willing to spend time with me, I just could not bring myself to say the words. I am so deeply sorry. For all of it."

Saira nodded.

Yogesh looked at Aneel. Her brother nodded.

"There's one more thing," Yogesh added. "I know that you have been in therapy for some weeks, and I know that Tyler is not part of your life anymore—"

Saira stood. "I'm not discussing Tyler with you."

"Hear me out. I want you to know that you don't have to go it alone."

"I'm not alone. I have my brother. I have Bhabhi."

"It's not the same. I can see the pain in your whole body because Tyler is not here. Therapy is a journey. There are ups. There are downs. It's not a straight line. If you are lucky enough to have someone like Tyler in your life already, you don't have to wait to be happy."

"I can't do that to him."

"Do what?"

"The days of not getting out of bed, the panic attacks…all of it. If I burden him with that, he will grow to resent me."

"Every relationship has challenges. Resentment can pop up from anything. Not just these issues. Besides, you're ahead. You have already started to put in the work way earlier than I did."

"Why do you care?" She nearly snapped at him. She wanted what he said to be true. But she couldn't be sure.

He shrugged. "I'm your father. I'd rather you learn from my mistakes than do them yourself."

She turned to Aneel. "Are you in on this?"

"Am I in on seeing you be happy?" Aneel nodded. "One hundred and ten percent. But it's your call."

Chapter Sixty

Tyler

Today was Raksha Bandhan. A celebration between brothers and sisters. Saira and Aneel were together today, for sure. Tyler had always been present on this day, when the two of them celebrated their bond. Even if they had been fighting, everything was pushed aside to celebrate that sibling bond. He missed the snarky banter. He missed watching Saira carefully tie a Rakhi on Aneel's wrist. He missed watching them try to shove as many sweets as possible into each other's mouths.

He had returned alone from New York, after spending a few days with Colton learning about the law practice he wanted to build. It was tempting, that was for sure. But he had come to realize that his home was in Baltimore.

Painful as it may be, and as pathetic as it may seem, he could not put that kind of distance between him and Saira as long as there was any chance that she might need him again. Even though he hadn't heard from her since the day she accidentally called him.

The sight of her face on his phone had given him a jolt and the sound of her voice had spread happiness through him. Happiness that was gone as soon as she hung up.

"Tyler, honey, come help with these crab cakes," his mother called from the kitchen. "And bring that wine."

"You got it, Mom." Tyler grabbed the chilled bottle of white wine and two glasses on his way to the kitchen.

He poured and they clinked glasses. "Didn't go to Raksha Bandhan today, Mom?"

She gave him a withering look. "Aneel invited me, but I couldn't very well leave you here to mope all alone."

"You could go. You can still go. I'm good, Mom."

She shook her head at him. "Get the frying pan out."

He spent the next few nights at his mom's to avoid going back to the empty condo. Everything about the condo reminded him of Saira. And Kiara. He told himself he was just being a good son and doing handyman stuff around the house.

But damn it, he missed Saira so much. He even missed the Beast.

The tune of "I Am Yours" by Andy Grammar floated to him in the morning, waking him from restless sleep.

That was Saira's ringtone.

He grabbed at the phone like a lifeline. He didn't care, even if it was a butt dial again. Any connection to her was better than none.

"Hello?" He was unable to take the grogginess from his voice.

"Were you sleeping?" Saira's voice floated to him as if it had never stopped.

"No. Yes. No."

"Simple question, Tyler."

"Nothing is simple, Saira."

Silence. But Tyler dared not speak, in case she decided to hang up.

"So, the thing is that in therapy, sometimes they ask you to bring along someone who has an important role in your life, to discuss things." She spoke fast, as if she might change her mind.

"Yeah," he said slowly. "I think I've heard about that."

"Aneel came once."

"Okay, good." It really was.

"I wondering if you would be able to come to my next session?"

His heart thudded. *She needed him.* "Yes." He managed, trying to keep his voice calm. "I'll be there. Text me the details."

"Will do."

"Saira?" His treacherous voice shook.

"Yes?"

"Thanks."

Silence floated as if she had more to say.

"I'll see you tomorrow." She ended the call.

Saira sat patiently across from Dr. Tam. Well, she might have appeared patient, but her insides were churning. Tyler was coming today. At least she thought he was. He was about three minutes late.

She was just about to suggest they check the waiting area when there was a knock at the door.

"Come on in," Dr. Tam called as she smiled at Saira.

Saira stood as she heard the door open. She hadn't seen Tyler for over six weeks. His hair was a bit longer, like he had skipped a cut. He was clean-shaven, however. Was it because he knew she liked him clean-shaven?

He was wearing jeans and a button-down shirt with the sleeves rolled up. He looked absolutely delightful, a breath of fresh air in a tunnel of strife. His blue gaze landed on her and he smiled. She had to stop herself from running up to him and jumping into his arms like the lovesick teenager she felt like.

He'd love it though, Bollywood fan that he was.

"Hi. I'm Tyler Hart." He shifted his attention momentarily to Dr. Tam.

"I'm Dr. Tam." She gestured to the chair next to Saira. "Please. Have a seat. Thank you for joining us."

Tyler smiled and took his seat. Saira couldn't stop drinking him in.

"Saira?" Dr. Tam said. "Would you like to have a seat as well?"

She flushed at having been caught staring at him. "Yes. Of course." She sat and faced Dr. Tam.

"Tyler," Dr. Tam began, "Saira has asked you here today because there are some things she would like to say to you. And we find it helps in therapy to include family as well as people with whom we hold close relationships."

"Which one am I?" Tyler asked.

Dr. Tam grinned. "That is for you both to figure out." She looked to Saira and nodded. "Whenever you're ready."

Saira turned to Tyler, her heart thudding in her chest. "I… uh… I heard you were moving to New York."

Tyler glanced at Dr. Tam, then back at her. "Um, no. Colton asked me to think about it, so I did. But I opted out." He gave her a small smile. Damn she had missed that smile.

"Why?"

"Why?" Amusement colored his eyes, and he raised one eyebrow, just a bit.

"Yes. Why?" She swallowed, bracing herself for his answer. His job was here. He loved his condo. But were those enough to hold him?

He sighed and turned his whole body to her so she was forced to look at him. "To be honest, Saira… I'm staying in Baltimore because home is…wherever you are. I don't want to leave Baltimore if you're here."

"But we're not together anymore," Saira said.

"That doesn't mean I don't love you." His gaze was vulnerable and open. "When I look at you, I see everything that I need, everything that makes me happy." He leaned toward her. "In your eyes, I can see everything you're hiding. Everything you won't say."

Saira stared at him. Her dad was wrong. Tyler was not merely a very good man. Tyler was the best man, the only man for her and she had let him go. She'd been a fool.

"I needed you to come here today to tell you I was wrong. When I broke up with you, I was trying to spare you all the bad stuff that goes along with all this." She made a vague motion at the room, unable to tear her eyes away from Tyler. "The truth is…that you ground me. Even when I push you away, you hold me tight." She let out a small chuckle. "I don't know how you do it, but you love me when I'm at my lowest." Tears burned at her eyes, and she gave him a watery smile. "One time, when we were in fake therapy, you told me you loved me and how that came to be."

Tyler gave her a half smile at the memory.

"Now, it's my turn." She wiped a tear that had escaped, and swallowed so she could speak. "I can't remember a time in my life that you were not around. I can't remember a time in my life when I didn't love you. But I can remember distinctly what it felt like to fall in love with you. Falling in love with you was like jumping off a cliff. It was leaving the security of the mountain of our friendship, for the free fall of loving you. It's the riskiest thing I've ever done. I certainly did not see it coming. I firmly believed in love, but I also firmly believed it was not for me. But all the same, I jumped. You caught me. And when I landed in your arms, I knew I was where I was supposed to be."

"What are you saying?" Tyler leaned toward her.

"I'm saying that this is a journey. I may never be done with therapy, or meds—this could just be how I am wired. But I've been working hard and I'm being honest, and I want to get better. It's a lonely journey. All I do after every session is fight the urge to call you and tell you all about it. I pick up my phone hundreds of times during the day to share some tidbit of my life, but then I remember that I pushed you away. I miss you, maybe it's selfish, but I need you in my life, by my side. When I lean into your strength, I'm better."

"Saira…"

"I'm saying, Tyler Hart, that I love you. That I would much rather traverse this journey with you by my side. The only promise I can make is that I will always love you. But I know this is a difficult road, and if it's not for you, I understand." Saira raised her chin. It was up to him. "I'm saying that you are real, very real to me. That I want you. That I need you. That I love you enough to burn the world down."

Tyle sat in silence for a moment.

"If I remember correctly, at this point you turned and ran." A smile twitched at his lips."

She nodded. "That I did."

He stood and took a step closer to her chair and put out his hand. "I'm not running. Not unless you're running with me."

Epilogue

One year later

"Bhaiya, are we all set for tonight?" Saira paced as she talked to her brother. Her belly was full of nerves. How would she make it to tonight?

"Oh, my god, Saira, ask me one more time and I'll snap." Aneel's patience was low. She heard the wail of a baby in the background. Aneel's daughter, Naya.

"I just want everything to go well," Saira said.

"It's Raksha Bandhan—I can pretty much guarantee all will be well. I gotta go. Tyler's on the other line." Aneel ended the call.

Saira dropped her phone on the bed and went over everything for tonight. This was Naya's first Raksha Bandhan. She was the cutest baby ever at four months old and Saira wanted it to be special. This day had always been special for her and Aneel, and they both wanted to pass that down. Saira made sure that she had her Rakhi for Aneel and also one for Baby Naya to tie on Veer.

Karina insisted on also celebrating the fact that Saira had passed the boards and was now officially a fully qualified veterinarian. Dr. Drew had wasted no time in offering Saira a partnership in her practice and Saira had never been so excited.

Her therapist, Dr. Tam, had been key this year in helping Saira navigate all that was happening in her life while at the same time dealing with her depression.

When it was time, Saira gathered Kiara and drove to Aneel's house for the celebrations. Aneel had everything else that she needed.

"Seriously, are you sure this is okay? I don't want to mess up Naya and Veer's first Raksha Bandhan," Tyler told Aneel.

"Tyler. For the one-millionth time, it's fine," Aneel answered. "Don't make me regret encouraging you to buy the house around the corner."

Tyler laughed. "Fine. I'll see you later."

Tyler had sold the condo six months ago. He and Saira still lived separately—he was trying to give her the space she needed, while still being there for her. The condo had been wonderful, but he recognized that owning it was part of his constant competition with Colton. He really wanted to live closer to his family, and whenever Saira was ready, he wanted to start a family with her in a home that they both loved.

She had helped him find the house and then move and decorate. The house had a fenced-in backyard that was perfect for Kiara, and any future children he and Saira might have. One day.

When it was time, Tyler walked over to Aneel's. The August day was hot, so he wore khaki shorts and a blue button-down shirt. He had taken the time to get a haircut and made sure he was clean-shaven.

He walked in to find that he was the last one to arrive. Colton and Rita had already come and were in a deep discussion with Karina and his mother about wedding planning. Their wedding was just a few months away. Chirag was there with his new girlfriend, a beautiful woman named Sejal. Saira and Aneel's father was also there with his wife.

Aneel was still tense around Yogesh Uncle, but he was coming around, for Saira's sake if nothing else.

"Hey." Saira immediately sidled up and kissed him. "Missed

you today," she whispered. Kiara ran through his legs and waited her turn. Saira was gorgeous in a fitted blue cotton salwar with a matching dupatta, her hair loose and free, the curls gorgeous.

"I saw you last night," he said softly. "A lot of you, in fact."

"It's never enough," she whispered into his ear, sending a thrill through his body.

"Saira, come on." Aneel called her.

She grabbed his hand and guided him to where Aneel and Veer were. "Hi, Bhabhi!" She hugged Karina and took Naya from her. "My niece is perfect, despite the fact that Aneel is her dad."

She handed the baby to Tyler. "She's going to tie her first Rakhi."

Tyler held Naya while Saira tied Naya's Rakhi on Veer's right wrist, wishing him a long and happy life. Then Veer and Naya hugged and exchanged gifts. Naya was too young for sweets, so Veer helped out and ate hers for her.

"That baby looks good on you, Ty," Saira whispered.

"Feels good too," Tyler said. Naya hadn't peeped.

"Aneel," Saira called out. Aneel stood in front of her while she tied his Rakhi, wishing him a long and happy life. They hugged, exchanged sweets and gifts. Tyler had seen this done many times over the years, but he never tired of it, and it always made him so happy.

After Saira finished, she nodded at Aneel, and he stepped back. Tyler caught Aneel's eye and nodded to Naya. Aneel came and took his daughter.

By the time he had done the hand-off, Saira had disappeared. Tyler turned to Aneel in question.

"Where did she go? I told you—"

Aneel grinned. "Relax. She's right behind you."

Tyler turned around to see Saira standing in front him, her

eyes teary, holding a small golden puppy. Kiara sat quietly at her feet.

"I had a bunch of things I planned to say," she said, a tear rolling down her cheek. "But I can't remember them at all."

Tyler's heart raced and pounded.

"You once said you would propose to me with a puppy." She shrugged. "I want to spend the rest of my life with you. You are my someone who I want by my side through the ups and the downs. I'm ready to take our journey to the next step. If you're ready too." She held out the puppy to him.

Tyler took the little guy and held him close. Without a word, he handed the puppy to Colton. Tyler stepped closer, reached into his pocket and pulled out the ring Saira had not been ready for the last time he gave it to her.

He held it out to her. "I'm ready."

* * * * *

Get up to 4 Free Books!

We'll send you 2 free books from each series you try PLUS a free Mystery Gift.

FREE
Value Over
$25

Both the **Harlequin® Special Edition** and **Harlequin® Heartwarming™** series feature compelling novels filled with stories of love and strength where the bonds of friendship, family and community unite.